GREEN EYED KEEPER

LEGENDARY STARS SAGA BOOK FOUR

DAI'JA S. ROSE

NOVA INK BOOKS

GREEN EYED KEEPER

LEGENDARY STARS SAGA BOOK FOUR

DAI'JA S. ROSE

NOVA INK BOOKS

Contact info: www.daijasrosebooks.com

ISBN (digital): 979-8-9891572-6-6

ISBN (paperback): 979-8-9891572-7-3

Edited by Susan Michaud

Map designed by: Luis Leopardi – Fiverr (leidolfr)

Nova Ink Books

For when the weight of destiny is heavy, when life is hard and you feel you are at your breaking point – endure. Everything you need has always been inside of you. Don't be afraid to reinvent yourself.

Kashmala

Wyndhm

Snow Tribe

Beach Tribe

THEYRA

Lower Ember

Upper Ember

Jungle Tribe

Kindle

PYROC

Mystic Ocean

BOOKTOK PRAISE

"This book was a breath of fresh air for fantasy readers. I'm excited to read more of the Legends story!" – @mblazer21

"Prepare to be captivated by this debut fantasy novel brimming with enchanting magic and extraordinary characters. Eagerly awaiting the sequel." – @bookswithambs

"Jai's character had me hooked from the very beginning! Navigating his impossible fate and accepting the reality of his new found purpose was an exhilarating journey. This is one for those who struggle to find intention and those ever faced with a life or death choice. " – @bookbehavior

"The Golden Eyed Legend is a riveting new fantasy series that I simply could not put down!" – @laurenslibraryyy

"Fun, adventurous, and fiery. It was a fast-paced, action pack. Our story is set in a world where some have lost their magic and others have kept and nurtured it. The story centers on a young man named Jai who was orphaned and taken in at a young age. One day he finds out he was gifted with a great power and must begin his adventure to control and protect his new found family and friends. I will say it is a nice debut. It is fast paced and to the point. Which I am always a fan of. It is also heavily ATLA inspired and I am loving the opportunity to jump into a similar world with fun and powerful characters all trying to move forward and discover themselves and their goals." – @theladyravens

"Golden Eyed Legend is the perfect book for a fantasy lover, and the perfect book if you don't know fantasy or are new to it. I love the world building and the characters arcs. Calida was my favorite! I love a strong willed woman! This book gave me Avatar the Last Airbender vibes in the best way! It was action packed and hard to put down as you wanted to continually know what happened next. For a debut novel, especially in fantasy, I can say this checks all the boxes, amazing world building, likeable characters,

great buildup and character arcs and an ability to keep you engaged from the very first chapter. If I had to use one word to describe this book it would be impactful, you feel something from every character and it adds to the story."
– @paristhebibliophile

"I really enjoyed reading this. It's not the typical genre I would normally read, but after reading this it's something I'm interested in reading more! I thought the description, the imagery, and the flow of the book was spectacular. It's very well written for a first time writer! I can't wait to read more from you in the future." – @cheyennetatikaaa

"The world building in the Golden Eyed Legend is intricate and intriguing. I found the magic system unique and an immediate draw. Instantly, I was curious about Jai's backstory and wanted to know more. If you're looking for the next epic fantasy read, this is it!" – @dmcancel
** @dmcancel is the author of *Blood & Sunlight* and *Shadows & Secrets*

Land sustains life.

It is the earthly tether.

You are the strongest.

Only you can carry the weight of all who exist.

Your way is one of stability and endurance.

The very fibers of your being yearn for work.

You welcome challenges and meet resistance head-on.

You are the keeper; loyalty is your honor. When all others

may waver, you stand and sustain.

LANDKEEPERS

SUBSTANCE | CORE | JUSTICE

B lessed Universe,

No one thinks of the end when they are beginning. No one. This doesn't even feel real. I'm a Legend. I never imagined that it could end this way. What was it all worth? What will my people remember? Will I be worth remembering?

For the first time, I admit, I'm afraid. I don't want to go. But somehow, these are my stars. Great Universe, may my successor be stronger than me. Give my successor great endurance to overcome trials. Allow my successor to see the beauty in the differences of the Earth Element. If it is Earth, it should have a home in Theyra regardless. The Landkeepers failed to understand that I was the first of many. I failed to understand why. Maybe because I was afraid of what I would find.

Basir, I'm so sorry. I turned my back on you when you needed me most. Forgive me, Basir! Forgive me, you were my only friend. Everything that made us different made our friendship more meaningful. We weathered many storms together from the outside. But the storms within us that we tried to pretend did not exist came and divided us. My heart wasn't in those terrible things I said. You are an incredible leader who will teach your people great things. If my life had any purpose, I hope it taught you patience. Of all of your strengths: wisdom, bravery, and negotiation, you were always so impatient. Hmm . . . that's what you had me for. Basir, patience teaches forgiveness, so despair not, I forgive you. Please forgive me. I miss you already. But despair not; our friendship was nothing short of destiny. The Universe ordained it. When you look at those mountains, remember me. I believe our friendship will be sustained through several lifetimes, and they'll be better than us. May the stars whisper when you sleep. I get it now! This is not the end, only the beginning.

-Ila

CHAPTER I

*T*he subtle sensation of blinking only garnered more confusion as to why everything was pitch black.

"Where did you go? Oaklee?"

A feminine giggle echoed from far ahead. "I'm over here!"

"It's too dark!"

He could not hear footsteps, but the soles of his feet could feel the vibration of Oaklee's steps. He could tell that she was standing in front of him. "Boaz, we have to hurry!"

"I'm trying! I can't see."

"Shoes off, that should help."

Boaz kicked off his shoes, gripping his toes into the soft ground. "Whoa! I can sense the tunnel walls."

"*Look at you! Come on,*" Oaklee grabbed his hand as they continued through the tunnels.

The tunnels were quiet except for their breathing. "*Do you think we are going to find something?*"

"*It has to be. The old sage said that there was an underground confinement. There was a blast of fire. The sages thought a volcano had erupted. When they investigated, they found corpses. But for some reason they couldn't continue searching.*"

"*Then why are we here?*"

Oaklee stopped walking, causing Boaz to run into her back. "*This war is getting worse. Maybe we could clear this place out and the Landkeepers can have a shelter in case we lose.*"

"*We won't lose!*"

She chuckled. "*Of course we won't. This is a just-in-case measure. Better safe than sorry, right?*"

"*Just in case,*" Boaz whispered.

Oaklee released his hand, "*I feel something up ahead.*" She grunted, "*It feels like roots!*"

"*Oaklee, wait! I can't sense anything that far!*"

Suddenly, a loud shrill filled the tunnels.

"*Oaklee! I'm coming!*"

"No! It's quicksand! Stay back!"

Boaz's heart raced with panic, "I'll go get help!"

"Boaz, it's too fast! Try to close the opening around me. It will keep me from sinking further."

Boaz gripped his toes deeper, "I can't feel it! I can't find you!"

"Don't panic. Try grounding," Oaklee's voice was calm.

Boaz took several deep breaths as he unclenched his toes. He stomped his right foot on the ground before sliding it mere inches forward. He could feel Oaklee writhing in quicksand!

"I know where you are! I'm coming, Oaklee!"

"Slow steps. I slipped forward; be careful."

As soon as his toes felt moisture, he scurried several feet back, "What do I do?"

"Feel for the dry edges and push them into my body; it will stop me from sinking."

Boaz felt the muscles in his legs straining. "Is it moving?"

Oaklee's voice was muffled, "You're doing great, Boaz."

"Oak-Oaklee? What's happening? Oaklee!"

"Don't worry. It's working! And the Landkeepers will win. It will be just like my parents said: when the mighty oak trees stand again, victory will be ours."

Boaz collapsed. He sighed and chuckled, "You're right! We'll win, and everyone will be safe. Oaklee, I think I did it! I'll go get help."

The reply was silence.

Boaz trembled, "Oaklee?"

There was nothing but darkness. "Oaklee!" Boaz slammed the ground with his fists repeatedly, praying to the Stars for the strength to split the earth to free her.

"Universe, help me! Oaklee!"

Boaz bolted up from his sand raft. He was soaked with sweat as he trembled. He choked back a sob.

I wasn't strong enough.

When he closed his eyes he could still remember her -those bright green eyes, long, curly black hair, skin like sun-kissed sand, and the obnoxious laugh that ended in a series of snorts he promised he would never forget. But with every passing year, memories start turning to fog. He shook his head free of the past, the present was ever-pressing.

I must get to Theyra!

Boaz glided through the sand-covered desert of Theyra on his raft. He was almost there. It had been two days since Aqila dropped him off at home. Those were the most challenging two days of his life. He told them that he had to go. His parents' arms were so warm, full of love and support. He embraced his younger brother and sister. He didn't tell them why, only that he must leave them. Boaz wanted to promise he would be back, but he could not. He would never make a promise that he could not keep. As he parted his lips, the distasteful metallic essence consumed his nostrils. He was close.

Pushing on until the desert turned into rocky terrain, he heard screams. The ground trembled time and again. If he hadn't been a Landkeeper himself, walking would have been impossible. To anyone else, they would have thought that Theyra was about to collapse from the quaking. However, Boaz knew better. The scary thing was this was normal to him. He looked around, and everyone walking by attempting to carry out their daily business seemed numb to the fighting. There were children headed to the schoolhouse, stepping over dead bodies like one would walk over a log in the street. Boaz thought about his siblings, Batu and Bali, going to school and stepping over dead bodies. It sickened him.

He recalled traveling to the Ember border with Sheraga, unable to smell the smoke or blood until he was right up on it. Even now, his nose had grown accustomed to the sight and smell of death. Boaz did not want this for his people any longer.

Up ahead was a grand metal fortress. When he squinted, he could see heavily armored soldiers on the lookout.

He sighed, "Here goes nothing." Boaz walked for nearly an hour. He could have made it faster, but he was thinking about what he would say. As he approached the line, a great divide in the rocky land wedged a mile deep, someone bumped into him. A tall, incredibly stocky man who looked no older than himself.

"Sorry about that, brother. Are you gonna fight? You're gonna need to put something in your hands. The Metallics don't play."

"How long have you been here?"

"Two months straight, my old man didn't come home some months ago. I'm taking every Metallic's head I can until I drop dead."

"Do you have a family?"

"Just my ma and sister now. I'm the man of the house!"

"You should go home, make your house a fortress. Make sure your family is all right. You know, they're going to worry for you. Please, don't leave them alone. If the enemy comes into your home, you can protect the people you love," Boaz advised him.

The young man, who towered over Boaz, thought for a moment, "You're not wrong. I'm Quillon. I haven't seen your face around these parts."

"Yeah, I'm a desert dweller, but I've been traveling a bit. I'm Boaz, by the way."

"Well, Boaz, you're welcome to come to the last mud house on the border between here and the desert if you need something. We'll fix you some food -that classic Landkeeper hospitality."

"Thank you, I'm honored."

Quillon nodded. Sincere appreciation was evident in his hunter-green eyes, "Boaz, take care. It can get bloody around here."

"I'll keep that in mind," Boaz called out. Boaz pushed through the crowd of shouting Landkeepers, curious to see what all the commotion was about. His shoulders banged against strangers. No one seemed to care about the physical contact. Their eyes were all focused forward.

The sharp scent of metal grew stronger with every step. The rancid smell offended Boaz's nostrils as he stifled a gag. Once he got near the front of the crowd, he saw Landkeepers ushering masses of rock against mounds of metal. Violent thuds against reverberating metal made Boaz's ears ring.

"This is it," he whispered.

The building ahead of him was a housing compound. It could easily house a thousand people. The metallic structure gleaming under the midday sun was blinding. He shaded his eyes with his hands, slowly allowing his sage green eyes to adjust. The building had several tiers and towers. Each building within the compound boasted towering, sleek walls of polished steel reflecting the light. The architecture was both imposing and elegant, with intricate designs etched into the metal surfaces. The massive gates, wrought from reinforced iron and adorned with complex mechanical locks, marked the entrance to the compound. These gates were flanked by imposing watchtowers, each manned by vigilant guards clad in armor. Their eyes scanned the perimeter with unwavering focus. The air thrummed with a quiet, almost palpable sense of control and authority. Rocks continued to slam against the compound. Suddenly, he heard a whizzing sound. The frontline was knocked to their knees as sheets of metal sliced their shins. The smell of fresh blood angered Boaz. The people in the compound were fighting back.

I have to do something!

Placing his hands on the uneven Earth, Boaz summoned his favorite ability. The moment he felt its presence, he captured it and called it forth straight from the Earth's core. He propelled himself upward into the sky with the fervent heat of lava under his feet. Gasps could be heard from both sides, and the fighting ceased instantaneously. Metal and rock fell to the earth with a clang. As Boaz stood on lava, he motioned a sandstorm to his left and a furry of rocks to his right. His eyes glowed green as he slowly descended to the ground. All eyes were on him.

"My name is Boaz, and I demand a ceasefire!"

"Legend" was being murmured after he called for a ceasefire followed by silence.

Several minutes passed, and murmurs rose again. He heard the clinking of metal; heavy footsteps were behind him. Turning his head, his lips parted at the sight of her. A woman was walking toward him. Her golden-brown skin glowed in the sunlight. Her piercing emerald orbs were emphasized by her malachite eyeshadow. The silver-like armor reflected the rays of the sun. The depth of her voice sent shivers down his spine, "Who are you to demand a ceasefire?"

Boaz turned to face her, "I'm Boaz, and I am a Legend."

The Landkeepers dropped their weapons immediately and kneeled behind him.

He could hear his name being whispered among the masses of people. The woman smirked, "What an interesting turn of events. Boaz, my name is Zuriel. Standing behind me here are the Metalkeepers. Now tell me, why should I listen to you? The last Legend was one of my kind; your people didn't listen to her. Ila was not respected by the Landkeepers. Instead, she was abused. They did not even give her a proper burial after her death. And now we are here; why should I respect you?"

"Because I'm your Legend too."

Zuriel laughed in scorn, "What is this, a joke? How do you intend to be my Legend and theirs? We're enemies, haven't you noticed? You can't be for them and for us. You have to choose a side."

"No, we are all one people. Land, lava, sand, and metal are all Earth."

"Boaz, that's sweet. It really is. But it's merely words. The blaring truth is the results of hundreds of years of trying to coexist have only brought misery to both sides. As the leader of the Metalkeepers, I'm trying to solve the problem. I am trying to give my people a separate state where we can live peacefully. Something that we Metalkeepers have never experienced. But your people don't want us to have anything. They were fine with us being kicked around in the street without food or homes. Deep in their hearts, they wish we were all gone. But after years of abuse, we're showing them we're not going anywhere."

Somewhere, a massive rock was flailed towards Zuriel. She extended her pauldron and caught it before quickly flailing it back. "See, we aren't the same. You should see that now." She turned to walk away.

"Zuriel, stop! Let's talk in private and see if we can find a civil arrangement for both sides," Boaz reasoned.

CHAPTER 2

"Stop? Make me," she turned on her heels, shooting multiple metal bars at him. Boaz covered himself with a rock shield before hurling it toward her. She used a metal beam to divide the rock, and foot swept a metal plate deep into his shins.

Boaz felt pain from the slicing impact, and the dampness of blood soaked his legs. He flipped into the air, kicking a stream of lava, which melted the metal in her hand. It liquified, and Zuriel attacked him with a shape-bending ball of liquid metal. Every time it touched his skin, it burned. She turned the liquid into a sword and attacked. Boaz was not prepared for her sheer strength and fluidity. This range of motion was nothing like the rigid form needed for utilizing rock. His range improved when he used lava, but he was outmatched by Zuriel's sheer speed and fluidity. He did not want to hurt her, but he didn't want to lose either.

They fought ferociously as the Metalkeepers and Landkeepers watched on. Zuriel made a liquid metal hand as her defense. Boaz knew he could trap her when she stepped forward by turning the ground to lava the second she moved. Boaz's plan would have burned her entire leg off if she stepped too quickly. He didn't want to make her his enemy. As he turned his face, there was nothing else to do but brace himself. The right side of his face felt like he had been slapped by the sun. The pain made him fall to his knees. The second he collapsed, she dug metal into his left leg with such force that he heard his bones crunch. He roared, magma meeting his fingertips. Mere seconds of blind rage and power that he knew could swallow her with lava.

However, his resolve was stronger. He was here to heal. That was his purpose. Zuriel hovered over him, "We are done here. Don't return unless you want me to teach you another lesson." Boaz's vision went hazy as he saw Zuriel's metal armor fade away.

Boaz pushed himself to his feet, relying on his right leg for strength. "Zuriel, this is just the beginning. You can't break me. We'll meet again, very soon."

"Typical Landkeepers, stubborn." Zuriel went inside the Metalkeeper compound. Boaz grimaced as he hobbled through the crowd. This time was different. Everyone was moving out of his way, lowering their heads in respect.

The Landkeepers began chanting his name. He continued hobbling through the searing pain. As his left leg began to tingle, he fell to his knees. *I cannot break.*

He pushed himself up. His body weight created more pain on his wounded legs. Boaz hobbled through. His vision began to blur as the crowd of Landkeepers morphed into elusive shadowy figures. Time seemed to slow, and words became distant echoes. His limp grew more unsteady with every step.

When Boaz opened his eyes again, it was nightfall. He was lying in a cot on the floor. Slowly sitting up, the searing pain in his shins was killing him. He looked down to see them wrapped in white cloth. There was a whisper, "He's awake."

Qullion barreled through the doorway, "That was epic! I can't believe that you're a Legend. The Universe is here to even the score!"

"Quillon, stop shouting. Mother is trying to rest." That gentle voice belonged to a young woman of average height with pretty olive eyes and rich brown skin. "Are you okay?"

"Yeah, I'm just kinda confused about where I am," Boaz rubbed the back of his head.

"I was headed home like you said, and I saw you level up on the huge spurt of lava. I heard you try to reason with the maniac lady. None of us have ever fought with Zuriel herself. I saw what she did to you and brought you back here. Boaz the Unbreakable!"

"What happened afterward?" Boaz asked.

"All hell broke loose. That divide where the Landkeepers and Metalkeepers fight, we call that the sunder line. The Metallics made the sunder line to split Theyra from us, and it became a blood bath. All the Landkeepers were fighting in your name! We took down her guards from the watchtowers." Quillon beamed with happiness at the violence.

I wasn't trying to encourage violence.

"I'm sorry, I was trying to prevent that from happening," Boaz shook his head.

"Bo, I respect you for trying to reason with her. But she's heartless! She can't be reasoned with, and she wants this war. Next time, don't hold back on her. She burned you and broke your leg! Next time, sever her head from her body."

The young woman flinched at hearing Quillon's violent words.

"Quillon, I can't just kill her."

Quillon's hunter eyes looked perplexed, "Why not? That solves the problem, right?"

"No, it doesn't! It just emboldens her followers. Besides, we don't want the young growing up believing that the only way to solve a problem is to kill someone," the young woman spoke up.

"Armani, you are not out there, so you don't get it. They took Dad from us," Quillon pressed.

"She's right. Killing Zuriel will only result in a complete killing spree where everyone is fair game. Besides, as I said earlier, I'm their Legend too."

Quillon huffed, "Well, I'm gonna protect my family. If Zuriel or her kind come through these doors, they will meet their end by my hands." He stood up and left.

Boaz sighed. Armani gave him some water in a clay cup and brought him some food. She sat several feet away from him, "He wasn't always like that. He's just beating himself up over what happened to our father and trying to keep it together. L-Like we all are. Thanks for trying to talk to Zuriel."

"I'm not done here. I'm going back tomorrow."

"What? But your legs?"

"I promised myself and those who are important to me that I wouldn't stop until I get a ceasefire."

"How much of this can you take?"

"If I don't try, I'll never find out. I have to keep going."

"Have you ever thought that we deserve this? The Landkeepers, I mean. As a people, we have oppressed them for something that they can't change. Now that anger is in their hearts, it is becoming a part of them."

"Armani, no one deserves this. I have a ten-year-old twin brother and sister who don't deserve this. Those kids who walk to school every day stepping over dead people don't deserve this. You, me, Quillon, we may all have kids one day; They don't deserve to see this. The Metalkeeper kids being kept in a fortress so they won't get killed don't deserve this. Innocent people are suffering. I'm tired of this."

"Why now?"

"What do you mean?"

"You said you're the Legend. Why are you just now showing your face? The people have needed you," she lowered her gaze.

After placing his empty plate and cup on the floor behind him, Boaz sighed and lay on the cot, "I've always known that I was a Legend. How it works is that in every Legend cycle, one Legend has a spiritual connection with the past Legends. In this Legend cycle, that's me. I've known that I was a Legend for as long as I can remember. I could not tell anyone my identity until all the other Legends had realized their destiny. I could not tell anyone who I was until the time was right. I knew immediately when other Legends came into my presence. I couldn't tell them who they were. I would get a sign that they figured out their destiny."

"I've been on this journey for a long time. Recently, I've been watching the other Legends fight for their destiny.

We would help each other, and I always felt guilty because there was a battle in my backyard that I couldn't do anything about. I had to wait to reveal my identity. I have to fix this because it's my destiny. I owe this to the people of Theyra and Ila. I owe this to the other Legends who are fighting for their destiny and the fate of their people. I'm not worthy to walk among them until I do this. So here I am at the ripe age of twenty, trying to stop a war."

Armani ran her hand through her ebony-colored long, slightly wavy hair. "Forgive me for my tone. Boaz, it might not mean much, but I appreciate what you're doing for us. Regardless, I have your back. I'm on your side. I believe in you." She grabbed the plate and cup and turned the light off in the room.

Boaz sighed. It felt like a huge weight lifted from his shoulders to tell someone what was on his mind. There was also a pang of guilt. The person who deserved to know the most, his best friend, was still unaware of his identity as a Legend. He had to survive so he could tell her face-to-face. He was thankful to Quillon and Armani for their kindness. His wounds were healing. He would be better by morning but did not know how much more of Zuriel's wrath he could take.

She was more powerful than he expected her to be. To be completely honest, he wasn't expecting a woman at all. She was incredibly gifted. He would have thought she was a goddess if he didn't know better. Beautiful, talented, and strong. He didn't know what to say to get her to listen. He just needed a ceasefire. Then he could ask about Neptune. He had to ask about Neptune and know what kind of business a Waterbearer had in Theyra.

As the night grew old, Boaz found sleep nearly impossible. Zuriel's words were ringing in his ears. The part that nagged him the most was that she was right. Ila was shunned and despised in her time by all Landkeepers. Her parents orphaned her when they realized her affinity with metal. She had a hard life. If it had not been for an early friendship with Basir, who knows how the Landkeepers would have treated her. He tried to convince her he was their Legend too, but to no avail. What would it take to convince her?

CHAPTER 3

In Kashmala, the night was growing quiet. Aqila looked over the beautiful land she called home. She smiled at the calming views of hilly valleys and dimpled mountains. She sighed and walked back inside, smiling to see her fiance pouring both of them some tea. She sat across from him. There was a simple peace between the couple.

"I think our parents were pleased with how the evening went," Kavi sighed after taking a sip.

"Thank Heavens," Aqila laughed. "It was a spectacular evening. Thank you for working so hard on this."

"*We* worked so hard for this. It felt like old times just being able to spend quality time together."

"Definitely," she whispered while drinking tea. Her mind was slowly becoming immersed in thoughts of Jai, Tiber, and Boaz. She no longer noticed Kavi's voice until he cleared his throat.

"What's on your mind?"

Aqila smirked, "How do you do that?"

"I could feel it. You get contemplative when something's on your mind. And . . . you stop listening to me." He tapped her nose with his finger.

Aqila giggled before knitting her brows, "I'm sorry! I promised that I wouldn't be preoccupied tonight."

"Well, your promise was that you wouldn't be preoccupied during the engagement gala. So, I'm not really sure if this counts in the terms in which you made your promise. Just saying."

She smiled, "Still, that's not why you're here. We're supposed to be spending time together."

Kavi reached across the table and placed his hand over hers, "What's on your mind?"

I never asked him about the wedding.

"Are you really okay with the new wedding date?"

"Yes, I agreed to it before we discussed it with our parents, did I not? We talked about it in full detail, or so

I thought. Is there something wrong with the new date? Something amiss?"

"No, I just started feeling like you didn't want to wait that long."

"Aqila, do you want to wait that long?" Kavi softened his usual firm gaze.

"Do I want to wait another year? No, I really don't. But so much is going on. I'm caught in a web of multiple visions. One thing leads to another and then some. I just wanted us to have some peace together. Then I was talking to Saar, and he made me feel crazy for asking you to wait that long," Aqila slumped in her chair, sighing.

"Why am I not surprised that my crazy brother had something to do with this? Our parents' ideal timeline was that we would marry next month. We both know that it is too soon for us. Is a year too long? I don't know. But trust me, I want what's best for us. In six months, we might say, you know what, let's get married before the month is out. If that happens, fine. We don't want to tell them we want to wait six months and then ask for another six months. That would be disastrous."

"You're right. I've been stressing out a lot lately," Aqila admitted.

"You're not the only one. That's why we need the time. We have been going nonstop. I hope we can have more time like this leading up to the wedding. Now, what was my crazy younger brother saying?"

"Basically, if it was him, he wouldn't want to wait. He wants to jump into his new life with his wife."

"Typical Saar jump first, think later. Let's revisit moving up the wedding date in a few months and see how we feel about it."

"Now, what's stressing you?"

"Hmmm," he hummed.

"You said that I'm not the only one stressing out."

"It's nothing I can't handle," he took another sip of tea.

"Kavi," Aqila placed her hand over his, "that doesn't mean we can't talk about it."

Assured by her touch, Kavi lowered his gaze and sat his cup down. "I've always known that the burden of rulership was heavy. The more I'm involved in the inner workings of things, the more intense it gets."

"I can't think of a more suitable man. I will be with you, supporting you every step of the way."

"I know."

Aqila lovingly gazed into his heather-gray eyes. Just then, there was a knock on the door. Kavi got up to answer it. As it swung open, it was Saar and Haneul.

"Really? Do you two know what time of night it is to come to Aqila's house?"

"Brother, trust I'd rather not be here at this time of night. I know you two needed some time alone, but I'm here in an official capacity as the Wind Guardian."

Haneul followed Saar inside, "I've intercepted some important information, and you're going to want to hear this."

CHAPTER 4

Boaz woke up early before the sun rose. He took the bandages off of his shins. His broken bone had mended and was just slightly sore. All of his wounds were nearly healed. Standing up, he could tolerate the weight on his left leg. He was going back to try to reason with Zuriel. He attempted to leave as quietly as possible.

"You aren't staying for coffee?"

Boaz looked at Armani, who was working on morning refreshments, "I guess I can stay for coffee."

Armani's eyes lit up, complimenting her soft expression. She went to pour Boaz his drink. He sat on the floor rug as she brought him his coffee.

"Thank you."

"You're welcome. If you were looking for Quillon, he already left. He escorts the children to school and then joins the riots."

"I was going to try and reason with Zuriel again," Boaz sighed.

"Be careful. She is a force to be reckoned with. This war has not been easy on either side, and everyone has a reason to be fighting. Please be careful. It would be horrible to lose another Legend prematurely."

"I'm going to fight until I have nothing left. But in the end, it will all be worth it."

"I have a lot of mixed feelings about this, but I know you're going to be on the side of right regardless." Armani admitted.

"Mixed feelings?" He questioned.

"Yeah, people wonder why you just showed up out of nowhere. As well as why you are so intent on reasoning with Zuriel instead of putting her in her place."

"What do they expect? I have to reason with Zuriel because I am her Legend, too. I can't just put her in her place when I don't know what her place is."

"Boaz, *I* get it," Armani whispered. "You don't have to explain yourself to me. Those weren't *my* questions," she gently touched her chest before turning away from him.

Boaz put the cup down and said, "I know, and I'm sorry."

"There's no reason to be sorry. Just keep trying your best, like everyone else out there. I have to help my mother. Take care of yourself," Armani retrieved the cups and placed them in the clay kitchen sink before disappearing into the narrow hallway.

Boaz stood up and sighed, "Alright, day two, here we go." As soon as he stepped outside, he ran as fast as possible to what Quillon called the sunder line. Pinkish-yellow hues danced across the morning sky as the sun appeared across the horizon. His legs carried him quickly. He was fortunate that he was a Landkeeper. Their bones naturally healed quickly. He could feel a tiny pull in his leg muscles, but besides that, it was as if he was never injured the day before.

Upon arriving at the sunder line, he put his hands on his knees and breathed heavily. There was no one else there besides him.

Thank heavens.

Unlike yesterday's palpable tension, the atmosphere was calm, and the Metalkeeper fortress looked quiet. Boaz slowly walked towards the fortress doors after shoving the metal gates open. Before he could knock, Zuriel appeared beside him. Her sudden presence nearly made him jump. He immediately positioned himself into a wide-legged stance.

"I had a feeling you would be back. I guess yesterday wasn't enough," she scoffed. She ignored his body language.

Boaz eased himself into a regular position with his hands at his side. "Zuriel, I just want to talk. I don't want this war and want to do whatever I can to end it. If we could just talk about a ceasefire, I will give you my word to end this war."

"Tell me, Legend, what did the Landkeepers say about negotiating a ceasefire?"

"We are technically all Landkeepers . . . ."

She rolled her eyes, "How about this, those who aren't gifted in metal, what did they say?"

"I haven't talked to them yet-"

"Why? Are you assuming that my kind are the only ones to blame? See, you are no different. Here you are, but we are the problem. That's been the issue since the beginning. Metalkeepers are the problem to the rest of you!"

"Zuriel, I never said that!"

"Not with your tongue, but your actions are clear!"

"I'm not ridiculous! I know it takes a mutual agreement on both sides to have a ceasefire. But I know that they will listen to me. So, I started with you."

"They won't listen to you," Zuriel scoffed, smirking ever so slightly.

"They will! If you lay down your arms first, they will follow suit without hesitation."

She threw her head back, "That's laughable. I wouldn't be a good general if I did something like that. Since you have nothing to say of importance, you must leave."

"This war has been going on for too long, Zuriel. I'm not leaving!"

She sighed, "Then I will have to remove you myself."

Boaz stood firm. Zuriel's gaze bore into Boaz.. He reflected on Aqila's words, *Be careful not to fan the flames of either side unless there is a clear right or wrong.* He didn't want to fight her again, "Alright, I'm leaving, but I won't stop trying to convince you."

Zuriel waved him off as if he was a child. It was irritating that she was so stubborn. When Boaz shifted his gaze upward, he saw multiple people crowding the sunder line. They were all looking at him, disappointed.

What should I do?

As he shuffled through them, they shouted their hate at Zuriel.

She stepped outside, her emerald eyes gleamed with defiance. "Back away from the Metalkeepers compound. Come any closer, and there will be *consequences*."

Several rock layers went hurling towards her from the Landkeepers at the line. Her arms turned in a fluid motion, and she deflected the attack with a metal sheet. Zuriel never flinched. The angry Landkeepers' assault continued. Boaz looked back. Zuriel was holding her own, but was he faithful to his word if he left them attacking her? This was war, yes, but she wasn't fighting them. She actually gave them a fair warning.

He turned around, "Stop, leave her alone. This is unnecessary!"

The Landkeepers ignored Boaz's request, and a violent onslaught of rock and lava made its way to Zuriel's fortress. The rock wasn't a problem to the Metalkeeper, but lava would begin to melt the metal and turn Zuriel's attack aggressive. Boaz tried to push himself through to stop the Landkeepers from attacking her, but they stood as a solid wall.

Boaz had no other choice. Slamming his fist to the ground and curling his fingers resulted in a massive earthquake. It seemed to ripple throughout Theyra. The Landkeepers and even Zuriel were knocked off their feet immediately. Boaz was the only one standing. "I said stop!" Raw power began to surge throughout his body. His discipline was fraying; he struggled to keep his eyes from glowing.

The sounds of his feral yell echoed. Everyone began to gather themselves. "You do this every day and end up in the same place. This is not working! The war is never going to end this way! So stop!"

Boaz took a breath as everyone stood up. He turned to leave. A loud uproar made Boaz turn around. The Landkeepers all turned on him. He was punched in the face multiple times. Rocks and boulders were being hurled at him from every direction. He curled his fingers; the pulse of magma was calling him.

No. These are your people.

He had at least a hundred people trying to attack him at once. Boaz used small rocks to cover his body and provide a shield. If he fought against them, they would forever be their enemy. So, Boaz did not. He allowed them to take all their anger and hatred out on him as he kept himself shielded. The Landkeepers split the earth in front of the Metalkeeper's compound. He was shoved into the deep dividing line, and the Landkeepers squeezed the divide together.

You must be joking!

It was bone-crushing pressure. Boaz's head felt like it was going to split. He let the little rocks fall away from his body so he could concentrate on not getting squeezed to death. He pushed against them, resulting in a stalemate. His face was turned upward, hands pressed against both sides of the rock. He saw multiple metal sheets being leveled toward the Landkeepers. Their shouts and screams were ringing in Boaz's ears. The distraction bought him time to escape the depths of the divide. He panted as he climbed upward back to level ground. His vision was beginning to blur due to the swelling in his face, and the smell of blood tickled his nose.

Zuriel and three more Metalkeepers were attacking the Landkeeper group. Boaz crawled low to avoid the rock, lava, and metal mass fury. He had not crawled out for too long before he was dragged back by his ankle in a metal cuff, right to Zuriel's feet.

"Looking quite pitiful, Boaz. Can't you see they are too far gone, Legend? I thought you said they would listen to you."

Boaz was angry. He breathed lava from his mouth, causing Zuriel to jump back. Angrily, she tossed him past the Landkeeper's riot and into a building.

Eyes fluttering, Boaz went to sit up, only to realize he could not. He reached his hand up to his face. His lips were bruised, sore, and split. His ribs were tender to the touch. He silently prayed that nothing was broken this time. His left eye was so swollen that it was difficult to keep it open. The swelling made his vision blurry, and he could feel a dull throbbing pain around it.

Whenever he closed his eyes to rest, memories of those striking, bright green eyes flooded back. He could also hear that obnoxious laugh as her words echoed through his soul, "It will be just like my parents said: when the mighty oak trees stand again, victory will be ours."

I have to be strong enough. Oaklee, I wish you were here right now.

"Boaz! You okay, man?"

His eyes fluttered open. "I'm alive. I guess that's what counts," Boaz could tell by the voice that it was Quillon again.

Having noticed that Boaz was not strong enough to sit up, he pulled him into a sitting position. "I didn't see everything, but what I did see was shocking and confusing. You defended Zuriel?"

"If I'm creating moral conflict for you, just leave me here. And don't bother to help me. I'm fine, really I am."

Quillon hung his head, "You're the Legend. I didn't mean any disrespect. I'm just confused, seeing you crawling out of the sunder line and getting tossed by Zuriel after having just defended her."

"I tried to talk to her. She was listening up to a point. Things got hostile when she told me to leave, and then I decided not to fight her because the Landkeepers had been fighting for years with the same result. Once I left, they started attacking her, and she wasn't doing anything. I told them to stop and reminded them that fighting Zuriel has gotten them nowhere. That's when the Landkeepers turned on me. They beat me up. Zuriel just saw it as her point proven."

"Why didn't you fight them back? Like, for real? Using all of your gifts!"

Boaz sighed, "Because I know that fighting like this will not solve anything. We are the same people! At the end of the day, it's all earth and land. People are dying because we can't seem to work together in peace. I understand Zuriel is trying to avenge the past. The Landkeepers don't like it. I get it. We are slow and stubborn to change. I'm trying to figure out who is the clear right and wrong. At first glance, it would seem like the Landkeepers are fighting because we hate metal. It just can't be as one-dimensional as land versus metal."

Quillon helped Boaz to his feet and supported his weight as the pair traveled back to his home.

"It is not one-dimensional. The Landkeepers do want the Metalkeepers to leave. But this started with resources. We dislike the Metalkeepeers because they don't have our work ethic. They can't handle the tasks needed to keep our land running, especially after the war with the Windmasters. It was all hands on deck. Food and resources are divided among those who work. The Metalkeepers are not as physically strong as us, so they couldn't acquire the same amount of resources as Landkeepers. This created division. Then we started arguing. Now, with Zuriel at the helm, the Metalkeepers leveled up and fought back. They decided they wanted their state and took the most mineral-rich area. We can barely supply enough minerals for trade, pushing us into Kindle. The Kindlers are mad because they already have the smallest territory. It's just a mess. We aren't going to let Zuriel and her agenda destroy us."

"How is she planning to destroy us?"

"Simple! We are forced out if we don't have access to the most mineral-rich area. The only other pockets are near the border of Ember and Kindle. Ember doesn't have enough to sustain us, and Kindle thinks we are trying to take their land. There's nowhere else for us to go."

"Well, I'm going to think about things for a while, and I am going back tomorrow," Boaz replied.

"Let's get you mended up. Your clothes are all tattered. I have something you can wear at home. Then we need to get some cool water on your face.I have great respect for you, Boaz. No one else has been brave enough to speak to Zuriel like that."

Boaz's head dropped, and Quillon practically dragged him. He could see what Boaz was trying to do, keep Theyra from an all-out blood bath. But things may already be too far gone for that. Either way, Legends are gifts from the Universe, and everyone living in Theyra needs all the gifts they can get.

"Thanks," Boaz groaned. He dug his heels into the ground and forced his legs to carry his weight."

"Man, you gotta rest up. You're looking rough."

"I'll be okay. I appreciate you."

"You're always welcome in my home."

Boaz nodded, pressing forward in the opposite direction, dragging himself through Theyra. Not wanting to draw any unnecessary attention. He heard someone call his name but refused to be confronted by another hostile Landkeeper. This time, if someone wanted a fight, he would give them one.

A hand touched his shoulder, and he nearly snapped. Locking the person's wrist, he twisted them and grabbed them by the throat. Only when he recognized the face did he release them, "I'm sorry," he groaned.

"What happened to you?"

"Everything and nothing all at once. What are you doing here, Tiber?"

The Waterbearer Legend looked concerned for Boaz's well-being, "Never mind that! You want me to make you some ice compresses?"

"No, I'm not hurt too bad, despite how it looks. This will be gone by tomorrow. So, what are you doing here exactly?"

"Oh, I just came from the Metalkeeper compound," Tiber shrugged her shoulders.

Boaz stopped in his tracks, "You went where?"

"The Metalkeeper compound. I got some intel from Zuriel. We may be able-"

"How the hell did you manage that?!"

Tiber stepped back, her eyes wide, "I acted like nothing changed. I've gone to the compound several times on Neptune's orders."

"There's a desert village a few miles east. Meet me in about an hour. We don't want to be out here talking about important stuff... you know Legend stuff," he whispered.

Tiber nodded and quickly left his side. Boaz sighed in relief. Things were spiraling out of hand, but if Tiber could help him negotiate with Zuriel, that would be helpful. He needed to gather three governing heads of the Landkeepers. Things might start looking up if he could get them to agree to a ceasefire.

Boaz welcomed the sandy heat that radiated through his sandals as he walked towards the village. He hadn't been to a desert village in years. Most of the Landkeepers in villages like this were called Exotics. They used sand as their element. The people were some of the most beautiful people he'd ever seen. The men and women had the most beautiful jade-green eyes. The Exotics didn't fight in the war. They were peaceful people. But everyone in Theyra knew better than to take their kindness for weakness. They were known to swallow people into the sand, killing them in a matter of minutes.

This would be the best place if he wanted to talk to Tiber privately. As Boaz approached the sandy meeting spot, Tiber had beaten him there. "How did you get here so fast?"

"Come on now, you walked. I've got a panther," Tiber gave Boaz a smug smile. Tiber had set up a tent already. The sleek, long tail of her panther gently waved in the air.

"Okay, what's your intel?"

"Well, I did a small mission for Aqila and Kavi today. I gave Zuriel a new formula to produce that tranquilizer. Kavi made some adjustments that negated the poison," Tiber explained.

"So, basically, it doesn't work anymore?"

"Exactly, and it will only tranquilize an animal for a few minutes. I told Zuriel that the new formula is what Neptune wants to produce now and to dispose of the old formula. She did exactly that, I watched her, and the Metalkeepers began producing the new formula."

"Could you ask her to rethink meeting with me?"

"Okay...," Tiber seemed hesitant. She formed water into ice and wrapped it in a cloth.

"What's wrong?"

"Nothing's wrong, but what do you plan to do afterward?"

He grimaced as she iced his face, "Meet with the three governing heads. All we need is for both sides to agree to a ceasefire."

"Once there's a ceasefire, we may be able to find out Neptune's identity!" Tiber's blue eyes widened.

"Exactly! Let's meet here tomorrow around this time. I'll let you know how things go with the governors, and you'll fill me in on Zuriel."

"Sounds like a plan," Tiber beamed with excitement.

Boaz was confident that a ceasefire was achievable with Tiber's help. His wounds were improving, thanks to the ice. He made his way to Quillon's house.

CHAPTER 5

Aqila and Haneul were hovering over the forest of Lower Ember.

"Are you sure you want to go in without me?" Haneul asked, his tan hand loosening its grip on the reins of his dasher.

"Yes, I know them. Besides, they are not going to want to discuss things with you. It's better this way, trust me." Aqila landed Talon and walked him over to the thickest part of the forest. "Stay hidden here, but call out if something happens," Aqila commanded. She ran to the well-camouflaged cabin and knocked on the door. She waited several minutes, and no one answered. She pressed her ear to the door. Everything was silent.

Could they all be out doing missions? I thought they always left a few people at the cabin.

Aqila quietly sighed. Before she could turn around, someone covered her mouth from behind. She elbowed them in the side. When they crouched in pain, she hit them with a sidekick. When she looked, it was Arrow. He quickly pulled her into the brush of the forest, dragging her by her foot. "Be quiet and stay down," he told her as she lay awkwardly.

Several minutes later, Aqila heard footsteps approaching the cabin. Arrow was peering in between the leaves of the brush. His arm flexed quietly as he readied his bow and shot a single arrow. A groan was heard, followed by the soft thud of a body hitting the dirt. Arrow made signals with his fingers. The rest of the Flamethrowers emerged from the bushes. Arrow helped Aqila to her feet.

"Suvan, take this body to the old hideout and leave it there," Arrow instructed.

"What's going on?" Aqila asked as she brushed the dirt from her clothes.

"I really don't know. The past couple of days, we've been experiencing ambushes in the morning and afternoon. They are Agni's soldiers, and we've had to kill them to ensure they don't take any information back."

"That's insane. How do they even know about the location? Arrow, where's Jai?"

"I don't know. He left with Arin a few days ago. Actually, it's been close to a week. I wasn't concerned for the first few days, but afterward, I sent Dysis to look for them, but she found nothing. I intended to send a search team, but then we started getting ambushed. I had already told Dysis to search for them again. But now she can't come back. We can't afford anyone tailing her."

"Something's going on with Jai. We were going to visit the Waterbearer tribes, and he lied about having something to do. Can you ask around about it?"

"If someone had any information on Jai, they would have told me already. Can't you have a vision?"

Aqila lowered her head. "I've tried, but recently, I can't have visions related to the Legends anymore."

"I'll ask around in good faith," Arrow agreed.

"Arrow, can I talk to Alena and Zay?"

"I don't see why not. They're over there," he said, pointing near the cabin's entrance. Aqila made her way over. The moment she came into view, Zay and Alena stopped talking.

"I hope I'm not interrupting anything," Aqila slightly bowed her head in respect.

"Of course not. Did you want to speak to us," Alena questioned. Her gaze softened at Aqila.

"I did. Do either of you know where Jai and Arin could be?"

"You do know Arrow already asked us about it," Zay huffed, folding his arms.

"I am aware that he asked, but I'm asking about possibilities. Are there any places that they could have gone? Were they talking about someplace specific? Maybe someone that they wanted to see?"

"Wait up, aren't you a Seer? How come you can't just ask the stars?" Zay was clearly irritated.

"Zay, stop," Alena hissed at him. "Jai and Arin were talking about something before they left. I didn't ask about it, though. I left Arin behind when we were looking for Zay, and she was still mad at me about it."

"I can't think of any place Jai would want to go. But there are people that he may have wanted to see. The only one that I know for sure is still alive is Arka, his guardian.

Others are just wild guesses, but it could be the reason for this wild duck chase."

"Give me the wild guesses," Aqila replied.

"Well, when Jai was young, he was separated from his family, and then he got amnesia around the time Arka found him. Jai may be looking for his parents. He had mentioned several times that his memory was improving and had vague memories of his early years before Arka."

"I'm not sure where Jai is originally from," Aqila sighed.

Zay tilted his head, "We grew up together in Lower Ember. However, he could be from Kindle. His eyes were normally light brown, like a sandy color. Only recently did they change to gold."

"Upper Ember is a good place to check, too. A lot of Kindlers settled there due to the overpopulation in Kindle," Alena chimed.

"Thank you, this has been a great help," Aqila returned to Talon. Her footsteps were ungraceful as she tried not to trip in the thick forest brush. As soon as she mounted Talon, they took flight. The owl's silent wing flaps propelled them into the sky at an incredible speed. Aqila spotted Haneul, "We're going to have to split up."

"They didn't have a location?"

"No, they had two possible areas, Upper Ember and Kindle."

"Let's just hit both of them together really quick. I don't like the idea of separating, especially since no one has heard from them," Haneul cautioned.

"You're right," Aqila sighed. She prayed to the Universe that they would locate Jai soon. They could not afford anything to happen to him. They still needed to find the Landkeeper Legend and prevent a worldwide war.

"Agni is concentrating his efforts on the Flamethrowers. That's the last thing I overheard from Neptune. The two of them met after that whole Tiber situation."

"Anything else?" Her question was laced with desperation.

"No, I haven't delivered enough Windmasters to convince him that there's a revolt. He doesn't trust me . . . yet."

"I hope everything is going well for Tiber and swapping those formulas. Neptune and Agni won't know something is wrong with them until it's too late. Should we go to Kindle or Upper Ember first?"

"Let's go to Kindle first, then Upper Ember; that way, we won't be far from the Flamethrowers in case we need to update them with our findings."

Aqila agreed as the pair hurried to Kindle. "What did you think about Saar's news?"

She reflected on Saar and Haneul visiting her home.

****

"I'm here because I've intercepted some important information. You're going to want to hear this."

Kavi pinched the bridge of his nose, "Well, don't waste time, elaborate."

"Sheraga just sent Pyre to deliver a message. Agni has made an attack on Pyroc's borders near a civilian city. Sheraga's preparing for war. He's asking for the Windmasters to pledge support. He wants an alliance. In the event that Kashmala and or Wyndhm are attacked by Agni, Sheraga has pledged to send reinforcements."

Kavi rolled his shoulders back slowly as he straightened his posture. "I'm assuming Sheraga would like some of our resources in exchange for military support if needed. I guess this is where you tell me, as the Wind Guardian, if we will need the support?"

Saar groaned, "I think we can hold our own."

Haneul shook his head. "Kavi, you should take it. Agni is involved with Neptune. We are still unsure as to how much support Neptune has. He has an alliance in Theyra. I think we should pair with Pyroc on this. Their military is the most powerful in the world."

"Do you have any idea how difficult that would be to get past my parents and the entire governing class?"

Aqila interjected "Kavi, after what Tiber and Nahal did to me in Avala. We should not ignore Sheraga's request. I know I'm unfamiliar with how the Capitol does things; it's just a suggestion."

"Don't misunderstand my intentions, love. I have every intention of supporting Pyroc, but we need to set the terms. I'll run everything by my father. However, my first order of business is to ensure that my tranquilizer can never be used as a weapon again."

Saar rolled his eyes, "That's lovely. Did you forget the part that Pyre is here? Sheraga's top general! What will I tell him?"

Kavi smiled, "Tell him that I'm interested in Sheraga's proposition. So much so that I want to hear more of it . . . in person."

***

"I think we should be preparing for war," Haneul sighed.

"The Windmasters aren't going to agree with that. Helping with supplies is one thing, but going to war is not something I see them on board with." Aqila replied.

"It doesn't matter. The moment we start helping Pyroc with supplies, we've taken a position. That automatically means we're in the war too. Is that what I want? No, that's why everything is hanging in the balance of what we do right now. Switching the formulas must be successful, and finding Jai so he can try to mediate this situation."

"I'm wondering if this move with Jai is exactly what Agni and Neptune want us to do," Aqila pondered.

"What's the worst-case scenario?"

"Worst case is that Jai and Arin got caught by Agni and are using active threats of war with Pyroc to lure the rest of the Legends out. The last thing Jai told me about Agni is that he wants to kill all of the Legends. What if this is his way of luring us out?"

"Even so, if he has Jai, we must try to free him. But, since you mentioned that angle, let's meet up with Tora while we are in Kindle. Besides, only a select few people know that you are a Legend that helps."

"Yeah, but being a Seer is not exactly a useful job for Agni and Neptune either," Aqila replied.

"No, but we are here together. Unity counts for something."

"You're right. Now, let's see if we can make it before sundown."

"At top speed, we can," Haneul wiggled his eyebrows.

"Go ahead and brag! At Talon's top speed, we should be able to make it with a few minutes to spare."

"Then what are you waiting for? Let's stop all of this chit-chat and hurry it up already!" Haneul and Vermilion dove at top speed, leaving Talon and Aqila behind.

CHAPTER 6

She shook her head before mumbling, "Show off." Talon flew as quickly as possible to stay within sight of Haneul. Aqila was in her head. Swapping the formulas was a big deal for their cause. Haneul has been investigating Neptune. A task that has yielded fascinating and perplexing results. The Flamethrowers are trying to rebuild and deal with Agni. Although that has been an ongoing battle, knowing that Cahya will have their back was comforting. The defective formula ensures a Pyrocean win if Agni does make good on his threats towards them. The Waterbearer tribes were working together, on alert for Neptune, but they had not seen him. Surprisingly, it did not seem like Neptune had as many Waterbearer followers as they had initially thought.

It felt as if a significant piece of the puzzle was missing. The why. Why is Neptune terrorizing the Waterbearers? Why is he working with Agni, a Fireheart, his natural rival? What are they working on? Do they share the same agenda? Why didn't he kill Tiber when he had the chance? If it is the Legends they are after, why let one slip out of your grasp? Aqila was near her wit's end. It was almost as if nothing was making sense anymore.

She took several deep breaths to refocus on what she could do: look for Jai. The predecessors taught them that they could not make progress divided, and they lived and died to prove that. Every Legend is needed. She had to find Jai or die trying.

After several hours of flying, Aqila landed Talon beside Vermilion.

"For riding an owl, you didn't make bad time," Haneul smirked. Aqila snatched him back by his long gray braid. "Okay, I was just joking!"

Aqila laughed, "I know, now let's talk to Tora. We're not far." The pair ran on foot until they reached his residence. Stepping carefully over the hot stones, Haneul knocked on the door.

A couple minutes passed before the hazel-eyed leader opened the door, "Who are you?"

Aqila slammed the door open and rushed inside, dragging Haneul behind her, "Sorry, no time for introductions!" Once inside, Aqila slammed the door behind her with a wind blast, "This is urgent!"

"Okay, well, since you're taking over my house, did you want me to sit down too?" Tora asked sarcastically.

Aqila gazed at him with piercing silver eyes, "Have you seen Jai?"

Tora sat on his couch and rested his right foot on his left knee, "No, but you're not the first person to ask me about him. What's going on?"

"He's missing," Aqila explained. "No one has been able to contact him. And Arin is with him, too."

Aqila felt her mind's eye calling to her. She heard Tora talking but could no longer understand what he was saying. Her consciousness was swept away as she stood. A scene played out before her. It was here, in this desert land of Kindle. Two young men growing up, division had settled in their hearts. One man would fall to the lightning of another. The scene kept repeating with two different young men each time. The faces were slightly blurry, but the eyes were always clear. The last two men bore a close resemblance to Tora and Jai. The eye color was different, but the expressions mirrored almost perfectly. Who were they?

"Aqila!"

She shook her head at the sound of her name, ushered back to reality at the sound of Haneul's voice.

Tora rolled his eyes, "I am not repeating myself."

Aqila could not stop staring at Tora, making him uneasy. She took several steps towards him.

"What Storm? I hope you don't think I had anything to do with this?"

"What's your father's name?"

Tora's hazel eyes widened in disbelief, "Roshan. What does that have to do with anything?"

"Do you have any uncles?"

"Yes, but I don't really remember him. I haven't seen him in at least fifteen years. I had overheard that my father and uncle had a strained relationship. Wait! Why am I telling you this? What does my family have to do with anything? You do know that my parents are deceased, right?"

"Yeah, I know that. I just had a vision. It was about a long-time rift between two men, one of whom looked like you."

"Well, I can't help you there. I don't have a long-time rift with anyone per se. I mean, the Landkeepers waltzing in my territory is a problem. Upper Ember can be a problem, but that's not an individual person. Anyway, I was telling your friend while you were mind traveling that a man came to me yesterday asking if I had seen Jai. I told him no and asked what I could do to help. He just said, 'He needs my help.' That was it. He left. He didn't leave a name or anything. I didn't take him seriously, though. Until now, that is."

"What's up with you and Sheraga not taking things seriously?!"

"Forgive me, mighty Seer! I shall grovel at your feet and beg for forgiveness! I wish the Universe told me you'd be paying me a visit. Still, the stars denied me," Tora said sarcastically as he exaggerated a bow to Aqila.

"Let's go," she whispered to Haneul.

Tora stood and grabbed Aqila's arm gently.

"Aqila, if I hear anything, I'll send for you immediately. You have my word," Tora vowed.

"Thanks, we appreciate it," Haneul waved as the pair left.

They walked in silence, both preoccupied with their own thoughts. Every now and again, their shoulders would bump into each other. They arrived at their respective dashers. As Aqila mounted, she groaned, "I didn't ask Tora what the man looked like!"

"Don't worry. He's in his fifties, tall, with black hair beginning to gray. He was in excellent shape physically. His eyes were brown, but I'm not sure what shade. That's all that Tora noticed. See, I had your back."

"Thanks, that vision really threw me off a bit. Why did we leave? It's past sundown. You want to stay at Tora's for the night?"

"Whatever you want to do, we could always sleep on our dashers."

"Let's go to Tora's just in case I have another vision," Aqila considered.

"That works. You go ahead while I tie the dashers down for the night," Haneul replied.

Aqila took her time walking back. She was still turning those images over and over in her head, asking herself what they could mean. She had an intuitive feeling that it was related to Jai somehow, but she didn't know how. All throughout the evening, Aqila wasn't herself. Was another vision coming? She felt like something was on the horizon. Hours passed, and she could not shake the feeling.

For the restless Aqila, night came quickly. Tora was sleeping in his room. Haneul was downstairs on the couch, and Aqila was in the guest bedroom. She couldn't sleep. Her body was dead tired, but her mind was running a marathon. This sensation was not new to her. She immediately thought of Zeroun. He would tell her to focus on her breath control. Ten-second inhales, followed by a ten-second exhale. Aqila took deep breaths, and her mind was beginning to clear. She was growing more and more tired. She felt the sensation, not of sleep, but of sight, banging behind her eye sockets. Upon closing her eyes, her physical body stilled as her mind's eye began to travel.

CHAPTER 7

Boaz touched his face as he woke up in Quillon's home.

The day before, he mentioned to Quillon that he would like to meet the governors to discuss the situation with Zuriel. Quillon told Boaz that was an easy task. He wasn't quite sure what he meant by that. Nevertheless, he was determined to have an audience with the governors.

I have to think of something to say.

Moments like this made him miss Aqila. She always knew what to say. She had this innate charm when she spoke. The words danced to the sound of her voice, urging people to listen. Unfortunately for him, the years they had spent together still did not allow the gift to rub off on him.

He prayed that Tiber would be able to convince Zuriel, whereas he was not. While walking in the hallway, Boaz heard voices in the kitchen area. Treading carefully, he intended to walk by without drawing too much attention to himself.

"Boaz! Everyone's waiting for you," Quillon shouted to him.

"Me," he raised a long, thick eyebrow. Upon turning his head, Boaz's mouth went agape. The governors were sitting there but did not appear pleased to see him. Boaz noticed that there were only two of them.

Armani was working feverishly, trying to serve breakfast to everyone. "Boaz, please take a seat with the rest of them."

Honoring her request, Boaz sat on the rug a short distance from Quillon and the two governors. Armani hurried to serve the food. Boaz could tell that she seemed uneasy, and she hastily served plates. He was shocked to see such an elaborate breakfast consisting of fish filets and rice with eggs and vegetable bits. Breakfast? This was a fancy dinner meal for Boaz. No one spoke as Armani poured the juice and hurried away.

As soon as she was out of sight, the older governor began to speak, "It is an honor to be in your presence, Legend. Quillon suggested we meet with you and discuss our outlook on the situation with the Metalkeepers."

Quillon wasn't joking when he said getting the governors together would be easy.

"Yes, thank you. I have been trying to obtain an audience with Zuriel about the situation. She has been somewhat difficult but realizes things cannot continue like this forever."

The middle-aged governor asked, "Why are you still trying to convince that woman? Do you not think that we have already tried to reason with her? She's unreasonable. Zuriel wants this war, and she has brainwashed her kind into following her. There is nothing that can change her mind. No words, at least. Zuriel is bloodthirsty and violent. She only understands violence. What we need is a Legend who is ready to help us topple her."

The older governor's gently pale green eyes looked disturbed, "Boaz, we are here, echoing the people's voice. We are tired of the Metalkeeper's occupation of our land and resources. Why are you being so lenient with her?"

The other governor slammed his hand on the rug, "If you don't start dealing with that woman as the threat to humanity that she is, the people will no longer support you!"

"Governors, please! Let's hear the Legend out. We should not disrespect him," Quillon supported Boaz.

"I am not being lenient with anyone. I understand the situation at hand more than you know. I understand what you want, but I realize that the way you want it will not solve your problem. You say Zuriel is a threat, but she is also the pulse of Metalkeepers. She has manifested what is in their heart. Killing her will only strengthen them, and more Zuriels will be born from the turmoil. Don't you see that? Zuriel is a product of the injustice that war produced. The only way to reason with the Metalkeepers is to reason with her. We've been fighting for a long time, and nothing has changed. What do you have to lose by doing something different?"

The middle-aged governor's bright green eyes were filled with fury. "Do you believe what we are hearing? He is saying that this is our fault!"

"I want to be perfectly clear: that is not what I said."

"He practically said it!" He stood and stormed out of Quillon's home.

The pale-eyed governor shook his head. Quillon helped him up, "Well, that's my cue to leave. Boaz, I heard you clearly. But what you are asking of us is nearly impossible. Both sides have suffered greatly. Many of us have lost families and friends. The Landkeepers will hear your voice but won't accept your words. I wish you good luck. We, too, are like Zuriel, unable to change what's in our hearts. Magnar's heart is in pain. His son was killed fighting the Metalkeepers. That was his only child. He heard your words as they burned his heart. My voice is not enough to sway the people. They won't change, but I will support your endeavors. I must go now. Good day, sons."

Quillon and Boaz watched as the elderly governor left the house. "Thanks, Quillon."

"I need to leave. Take care of yourself, Boaz," Quillon never looked at Boaz as he followed the governors.

Boaz sighed in frustration and began stacking the plates. No one really had an opportunity to eat. He felt terrible that Armani worked so hard and no one ate her food. Boaz took Quillon and the governor's plates to the small counter before returning to eat himself. He decided that after today, he would not be returning here. He clearly saw that he was asking too much from Quillon's family and didn't want to bring them more hardships than he already had.

Armani walked into the kitchen, "I was expecting it to take longer than that. They didn't even eat!"

"That's my fault. They disagreed with me, and Magnar was so furious that he left."

"What about the elder Othniel?"

"He understood, but he says that the Landkeepers will neither agree nor support me. He wished me luck."

"Well, that was not a complete loss?" Hope twinkled in her olive eyes.

"I'm supposed to meet with Zuriel again, and I failed. Zuriel was right about the Landkeepers not listening to me. I am truly sorry for any hardship I have caused you and your family. This is the last time that I'll be here. I promise."

"Why? Have we made you uncomfortable?"

"No, not at all! But I can see how hard this is on Quillon. He wants Zuriel dead, like many other Landkeepers, and I'm not delivering that. And I will not deliver that. This is hard on him. I appreciate everything your family has done to help me, and I will not inflict injustice. It is not just for you to help me when I am not helping you."

"Quillon's not upset with you. Our father was a governor - the last governor. His death has been difficult for us. Our mother is grieving herself to death."

"I am so sorry," he whispered.

"She is losing the will to live in this world without him. Quillon is just beating himself up. Father always told him to take care of the family if anything happened to him."

"If there's anything I can do-"

"Yes, do what the Universe wants," She sat beside him. "You have been blessed. You are our gift. Boaz, this change is meant for us. Change is the opposite of our strengths: stability, consistency, and endurance. Land and Earth will only yield to a mighty force or constant pressure. Don't stop fighting for us. Please, don't give up on us." Tears slowly streamed down her face.

His heart hurt seeing her like this. Boaz wiped every tear that fell from her beautiful eyes. She cried, and he embraced her. He thought about his family and what life would be like for Batu and Bali without their parents. He gently pats Armani's sleek black hair, "I will never give up on you."

She sat up, wiping her eyes with her sleeves, "Thank you, Boaz. Please feel free to come back. You're welcome here."

Boaz stood to leave, "Thank you. Armani-"

"Yes?"

"Your food was good," he smiled. Although her eyes were red from crying, she smiled. Their eyes lingered on each other as if this was goodbye. Vibrant olive met soothing sage for several moments before they drifted apart. Afraid to say too much, Boaz turned to leave, and reluctantly Armani let him go.

Boaz set up his sand raft and proceeded to the agreed-upon meeting place. He took his time going to meet Tiber. His mind was swirling with thoughts. He reflected on Aqila's words. He was trying not to fan the flames of either side. He was trying to see who was clearly in the wrong. The blame could not be pointed solely to one side. He saw Tiber in the distance and went to greet her.

"Why do you look so down?"

Boaz groaned, "Do you have good news or bad news?"

"Good for the most part."

"Then please go ahead and start," Boaz plopped down on his sand raft.

"Well, I told Zuriel that Neptune heard rumors about the Landkeeper Legend coming to visit her, and he wanted an update. Zuriel could not answer any questions, so I suggested that she may want to learn more about why the Legend was visiting her, especially if Neptune has more questions in the future. Initially, she seemed hesitant, then agreed to investigate the issue further."

"That's good news. I appreciate all you've done. I'm just furious that I'm not holding up my end."

"Sounds like the meeting with the governors didn't go too well," Tiber's navy eyes wandered.

"The conversation didn't go anywhere. Actually, there are only two governors. The third is deceased due to war violence. One governor was so infuriated by my perspective that he cut the meeting short. The elder said he would support my efforts, but not much could be done to change the Landkeepers' minds."

"At least you have the opportunity to have a real conversation with Zuriel."

"Yes, that's a positive. But I don't know how far that will get me now."

"Go as far as it will take you; Maybe you'll have another idea along the way."

"You're right. Well, what's next for you?"

"I'll be here for a while until Aqila sends another message. Once I hear from her, I'll leave. She mentioned having important business with Jai."

Boaz was surprised by Tiber's comment, "She's been in touch with him?"

"She didn't say, so I'm not sure."

"I hope things are okay - I meant going well for them."

"You know what would be awesome? If the Landkeeper Legend just came in and sorted all this mess out! Wouldn't that be great? There's only one more to be discovered now, so it's definitely not a far-fetched idea. The Legend would probably know exactly what to do about everything." She had the same expression that Armani had towards him, hope.

Boaz watched Tiber get excited about the Landkeeper Legend. " It would be great if the Legend had the answers. Legends are just people you know. Yes, they are very powerful people, but they must learn and grow like everyone else. And there's also the possibility that they may not know they're a Legend yet."

"Well, you do have a point there," Tiber reflected. "You've got this! Look at it like this, you've already been beaten up by everyone, so you're familiar with what they have in their arsenal. You won't be surprised by anything."

Boaz wasn't entirely sure how she arrived at that conclusion, but he decided to let it go. "I have nothing to lose by trying. You want to meet later so I can tell you how things went?"

"Sure! You know I'm set up near the Exotics, and there's plenty of room if you need a place to stay. The best part is they have this music and dance thing they do when the sun sets! It's really-"

"Thanks, but I have a place to stay for a couple of nights."

Tiber shrugged, "No problem, now go on! I wouldn't keep Zuriel waiting."

"I'm going! You take care of yourself while I'm gone," Boaz smiled at the Waterbearer before boarding his sand raft. He was a little frustrated that even Tiber, a Legend herself, believed he should have the answer to this problem. Boaz hurried to the Metalkeeper compound to talk to Zuriel, praying that not too many people would be present. He was tired of the constant barrage of insults and expectations thrust upon him. If everyone has an answer, why aren't they doing anything other than fighting and killing each other?

He took a breath and calmed his nerves. He didn't want to go into the situation angry. Boaz went back to Quillon's house to get his sand raft. He rode through the sandy desert for almost an hour before the terrain naturally began to change to a consistent grassy mass with rich soil and multiple rocks. Leaving his raft, he headed to the sunder line, once again to deal with the mighty commander herself, Zuriel.

CHAPTER 8

Unfortunately, there was already a crowd. Zuriel and several other Metalkeepers were expertly handling themselves. Rock clashed with metal. The sounds of hate-filled screams rang through his ears as Boaz made his way closer to the compound.

He briefly caught Zuriel's attention. Her emerald eyes flashed with an annoyed expression. She ordered her soldiers back. She liquified a metal sheet from her compound's gate. She surrounded every Landkeeper on the sunder line and solidified the metal within seconds. The Landkeepers were completely encased. Their screams just echoed against the clanging of the metal.

Boaz was furious! He stormed towards her.

"Relax, Legend, did you really think they would just allow you to come here without trying to maul you? We would hate to have a repeat of last time, wouldn't we?" Her tone oozed mockery as she motioned for him to follow her.

He took a deep breath and followed her and the soldiers inside the Metalkeeper compound. The smell almost brought Boaz to his knees. The air tasted metallic. It was disgusting. Struggling to compose himself, he gulped air, trying not to gag. Inside the compound was a massive assembly line. Several things were being made. There was an assembly line for weapons, pots, and pans, the metal shields on their uniforms, and it seemed like many other things were being produced. Hundreds of people were working on the parts of the assembly. The Metalkeepers were laser-focused. The loud clanging of parts in constant movement echoes throughout the compound.

"Who came up with all of this?"

Zuriel motioned for the soldiers to leave them alone once they passed the assembly lines, "I did."

Boaz was taken aback. He was surprised by Zuriel's response but was in awe over the living facility he was looking at. It was likened to a mansion made of metal. He followed Zuriel inside. There was so much activity that Boaz had to run to keep from being separated from her.

Do all of the Metalkeepers live here?

He stayed on his toes, never letting her back go from his sight. She stopped at the door and waited for him to catch up. Boaz bumped shoulders with someone. A sweet floral scent imprinted in his nostrils. His attention immediately turned; it was a young woman. She turned, glaring at him with piercing eyes. They were soft emerald in color. Her armored clothes were covered with a dark green cape. Her straight black hair fell right below her chin, framing her bronze-skinned face.

"Forgive me," Boaz lowered his head.

The young woman's gaze softened, "Forgiven."

Zuriel cleared her throat and tapped her foot impatiently as she opened the door, allowing them to enter.

This had to be her room. It was small. There was a bunk bed over to one side, a desk, and a dresser. There was a door leading to a small bathroom as well. Zuriel pulled a chair up to the desk and sat down. Boaz's eyes traveled to the relatively small window. There appeared to be children playing behind the mansion. Then, a tall metal wall shielded one's view from what was directly behind. Were those trees? He focused on Zuriel after hearing her clear her throat.

"Isn't this what you wanted? To meet with me? Well, here we are," she shrugged.

"Yes, it is, and I thank you. You have done an excellent job of trying to secure your people. But is this the life you want for yourself and your people?"

She raised an eyebrow, "I must admit that things have the potential to be better, but this is the best we have ever had. I won't give up everything we have worked for so easily."

"Zuriel, there can be more for everyone! I don't want you or anyone to have to live like this. This war is taking a toll on everybody. I'm tired of walking the streets and seeing dead bodies piling up. The yelling, the riots, the killing, we have the power to stop this. I want us to live together in peace. I want you to agree to a ceasefire."

"You're bold and brave and can take a beating. I admire that. In some ways, you remind me of myself. But you are insane to think I'd agree to a ceasefire."

"If you would ever walk through Theyra to see what this war is doing to innocent-"

"Oh no, no, no," she cut him off. "I'm in my mid-thirties. I don't think you really have a clue what this war has done to innocent people! My family, my people, we were innocent! We've been oppressed for hundreds of years. No one cared when it was us!"

"*I* wasn't here hundreds of years ago. I wasn't even born. But I'm here now. I'm showing up now! I'm trying now! If I don't understand, make me understand; spell it out."

"Fine, I will spell it out. Then I'll make you understand. When I was young, the streets of Theyra were never safe for me. My parents were Metalkeepers. The only ones in our village. The villagers would raid our home weekly, taking the little food and coins that we had. My father worked in the mines for three coins a day. He had a family that he rarely spent time with. He had to work over fourteen hours daily to bring home six coins, which was never enough. My brother was allowed to go to school. I was not because my parents couldn't afford the clothes to put a girl through school. I wore my brother's hand-me-downs every day. I never had my own clothes. My father was killed in a mining accident, and my mother was pregnant at the time. Then my brother was killed on the way home after school."

"I'm sorry, Zuriel-"

"Let me finish! I tried to find work after my brother's murder and was met with abuse day after day, coming home with a bloody face as a testimony. And when it was time for my mother to have the baby," she looked away, holding back tears, "no one would help me. I tried to help her deliver the baby. She made me promise that I would take care of my baby sister. And...my mother died the next day. I was sixteen years old with a newborn baby. And you would think that people would see you suffering and try to help. But no! Day after day, I would walk through the streets of Theyra and see *my* people's bodies piled up," she stood from her seat and came eye to eye with Boaz.

When he looked into her eyes for the first time, he saw her pain. How could he have not seen it before? How did he miss it?

"This now is justice. Your people's bodies are tossed about in the street. It's justice. I got tired of watching my people getting kicked around, so I honed my craft. I spent most of my time exploring everything about my gift. I taught myself the nuances of metal. Through practice, I saw how it could be used as a weapon and a defense. I grew stronger and stronger as time passed. Then I started teaching other Metalkeepers. The oppression did not stop, but we had a leg to stand on this time. We could fight back. I learned that the ones who learned the fastest are the ones who suffered the most. We had to steal food and livestock to get by day to day.

"Your people started blocking us from the river, keeping us from getting water. The very river that lies behind this compound. We started sneaking to get water. Then we started fighting along the river. Next, we killed each other along the river. I told the Metalkeepers that if they kill us, we kill them. That day, none of the Landkeepers who came to the river made it home to their families. My people rallied together, and in one night, we made the shell of this compound. Within a month, we had finished. And for the first time, we had a safe home. And now *we* have control over the river."

"Zuriel, it doesn't have to continue to be like this-"

"I will not agree to a ceasefire. Boaz, I admire your tenacity. But we are too far gone now. Landkeepers and Metalkeepers cannot exist without fighting."

"The governors agreed to a ceasefire and wanted to know what would satisfy you."

Zuriel stepped back a bit, "What? You... you actually managed to convince them? Well, now that's something. I never believed that would ever happen in my lifetime. I will make a request on behalf of my people. We want a separate territory of our own and two years' supplies for livestock and crops. We want to be independent of the Landkeepers. That is what we as a community need, so that is what I want. That is my request."

Boaz's heart dropped, "I'll relay your request to the governors."

He nodded in respect. Zuriel turned her back to him as he left the room. He sharply turned the corner. The young woman from earlier was leaning against the wall. He felt her gaze upon him as he walked by.

"How was it?"

Boaz turned. The sound of her voice caught him off guard. Her voice was deep and melodic. "Excuse me?"

"How was it? Your talk with Zuriel?"

"It went." Boaz had nothing else to say, but he felt uneasy about her questions.

It was almost as if she could sense his apprehension. Her gaze softened, "I'm Fayruz."

"I'm Boaz," he extended his hand. She accepted; her grip was firm.

"Now get yourself out of here." She turned to leave.

Boaz's feet didn't move. He was at a loss. How her gaze would soften, the depth of her voice, and the way her name fell off his lips with ease as he whispered, "Fayruz." Boaz took a breath and focused on leaving the compound. He noticed some of Zuriel's soldiers following him.

He was heading towards the assembly line when he heard his name being called. Boaz turned, and everything went dark.

CHAPTER 9

The crashing thumps of horses racing made the ground tremble. The four-legged beauties neighed as they came to a stop.

"I've never been to this part of Upper Ember. It's beautiful!" Arin gasped at the sight before them.

The town ahead was a sight to behold. The houses were modest cottages ranging from off-white to terracotta in color. There were wooden poles embellished with delicate little golden lights that climbed the poles in a spiral. The subtle yellow glow cast a peaceful atmosphere against the teal blues of the sun setting across the horizon.

Arin glanced at Jai through the corners of her eyes. His eyes never lost focus on the beautiful Comet Town. Her heart twisted to see fine lines creep across his forehead.

"Do you want to try again tomorrow?" She asked.

Jai hung his head, "No, we should be getting back. Everyone is probably wondering where we are."

"We'll find him, Jai."

"Maybe this was for the best. There's a war, and I shouldn't get him involved."

Arin opened her mouth to speak when she noticed a dark figure moving about in town. "What's that?"

Jai's expression immediately became alert at Arin's words. "It's not what, but who. Let's take a look."

Arin pulled Jai's sleeve, "Jai, let's not be rash. Maybe we should go. You're . . . you remember?"

Goosebumps rose on his skin. Something didn't feel right. "Just a quick look. Five minutes, then we can leave."

Arin nodded as they rode their horses back into town. The person wore dark clothes and a hood, similar to the hood that Jai kept with him. Jai rode slightly ahead of Arin. Several minutes passed, and they were gaining on the person.

Are they slowing down?

Arin peeled off, approaching the right as Jai continued pressing on their left. Suddenly, a piercing swoosh claimed the silent evening. Jai leaned back, something sharp grazed his nose. Arin groaned, grabbing her arm. Flames darted in their respective directions. The hood fell, revealing a woman.

"Sitara?" Arin questioned.

The woman turned towards her, "Arin!" She ran towards her, gently pulling her off the horse. Jai rushed towards them.

"I'm sorry. I noticed I was being followed and reacted."

"Hold still," Jai clutched Arin's arm. Rolling her sleeve until he carefully moved her hand from the wound. She grimaced upon seeing how deep the cut was.

"It's okay," Jai whispered as light flecks gathered near her wound until it became a soft beam that pulled it back together. Arin's hands were still bloody. Jai removed his vest, allowing her to wipe her hands.

"You okay?" He asked her, clutching her face in his hands.

She nodded.

Sitara honey-colored eyes brimmed with concern. "Forgive me again. I must ask what are you two doing here?"

"Just heading back to the Flamethrowers. We saw something odd and decided to check it out. Thankfully, it was you." Jai answered her.

"You can't go back there! The Flamethrowers have been ambushed by Agni several times a day for about a week. If you return, you may lead his soldiers to all of the cabin locations."

Arin's eyes widened, "Jai, we have to help them!"

Sitara cupped Arin's face, "I know you want to go back, but it would be unwise. I must be on my way. Just be careful."

Jai helped Arin back up on her horse as Sitara rushed into Comet town. The sun had completely set. But the glowing lights made it easy to find their way out of the town. He noticed Arin's hand fidgeting on the reins. He opened his mouth to speak, but no words came out.

This is my fault. I should have gone with Aqila. Then this wouldn't have happened.

"What do we do now? I want to make sure everyone is okay, but Sitara's right. We would only lead Agni's soldiers to all of our cabins." Arin hung her head as she spoke.

"I need to see Aqila; we may have enough information for her to provide insight."

"How do we know where she is?"

"I'm taking a chance that she may be in one of the Fireheart territories. I lied about why I could not go with her to the Waterbearer tribes. I'm thinking she would have gone to the tribes then returned around these parts."

Arin was puzzled, "What if she's angry?"

Jai sighed, "I guess I'll deal with that when we get there. Let's try Kindle first. Aqila wouldn't be here, and if the Flamethrowers are being ambushed, I'd guess that she isn't in Lower Ember either."

The pair rode through the villages of Upper Ember, hurrying to get to the border of Kindle.

Suddenly, a thought dawned on Jai as he reflected on Arin's injury, "Arin, I never asked if you were okay with this. I won't have any hard feelings if you are not."

"Why are you suggesting this now?"

Jai sighed, "Because I can't make any guarantees . . about anything. I made up my mind that I wanted this destiny so I could save my people. I'm tired of watching my people die. Agni is a threat, and the Flamethrowers are being attacked. Your sister is there. I don't think I'll be able to forgive myself if something happens to you. This is all my fault. I can't bear to watch you get hurt again."

"Jai, this isn't your fault! Agni would be after us regardless of what we do. I'm here because I believe in what you're doing. I don't want to just sit around calling myself a Flamethrower, all while doing nothing. I believe in the Legends, their purpose, and their destiny." Arin pulled her horse in front of Jai, causing him to pull his reins. "If I die for this mission, bury me with honor, forgive yourself, and live your life as if I'd never died. And know that anything less would be a stain on my memory."

She never moved. Jai swallowed hard. He didn't want to think about people dying. He wanted to believe that he could save them all. His heart didn't want to promise her that. But that blazing fire in her eyes was mesmerizing. Arin was such a spectacular woman. He hadn't met anyone like her before, kind-hearted and brave at the same time.

"I promise."

With a big smile, she rode off, saying, "I knew you would!" Her smile made Jai smile, and he hurried to catch up with her.

CHAPTER 10

Haneul paced around outside of the room Aqila was in.

"I don't see why you can't just open the door!" Tora growled.

"Hush, she's having a vision. I don't want to disturb her."

"Well, walking a hole through the floor isn't helping anyone. You're gonna fall through the hole and land on your back, and that'll wake her up."

"I'm a Windmaster. I don't land on my back."

"I'm tired of this! I think we should just wake her up," Tora pressed again. "I mean, she's been quiet for nearly four hours."

"Even more of a reason for us to be patient. She is a new Seer."

Tora sighed and stretched his back. "Well, Pacer, I'm going to make something to eat. Want something?"

"No thanks, I'm not hungry." As Tora headed downstairs, Haneul sighed. He's not sure what kind of vision Aqila is in, but it's obviously important. If she continues this way all day, it could hinder finding Jai.

That evening, when he and Saar visited Aqila, he informed her of Neptune's desire to increase the production of that tranquilizer. He discovered that the Metalkeepers manufactured all kinds of weapons for Neptune. He would pay the Metalkeepers for the weapons, and Agni would pay for the batches of formula. Zuriel, in turn, supplied Neptune's soldiers with resources. It was a complete cycle.

Saar had reported that Agni was battle-ready and preparing to attack Pyroc. That was a surprise, especially since Agni had lost hundreds of soldiers fighting the Flamethrowers. He must indeed have the pulse of the Firehearts anytime they were ready to fight beside him so quickly after knowing how his former soldiers met their end.

As the current head of foreign affairs, Kavi confirmed the Windmasters' long-standing allyship with Pyroc. He and Aqila devised a plan that allowed a switch of formulas to take place. However, everyone knows that a previous batch of the tranquilizers was still floating around with Agni and Neptune. Upon finding Jai, Aqila could help him locate Agni's supply. Haneul would return to Neptune and inquire with his men about the supply.

Haneul couldn't stay here too long. It took a while to gain the trust of Neptune's men. He had to show Neptune a supply of Windmaster soldiers soon. Haneul planned to use the masters at his dojo, all agents for Kashmala and Wyndhm. This kind of dangerous endeavor was enough to get anyone anxious. He knows that a single misstep could cost him his life.

Aqila, staggering through the door, immediately pulled him from his thoughts. She was drenched in sweat and feebly holding on to the doorframe. He hurried to support her.

"Jai, bring him here," she gasped for air. "The border, bring him here."

Haneul picked her up and laid her back on the bed, "Are you okay? Do you need anything?"

She strained her neck to sit up, "Just bring back Jai."

Haneul's heart started to beat out of his chest. "I will, Aqila. I'll bring him," he said as he ran downstairs at lightning speed. "Tora!"

"So, I guess she's up, seeing that you're yelling now," he continued eating.

"Yes, she's awake, and she looks horrible. She needs me to leave and bring Jai back here. Watch out for her!"

In between chews, "Got it. Does she need anything? Is she sick?"

"I think she's drained from exhaustion. She seems very weak right now. Just watch out for her while I'm away!" Haneul hurried and left.

Tora put his plate in the sink and walked upstairs to check on Aqila. Haneul was right. She seemed tired and weak. Her skin was sweaty and clammy. However, she was in a deep sleep. If anything happened, she would be defenseless. He would watch her until Haneul returned.

Haneul was flying on Vermillion high in the skies of Kindle. With the dry evening heat of the desert and the sandy terrain, it would be easy to get lost. It was dark, except for the soft, glowing light of the moon. He couldn't push Vermillion at her top speed because he would be bound to miss Jai. Haneul was not wholly confident about where Jai was or what he looked like. The only thing Aqila said was the border, and she was not in any shape for him to have asked her any more questions. There were three borders, Kindle-Pyroc, Kindle-Ember, and Kindle-Theyra. Based on Aqila's thought process, it made the most sense for Jai to be near Kindle-Ember.

Deciding he would check there first, Haneul took his time riding over Kindle in case Jai was already here. He was confident that Aqila was safe with Tora. Still, she would be defenseless in her current state if anything were to happen. Then Kavi would kill him indeed.

Yes, it never hurts to be careful.

He still wondered. What kind of vision did Aqila have that drained her strength like that? Haneul prayed to the Universe for those who he believed could use some relief. Then, there was the man who had already come to Tora looking for Jai. Whatever he did, he had to be careful.

***

"Jai, we've been riding for hours. Let's take a break," Arin suggested.

"I know you're tired. I am, too, but we can't take a break yet. We must get to the border by sundown, and it's too dangerous to idle around here."

"You're right. I'll be okay."

Jai knew she was tired. Arin was the superior rider, but her horse was lagging. Her eyelids kept fluttering as she struggled to stay awake. They had to get to Aqila. The Flamethrowers were in danger.

"Are you sure that Aqila will want to help? She may be upset that you didn't tell her about this."

"I don't think Aqila would refuse to help even if she's upset about us leaving. I just hope she's not *too* upset about it." Jai signed as Arin's question continued to play in his mind. Jai's stomach started growling excessively loud.

"I'm not the only one who wanted to stop and take a break, huh?"

"We can eat as soon as we get to the border," Jai laughed.

"As soon as we get there? How's that supposed to happen? Do you know of any places to eat on the border?"

"No, but you've been there a hundred times. Anywhere we can eat?"

"Nowhere that delivers on the 'as soon as we get to the border' promise you just made."

"I mean... it wasn't a promise. We need to get to the border as soon as we can. I know you're tired and hungry; so am I but-"

"No, if that's how you feel, we keep going. I am more hungry than tired, but you're right. We should keep pushing forward. Besides, if we stopped to eat, we would probably get more sleepy."

Jai was thankful that Arin decided to hang in there a little longer, but he felt uneasy. Something was urging him to get to the border as soon as possible.

"Do you feel okay?" Arin asked.

"I'm just worried about the Flamethrowers."

A soothing silence fell between them for several minutes as they pressed their horses onward. It was the dark of night. The lonely moon was painted across the sky without any stars in view. Arin pulled ahead a bit. Jai could tell by the way she was seamlessly weaving through the town's dirt roads that she was heat sensing.

Arin looked back, "Once this is over, this Agni/Neptune madness, what will you do with your life?"

"I'm going to rebuild this place. Growing up, Lower Ember was all I knew. Now that I have seen places like Kindle, Pyroc, and Upper Ember, I also want something like that for Lower Ember. Maybe get rid of the divide altogether and just call it Ember. I know that's a huge undertaking, but that is where my heart is."

"Nothing is too big of an undertaking when you have a team and the Universe backing you up," she smiled at him. "One Ember sounds nice, though. I'll be supporting you until the end."

"You don't have to. Don't you have a big dream you want to accomplish for yourself?"

"My dream was to live to help the Golden-Eyed Legend, and that's what I'm doing."

"Don't you want to settle down? You know, getting married and having a family is what most women dream of."

"I could ask you the same thing. Men have dreams like that, too."

"True, I haven't thought about it. I would like to settle down and at least get married. But, I feel like being a Legend will make being a husband and a father difficult."

"I don't know. From the last Legends, only Cyra and Aenon got married and had children, and we probably shouldn't gauge the future from them . . . just saying."

Jai laughed, "Yeah, you're right about that one. I answered, now it's your turn."

Arin smirked, "Maybe one day after the thrill of being a Flamethrower has settled in my life, I could see myself as a wife and mother."

"When this is all over, I hope we can see all of our dreams become a reality."

"Me too," Arin murmured. "After we get to the border, will we know how to contact Aqila? It probably won't be as simple as arriving at the border, and she's just standing there waiting."

"I thought we could get to the border, catch our breath, find something to eat, and then head to Tora's house. Aqila and Tora know each other, so we may be able to get in touch with her from there."

"Sounds like a plan. I think we can make it in a few hours if we push a little more," Arin said, looking at the sky. "It will be morning soon."

"Yeah, let's try and make some time," Jai snapped the reins, urging the horse to go faster.

"You know that Tora's house is far from the border. It's nearly night now. Do you really think we will make it?"

"The way I see it, we don't have much choice," Jai answered.

CHAPTER II

The pair pressed on toward the border. As an hour slowly escaped them, Arin noticed something peculiar. "Jai, maybe I'm tired, but do you keep noticing a shadow over us?"

"Hmm? I haven't noticed anything, but I can't say that I've been paying attention."

"Jai! Are you kidding me? Why aren't you paying attention?"

"Uh, because I'm the one who has to figure out what to tell Aqila," he groaned.

"Yeah, because you are the one who lied to her," Arin muttered.

As they reached the border, a massive bird dove right in front of them. Arin blasted a fireball, only for the rider to casually dodge the blow. Jai followed her attack with a bright light beam and rapid-fire punches. The bird screeched, lunging forward, which startled the horses. They were wild underneath the Firehearts. Jai was flung off his horse. Arin calmed her horse down. She spewed fire at the man, but the flames died several feet in front of him.

With a sweeping motion, the man moved his arm, casting a turbulent wind pushing them back several feet. The Firehearts huffed to catch their breath.

"Firstly, it would be unwise to continue your feeble attacks. Secondly, I believe Aqila the Seer has requested your presence," the gray-haired rider calmly spoke.

Jai's eyes widened, "A Windmaster! Aqila wants to see us? Where is she?"

"Jai, we shouldn't just trust anyone. What is he doing here anyway?" Arin questioned. Her hand ignited fire, but before she could attack. Jai grabbed her hand.

The Windmaster smirked, "Well, allow me to introduce myself. I'm Haneul, an ally of Aqila and Kavi, and she has only requested Jai's presence. You can decide for yourself whether or not to follow me." He eyed Arin as he spoke.

Haneul leaped from the back of the massive bird and clicked his tongue. The winged creature took to the sky. Haneul followed on foot, walking back toward the heart of Kindle.

"I don't know, Jai," Arin sighed.

"We must follow him," Jai mounted his horse, giving it a gentle kick in the side. As he followed Haneul's shadow, he noticed that Arin wasn't following.

"What?"

She folded her arms across her chest, "I just don't trust it, Jai. I'm tired! I don't want to get my hopes up of feeling like we have refuge somewhere for it to be a hoax."

Casting a soft light in his hand, he rode toward her. "My poor baby is tired and hungry?" Jai watched as she pouted. "Let's just say, using logic now, if Aqila's here, we're probably heading to Tora's house. She does not live here, so we'll take off if this guy leads us anywhere other than Tora's house. How does that sound?"

"Fine, if we're going to Tora's, I want to eat and sleep before we go anywhere else!"

Jai smiled as he hurried to catch up with Haneul, "Finally, a promise I can keep."

Arin sighed and pulled the reins to follow Jai and Haneul in the quiet of the night.

CHAPTER 12

It didn't take them long to arrive at Tora's house. Haneul had already gone inside while Jai tied up the horses. The door was cracked open as Jai and Arin cautiously went inside.

"Didn't know we'd be back here so soon," Arin whispered.

Haneul walked into the kitchen, "How's she doing?"

Tora sighed, "Stable. You can go up if you want."

"Tora, it's good to see you again," Jai shook his hand.

"Likewise," replied the hazel-eyed Fireheart.

"Jai, Aqila requested your presence. Her last vision left her quite weak. I just thought you should know," Haneul explained.

Jai gulped as he walked toward the stairs. He knew this would eventually happen, that he would have to face her. He silently prayed to the Universe as he proceeded upstairs.

When he reached the top step, he was immediately drawn to the room where she resided. The door was slightly open. He pushed it gently to allow himself to enter.

"Jai," Aqila acknowledged him immediately.

She seemed like her usual self, although her eyes looked tired. "I heard you had a rough one. How are you feeling?"

"I'm better now that I've rested. I had the sight all night, so I was fatigued. But I'm glad you're here. We have lots to catch up on."

How could she just move past the fact that he lied to her so quickly? The guilt was swelling up inside him, "I'm sorry-"

"For what?"

"For lying to you. I know you wanted me to go to the Waterbearer tribes with you. But I pursued my own leads instead."

"It's all fine. You told me you couldn't go because something important had come up. And you offered to meet me there, which I declined. You're a Legend, and I'm a Legend. We aren't slaves to each other. We're allies. If something was important enough for you to change your plans, then it was important. I'm not mad at you. I was frustrated at first because I didn't understand. Then I couldn't have insights about you for a while. I started to doubt my abilities, my place, and my destiny. I'm a new Seer with much I need to prove. That's not your burden, and you don't need to apologize for what you felt you had to do."

"Well, I did feel bad about not being straightforward, but knowing that you aren't mad at me is a relief. What did you want to see me about?"

"To reveal the Waterbearer Legend. She's the girl that captured and poisoned me. Her name is Tiber, and she's on our side now. The past is the past, and we are moving forward with a fresh start."

"Wow, what a change of events. So, we just have one more to go, right? What is Tiber doing?"

"Yes, there's one Legend left, but that Legend is the One Who Knows. I have found it odd that they haven't sought us out. But there's nothing to be done about that. As for Tiber, since Neptune's allies don't know that she has cut ties and reformed, she is switching the weaponized tranquilizers out with regular tranquilizers. Agni was planning on using them to attack Pyroc. That is the only way he could clinch a win."

"What? He actually had a plan to take over the Firehearts. Aqila, if Tiber hadn't poisoned you, it might have been too late for the Firehearts. With Agni's plan, he can overthrow Pyroc, and then Kindle will be easy work for him."

"I know. This is why we must stay alert. Agni could have easily taken over every Fireheart territory, so we can't underestimate him. We all must be careful. Haneul should be leaving to meet Neptune in person."

"What? When did this happen? You mean the Windmaster downstairs is meeting Neptune?"

"Yes, he is going undercover and is reporting all of his findings to Kavi and myself. It's been giving us an edge."

"And it's dangerous."

Aqila lowered her head, "We know." She sighed, "Now things are more complicated. Before Tiber realized she was a Legend, I had a vision saying, 'The sea has one set of eyes, but two faces, so what is in a name?' I didn't understand at the moment. Not until one of the governing Waterbearers admitted to being Neptune. But he's not the Neptune who we're after. Someone knows that Mahak is Neptune and uses the same name, so if found, Mahak would fall."

"How does that tie into anything?"

"Let's go back even further. Kavi rescued me from the Snow tribe. Tiber and all surviving attackers are brought back to the tribe. The Chief, Tiber's father, was murdered, and the succession scroll went missing."

Jai frowned, "Someone wants control over the tribe. But why that tribe? It's the smallest and weakest tribe; they aren't as advanced as the other two."

"The Snow tribe isn't the weakest. They've been mismanaged. All Waterbearer tribes are equal in strength and they all intermix. Mahak learned of a resource that he'd been selling to another tribe in secret. He did this to help his struggling tribe survive through the mismanagement of generations of chiefs. But because of his lineage, he couldn't tell people his true name, so he developed a trading name called Neptune. He was unaware of the atrocities the evil Neptune committed."

"But why would someone want to take over that tribe?"

"For the resource! It is a liquid mineral formula. One of its obvious benefits is that it slows aging. For Mahak's age, he does not appear a day over twenty-five years old."

"You're kidding," Jai gasped.

"Nope, he sells it to Marina, the Chiefess of the Beach tribe. She looks like she hasn't aged a day, either. Marina sells it within her tribe. Mahak also recently started a business deal in Theyra, helping the Metalkeepers. A part of the deal is to manufacture weapons. The Snow Tribe men now have crossbows with metal parts. Tiber told me they make the poison in Theyra and sell it to Agni. Mahak knew nothing about selling anything to any Fireheart and was completely against the idea."

"Makes sense, Firehearts and Waterbearers are long time enemies. So, what Haneul finds out is critical. We don't know who Neptune is without it."

"Well, it will help. We still don't know who Agni really is and why he's after complete control. The same with Neptune, but I think I've come closer to the why. Neptune has to be from the Snow tribe, and he has to know Mahak closely to trail his business dealings so flawlessly. But he also hates Mahak to set him up to take the fall for his crimes."

"He? You're sure it's a man?"

"Yes, evil Neptune attacked Tiber and the Beach tribe about a week or so ago. Neptune probably thought that Tiber had the succession decree. She was framed for her father's murder. Neptune was clearly a man. All accounts of his crimes that I've researched confirm that he's a man. He strong-armed two chiefs and killed them."

"You've really outdone yourself. You've been working hard to save the world while I've just been wasting time." Jai hung his head, unable to look Aqila in the eyes.

"Jai?"

"What? It's the truth. I found my father, that's why I didn't go with you. I wanted to go and spend some time with him. The moment was almost magical. My whole life, I've just wanted to belong somewhere. I thought that he was my answer. I just wanted closure. I just needed to know what happened? I know it sounds so stupid. I'm in my twenties, and this is what's important to me, but-"

"Sometimes you just want to know, right? Want to know whose nose you have, where your height came from, and why your eyes are shaped like that? Hmm? I know Jai. I was taken from my mother's arms right after I was born. I know, I know what it's like to be different. I didn't know

I was a Legend, and being a Seer isn't much easier. I don't know how I would have made it without Kavi and some amazing friends. Nothing's wrong with needing closure. We all have a right to seek that which will bring us peace."

"I guess. Nothing went as planned, though. Arin came along as we searched the town with no luck at all. Then we learned from Sitara that the Flamethrowers were being attacked. She told us not to go back. What if Agni's soldiers saw Arin and me leave the forest? What if it's my fault? All because I couldn't wait."

"I was aware of the attacks, but the Flamethrowers are okay. They are working to move locations."

"You knew already?"

"Yes, I went there looking for you. Everyone is doing okay. Everyone is safe."

Jai took a long breath. The hairs on his arms stood up as Aqila spoke. He was relieved.

"Jai, do you happen to remember having any siblings?"

"No, I just remember glimpses of my father. But I vividly remember the sound of his voice. I don't recall anyone else."

"When Haneul and I got here, I had a vision, but still don't fully understand it. It was about a rift between brothers. The strange part was at the end, the last pair of brothers looked like you and Tora," Aqila explained.

"Me and Tora! We don't have any issues. We're not even related!"

"You can't say that, Jai. You don't know that for sure. Before your eyes stayed gold, they were light brown, a Kindler color. And besides, you two somewhat favor each other," Aqila argued.

"Tora and I look alike? You're joking. We don't look anything like each other."

"If you're positive about it," Aqila dropped the subject. "I felt like I needed to see you because the vision I had last night was disturbing, and I wasn't sure if you were in any danger."

"What do you mean?"

"I saw how all the Legends died," she whispered.

"Legends as in the previous ones or us? I don't want to know how I die, so if you know, don't tell me."

"No, the previous Legends."

"Well, don't we all know that? Aenon was murdered by his wife, Ila was murdered by Basir, Cyra died in battle, and Basir died of old age. We all know that. Why did you need a vision?"

"It's not as simple as that. First, Aenon and Ila's deaths were accidents, and Basir died of old age. However, Cyra didn't die in battle; she sacrificed herself. In doing so, she made a prophecy. Because she knew that her legacy would create a curse."

"Slow up. Her legacy created a curse, so she sacrificed her life to make a prophecy, and the Universe accepted this?"

"The Universe wants us all to turn, accept its presence, and acknowledge its true power. In her repentance, her prayer was answered. Jai, you're the answer to her prayer."

"Why me?"

"Everything that happened to you happened for a reason. Being separated from your family, being raised in the World Order, your eyes not being gold at first, the problems with your element. Everything. Cyra prayed for you specifically. 'Give my successor a light greater than mine. Make his light undeniable. Let his soul reflect the essence of the Sun: light, warmth, love, and life. Most importantly, life, for without the Sun, there would be no life. Let him embrace this power and cherish it.'"

Something about the words Aqila spoke triggered a sensation deep in Jai's mind. As they fell from her lips, he clung to the words, "'Universe when he rises, guide him and light his path, as you lit mine. Universe, control the raging wildfires. Restrain the fires of anger, fear, hatred, and pain, and make them bow to the light and the fire of life. Rise upon him gently, show him his worth.'"

"That's what she prayed for? How did she know that I'd be a man?"

"After Basir's exile, Zeroun told him that the Legends alternate genders every cycle, just like Seers. Aenon was killed while Basir was in exile, and he grieved for him. After the exile, Cyra visited him and asked for his help in trying to restore balance. They had an intimate talk about their fears and flaws. Basir told her that he prayed his successor would be different from him. He said, 'By the grace of the stars, remove all obstacles from her vision. Let her eyes be clear always. Grant her powerful wings that create hurricanes in battle and add a gentle understanding to her ways. Let her voice not be a whisper. Let it echo. Help her to find truth, knowledge, and understanding in whatever she seeks. Challenge her, so she will feel worthy.'"

"That's what he told Cyra? In a way, he almost prayed for you to be a Seer."

"I know Cyra and Basir lived the longest and prayed for their successors to have different qualities, the ones that we have. Aenon and Ila had desires for their successors, but it wasn't as intimate as Cyra and Basir. Cyra's sacrifice allowed all their prayers to be answered, including Basir, Aenon, and Ila."

"So with this, we know what our purpose is. We had to be the answer to our predecessors' prayers. We have to settle the unrest between our people, and that's our purpose as Legends. But now we know that the Landkeeper Legend is a man because genders alternate. Speaking of Landkeepers, where's Boaz?"

"He went home to see how he could help end the civil war. I hope he's doing okay," Aqila sighed, missing her friend.

"Boaz is strong, Aqila. He'll be okay. What are our next steps? We have a lot of information to use."

"Haneul is meeting with Neptune and will follow up with Kavi on his findings. The WindGuard are prepared to deal with an assault from Neptune and are tailing him to the best of our ability. For Mahak, we are acting like he will be tried for "Neptune's crimes". This is just a ruse, but only a few people know it. Nahal is in forever ice, so we don't have to worry about him for a while. Tiber should have switched the formulas by now and should be overseeing the destruction of the previous product. The Jungle tribe and Beach tribe are fortifying themselves against any attack. Our bases are somewhat covered with Neptune, but Agni is a different story. Agni is planning an attack on Pyroc, but we don't know how much of the original tranquilizer he has left. We need to stay cautious of the situation with the Flamethrowers, and I'd keep my eyes on Sitara too. We don't want anything to happen to them. I will continue trying to get to the root of things and discover the why behind all of this."

"Does Sheraga know about Agni's plans?"

"Yes, he does, but he doesn't see it as a threat. That's how he is, and you can't change his mind."

"I can investigate Agni," Jai volunteered.

"Whatever you do, don't go alone. Agni wants you dead. Never forget that."

Aqila stood up and headed to the door, followed by Jai. After they came downstairs, they were immediately met by Arin.

"It's good to see you're doing okay, Aqila!"

"Thanks, Arin. It's good to see you."

"I'm glad you're looking like yourself, Storm," Tora shouted from across the room, "Your boy left about thirty minutes ago."

"I have to go. If anyone needs me, I'll be in Theyra," Aqila walked to the door, "Tora, thank you for everything. If you need anything, I will be at your service. Good luck, everyone."

"She's always so classy. I like it," Tora smiled. He noticed Jai and Arin's bewildered expression, "Cool it, she has a fiance. Wow, I can't even compliment anyone these days. What is the world coming to? Don't you have somewhere to be?"

"Yes, we do-" Jai started.

"Yes, tomorrow, after a good meal and some rest. Right, Jai?"

He swallowed hard, "Yeah, she's right. Everything can wait until tomorrow."

CHAPTER 13

Boaz lay on his raft in the middle of the desert. He was far past his house, closer to the Kashmalan mountains. He rubbed the knot of his head from where he was knocked out. He felt like the worst Legend ever after getting tossed out of the Metalkeeper compound.

Everyone else has been progressing and growing, but he hasn't changed. He's remained the same. It was frustrating. It was a suffocating feeling, knowing that you're supposed to be destined for great things but, in actuality, accomplishing nothing at all.

"Ugh, I hate feeling stuck like this!" The wind carried particles of sand past his face. "I didn't even find them. They literally just fell in my lap. I didn't find Aqila, Jai, or

Tiber. They all came into my presence in their own time. I'm a Legend. I never ran from my destiny but ran to it."

"Are you okay?"

Boaz sat up and squinted his eyes. It was Tiber. Her sleek panther was not far behind her.

"What are you doing here?" He asked.

She sat beside him on his raft, "I finished everything Aqila wanted to be done, so I'm just waiting to receive my next steps. I don't want to lie to you. I overheard you talking to yourself."

"Sorry you had to meet this lame Legend," he scoffed, "it seems like there's one in every cycle, huh?"

"I can't speak for other cycles, I wasn't there. But I think you're a great Legend. This war has been going on for a long time, and one day isn't going to change them. But, you're trying, and you're the only one trying because you're the only one brave enough to try."

"Or I'm dumb enough to think I can make a difference. Are you just now finding out about me?"

"No. Aqila had just learned about me being a Legend. When we met, you said you wanted to talk about Legend stuff. You couldn't have known I was one unless you knew all along. You got all uneasy when I told you that the

Landkeeper Legend might know what to do, and I pieced it together. Does Aqila know?"

"Of course not-"

"But you two are so close!"

"It doesn't work like that. I can't tell them my identity. If they figure it out, that's one thing. However, I can't uncover my identity nor uncover theirs. I have to wait until the Legend of each nation knows and accepts its identity. Traditionally, the Legends before me went on quests to find and unite all Legends."

"What else can you say other than that wasn't *your* destiny. Obviously, there is something different in store for you. Like you said, you met us before you had to go on a quest, and there's nothing wrong with that."

"I know nothing's wrong with it, *per se*. It just feels like I'm missing that experience. Besides, I'm doing a terrible job. The governors are mad at me, my people are mad at me, I lied to Zuriel-"

"You lied to her?"

"Yes, I told her that the governors agreed to meet with her. You don't understand. She's hell-bent that the common Landkeepers are against her. I had to tell her something, or nothing would change."

"What will you do now?"

"I have to secure a meeting by force if necessary. Aqila told me not to fan the flames of either side unless there was a clear right or wrong. She was right, but in this case, both sides are clearly wrong. At this point, it doesn't matter who started what. The point is that innocent people are dying. Theyra can't be a land of a free-for-all killing spree. I won't allow it. Change is hard for us. We won't do it unless we're forced to."

"I hope that doesn't include destroying things to make your point," Tiber grew wary.

"I don't know, I tried coming in peace. But they won't listen. They won't change until they feel forced to. They'll keep digging for another option. When they dig this time, there won't be another option. Don't worry, I won't destroy everything . . . I'll try not to," Boaz winked a sage eye at Tiber as he nudged her off the raft and hurried back deep into the heart of Theyra.

CHAPTER 14

Tiber stood as sand flew past her face and watched until she could no longer make out Boaz and his raft. She smiled. He was such a good person with a heart of gold. It was sad that his people couldn't see the blessing in him. After all this time, no one has tried to quell the violence like he did. Boaz was braver than most. She knew that without question. She mounted her loyal companion, Mika. Slowly across the desert sand, they went. Staying busy with her mission from Aqila and Kavi took her mind off the pangs of regret she constantly fought to push away.

Not a day went by that she didn't miss her Tribe. She hadn't seen her sister in so long. The motherly comfort and consoling she sought from her was only a memory.

Tiber knew that she had made the decision that would best protect her people - all Waterbearer tribes. Though they called themselves by different names, they were still interconnected people. When she closed her eyes against the hot sand and relentless sun, all she could see were his eyes. Those piercing yet gentle teal eyes were likened to being pulled into an oasis. A lush safe haven that was Cove. Tiber wondered how he was holding up with everything going on. She also wondered if he missed her. Does he think about her every day, like she thinks of him?

She shook her head to clear her mind of such thoughts. Everything that happened was for the best. Wasn't it? Tiber never thought that she would feel so empty away from the Waterbearers. The desert was a harsh contrast to the cold snow or the vibrant jungle life.

Nevertheless, she pressed on, awaiting her next instruction. She was sure that all the tranquilizers had been destroyed by the Metalkeepers. The production of the harmless version was well underway. The Metalkeepers moved so fast that if any other Neptune soldiers came through, they would never know the difference. They still did not know how much of the original formula Agni had in his possession. It didn't take long for her to reach the tent she was staying in. However, when her tent came into focus, she got an odd feeling about things. The yak pelt tent cover was intact, but something felt off, and she couldn't put her finger on it.

Had Neptune found her so quickly? Did one of the Metalkeepers recognize she was a fraud and track her down? She was worried. Tiber slowly dismounted Mika.

"If I yell, ambush the intruder. Stay here until I give you the signal."

Mika stayed as her master directed. Tiber slowly approached the tent. She didn't hear any noise, but as the sun's light cast down the tent, she could see a person's shadow. Tiber snatched the yak pelt back and caught the intruder.

"Ahh," Tiber screamed.

The gray-haired woman turned around, "What are you screaming for?"

Suddenly, the tent collapsed. Thrashing and kicking, Tiber groaned, "Easy, Mika, easy, girl!"

The panther backed up before licking her paws. "Sorry, I thought you may have been with Neptune."

"Really, I don't think he's capable of planning such an uneventful attack," Aqila slightly coughed up sand.

"Did I miss a message from you? You came unannounced," Tiber inquired.

"No, I was just positive that you would still be here. I knew you wouldn't be staying in the heart of Theyra. That place is like a minefield. So I checked the outskirts first. I also thought that Boaz would be home. It was odd. His parents hadn't seen him for weeks. I hope his mission is going well. Anyway, how did things go?"

"Everything went well. The old formula is destroyed, and the new formula is full speed ahead."

"Anything suspicious going on?"

"I didn't notice anything. I attempted to inquire about the quantity of the last shipment. Still, Zuriel suspected Neptune was starting to have a breakdown in communication."

"What was Zuriel like? Calm about the changes or uneasy?"

"She seemed calm about everything but slightly distracted. She normally makes intense eye contact but avoided my gaze this time. I asked if everything was okay, and she brushed me off."

"Interesting," Aqila reflected. "Well, now, onto the next phase. Can you pick up the antidote and drop it off at Pyroc? Meanwhile, I will be doing some research to try to trace Agni and Neptune's background using the information I have."

"How? I don't mind doing what's necessary to ensure we win, but Pyroc? Will they even accept me? I am a Waterbearer, you know. Do I need to tell them that I'm a Legend?"

"Well, I was going to ask Jai, but our plans changed. You won't be going alone. Kavi sent the antidote to the Jungle tribe. Since Cove is a chief, he's willing to go to Pyroc. Jai will meet you there. I will be in the great library far off near the border of Kindle, awaiting your return. I am hopeful that afterward we can try and find the last Legend. Once we ensure that Pyroc is not caught off guard by Agni's plans."

"Do you think it's a good idea to go with Cove?"

"Why not? You need a Chief to go with you. DragonLord Sheraga will immediately open his schedule to accommodate anyone with an official position. Yes, Legend is an official position. I know Sheraga personally, he's going to ask you to prove yourself. We don't want to attract Agni's nor Neptune's attention to you, especially since Agni wants all of us dead. We don't want to fuel him if we can avoid it."

"I see what you're saying. I didn't tell Cove goodbye before I left, and I don't want us to have a misunderstanding."

"You don't have to fear misunderstanding, Tiber. Just be willing to open up."

"Yeah, you're right. I shouldn't keep avoiding him," Tiber sighed.

Aqila smiled, "It will be okay. If things go downhill, you can come back and blame me as much as you want."

They laughed, "Okay then, well, I'm ready!" Tiber and Aqila walked outside the tent and began disassembling it. "Aqila, do you really think we can win? I'm not trying to sound doubtful, but Agni and Neptune are everywhere."

"The more appropriate question is, can we afford to lose? Agni wants us Legends dead. He thinks he can break the cycle. Maybe he can. Why would we sit around waiting to find out? Can the world handle much more of this? No, it can't. If this keeps up, we will have another world war. Did we start this problem? No, but that's not the point. We are blessed with the power to finish it. The power that our predecessors didn't have."

"I know you're right. I'm a little worried."

"Bravery starts with admitting your fears. I have fears too, but my faith in the Universe is stronger than my fears, so I keep going." Tiber was rolling the tent as Talon dove from the sky.

Aqila mounted her dasher, "Tiber, if all goes well, Jai will meet you in Pyroc. Don't tell anyone you're a Legend. We don't need extra targets on our back, especially since Neptune already knows about you. Afterward, I'll meet you on the Kindle-Theyra border."

Tiber pat Mika's black pelt, "Sounds like a plan. Good luck to you!" With that, the women went their separate ways.

CHAPTER 15

Boaz hurried to Quillon's home and knocked on the door.

"Who is it?"

"Armani, it's Boaz," he tried to catch his breath.

"Come in. Are you okay?"

"Yes, I'm fine. I hurried here as fast as I could. Is Quillon here?"

"Yeah, I'm here," he bellowed from across the room, "I almost thought you left us for a minute."

"No, why would you think that?" Boaz asked.

"Well, I thought your work was done, man. Zuriel and the Metalkeepers didn't meet us at the sunder line like they usually do. So everyone just left. Whatever you did got her scared of us big time!"

Armani shifted uneasily. "I'll leave you two," she said, bowed slightly, and started to leave the front room.

"Quillon, I convinced Zuriel to meet with the elders."

Quillon and Armani stood still as statues for several minutes. Quillon shook his head violently, "How did you do that? Does she actually want to talk this out? After all of these years? She really wants to talk?"

"Yes, Zuriel really wants to talk. But I have to tell you the truth. I convinced her on a lie."

"What?" Armani and Quillon asked in unison.

"Because I needed to prove to myself that Zuriel is not a war-loving, bloodthirsty manic like everyone is making her out to be. I talked to her. She's in pain, just like everyone else. The Metalkeepers follow her because they find hope and security in her strength. She's like a mother to them. I told her that the elders want to meet with her to attempt to negotiate a ceasefire."

Quillon's hunter-green eyes went wide, "But Boaz, they don't. They don't want to talk to her!"

"Almost true," Armani spoke. "Magnar won't hear of it. But Othniel is willing to support Boaz."

"A fifty-fifty split won't help," Quillon groaned.

"No, it won't, but what about you? Quillon, stand in for Father! Tip the scale in Boaz's favor!"

"I'm not a governor!"

"It doesn't matter when the governors aren't doing anything! They aren't helping! Something, someone has to yield, or we are all going to just kill ourselves. What would Father do?" Armani pleaded with her brother.

"Quillon, I wasn't suggesting you try voting with the governors. I understand that I might be asking too much from you. I just want your good word and support," Boaz extended his hand.

Quillon accepted, "You have my support. I will go and put a good word in for you and inform the governors that Zuriel wishes to meet and discuss a ceasefire."

"Good, we'll meet at the sunder line as soon as possible," Boaz confirmed.

Quillon left immediately. Armani smiled and hugged Boaz, "I'm so proud of you. For a minute, I thought you really fought her. But I'm relieved now. I haven't seen someone so committed to peace. It's refreshing. You remind me a lot of my father. I just wish he could have met you."

"I've had a lot of doubts about being a Legend. But I've never wanted to win something so badly. We can beat this, but peace won't be attained just yet. We've got another battle ahead; if we aren't united, we'll never win."

"Another battle?"

"Yes, some people won't be happy to see us stand together. So they have been doing everything they can to ensure we don't. I have to go get Zuriel now. Thank you for your support, Armani."

Boaz turned to leave. He didn't look back to see her expression. He wasn't quite sure why he told her that. Something just made him believe that it needed to be said. Armani smiled at Boaz's words.

CHAPTER 16

Boaz was traveling through the desert. Flecks of sand danced in the wind, and a whiff of metal tinged the air as he continued riding through the sand dunes. His muscles felt stiff; he hadn't had a proper night's rest in several days. His mental state wasn't making anything easier.

"I have to devise something to convince the governors to talk to Zuriel. I could tell them that she agreed to meet them and discuss a path to a ceasefire. That worked with her, maybe it will work again. The only issue is that I know that she wants an independent state. Zuriel may expect me to vouch on her behalf. Hmm, it's not a bad idea. I just don't know how to make it happen."

Suddenly, Boaz's sand raft lurched forward and began to spin out of control. He dug his heels into the ground. The spinning abruptly stopped, tossing him from the raft. With a loud slam, he was completely encased in a metal box. The box tilted upward, causing Boaz to tumble into a corner as it was sealed with a metal sheet.

Bracing himself on one of the metal walls, Boaz staggered as the box began to move at a pace that didn't allow him to keep his balance. His head crashed into the metal walls over and over until he had bruises all over his face. His vision began to blur, and his throat burned with acid as he struggled not to vomit.

Boaz hated the feeling of tumbling endlessly. There was nothing to ground him, nothing to hold onto. His connection to the earth was severed by metal. He closed his eyes against the remaining flecks of sand.

He subconsciously called for Ila, and images of Basir, Aenon, and Cyra glitched in his mind multiple times.

Ila!

Her name was a distant echo in his mind as his sanity was beginning to fray.

Try grounding.

He heard her voice, but those words reminded him of her.

Was this how she felt, with nothing to tether her to the land in her final moments? Oaklee, forgive me.

Tears burned against his eyelids as his body slammed against the metal floor. It was quiet. The tumbling had stopped. Boaz's arms trembled as he attempted to stand up. Coughing violently, he threw up. Clutching his stomach, he fell to his knees. Wiping his mouth on his sleeve, he charged at the walls, kicking with all his might.

He didn't even dent the metal. Boaz placed his hands on the wall. He went to withdraw due to the fervent heat, but cuffs appeared. He twisted around as best as he could with both hands subdued.

"Let me out of here!"

Yanking with all of his strength was futile. He was stuck. The heat of the wall was beginning to bake his hands and back.

Near the top of the metal box, a small opening was torn. There she was, Zuriel!

"Let me go!"

"Oh, Boaz, now why would I do that?" She smirked, her emerald eyes narrowed.

"What are you doing? Why would you do this? I was setting up a meeting with the governors on YOUR behalf!"

"Were you? I've been at this for a while. No governors have EVER been interested in meeting. The thought hit me, had I been an idiot to invite you? I thought I killed that soft part of myself a long time ago. But apparently, I missed a spot. You weren't setting up any meetings! You intend to trap me! To lure me away from the rest of the Metalkeepers! Your agenda is to try and topple me, but that will never happen! I will end you! I will make you feel the depth of my people's suffering, and afterward, you'll have the clarity to decide if you truly want peace with me."

The metal was starting to burn Boaz's skin. He grit his teeth and groaned at the pain.

"Zuriel! I have no ill will towards you! Ahh!"

"Lies. I sent my most loyal soldier to follow you. You've been residing with a family who are staunch supporters against the ideas of independent Metalkeepers! Staying with a governor, huh, Boaz! Is that why you thought you could deceive me?"

With a swift motion of her arms, she chained his feet to the ground and dug the metal into his skin!

"I was negotiating for you," Boaz couldn't feel any earthly materials for him to summon. He groaned against the pain. His muscles grew limp as he felt his strength leaving his body.

"For me or against me?"

Zuriel flung multiple metal knives directly at Boaz. He howled in pain as his shoulders, chest, and legs were stabbed simultaneously. She guided her hands backward, pulling the knives from his flesh as his blood ran all over his clothes. Seconds later, she stabbed him again, simultaneously in new areas on his body.

Boaz willed the little specks of sand towards him. Zuriel cast her gaze down. Balling her hands into fists. Long nails with dull tips pierced through Boaz's hands and drove through the metal walls. He screamed at the top of his lungs.

"I gave you a chance to be honest, but you're no different than the rest of your kind. I heard that the governor had a daughter. Let's see if her pain will draw the truth from you. Can you do it, Boaz? Can you handle hearing her scream? She may even cry for you to save her."

His eyes glowed green, "Don't touch her!" Instead of power, pain seared through his body. Without any contact to his element, he could not ground himself to heal or surge his power.

Armani was in danger. Boaz became aware of his mind and his fears.

I can't save her!

He closed his eyes. Those bright green eyes, long curly black hair, skin like sun-kissed sand.

Oaklee!

"Oaklee, I didn't save you. I wasn't strong enough. Aqila, I didn't save you. I can't save her! I can't save her! I can't-"

Blood dripped down his wrist as he writhed, still trying to free himself from Zuriel's clutches, yelling in anguish at the top of his lungs.

A loud clang reverberated against the metal box, and his vision began to double. An armored foot crashed into the box.

"WHAT ARE YOU DOING?" A deep, melodic voice echoed against the metal.

Zuriel's eyes widened. "Get out of-"

"NO! We agreed that you wouldn't do anything until I returned!"

"Fayruz, I am just taking necessary action-"

"Undo this now!"

Zuriel leaped from the opening down to meet Fayruz eye-to-eye. "I am ending this. Our people have suffered enough."

"He didn't lie, Zuriel! I went to the desert, and I saw all the governors leave that house! Then Boaz left. He *did* talk to the governors! But look at what you've done!"

Zuriel touched Fayruz's shoulder, but her hand was slapped away. "UNDO THIS NOW!"

"My Fay! We don't need the governors anymore. I've subdued the Legend. I will make it all go away."

Pulling metal from the box floor, Fayruz made a metal scythe. With the same motion, Zuriel made two swords.

"My Fay, do not be unwise. You are not a match for me. Do not stand in the way of our cause."

"I'm not raising an arm against you. What's become of you, Zuri? What happened to your sense of justice? Why does the truth not matter to you? You've acted on a lie, and you are hurting people. You are becoming a monster. What vile has set in your heart? Do I have to die for you to listen?"

Fayruz's scythe made its way to her own throat.

"No!" Zuriel dropped her swords and snatched the scythe away from Fayruz. Her eyes began to water. "Please, don't ever-"

"Undo this now," Fayruz growled.

After wiping the corners of her eyes, Zuriel sighed. The metal cuffs dissipated. "The cuffs are gone. You can handle the rest. You seem rather invested in this." She stormed off, knocking her shoulder into Fayruz.

Fayruz ran to Boaz. The metal nails in his hands still caused him to be immobile.

"Boaz, hold on!" Fayruz quickly pulled the knives free from his body. Her hands trembled as she pulled on the nails until he was free.

The pain was no longer registering for Boaz. His bloody body fell limp into Fayruz.

"Oaklee. Oaklee. Aqila. I didn't save them. I was too late. I wasn't strong enough." He muttered in distress.

Fayruz's eyes watered to see him in this state. With his blood staining her hands, she cupped his bruised face, "Shhh." Her voice was a gentle whisper. "I'm getting you out of here. You will touch the earth again, and you will heal. Shhh. Your mind, let it find quiet."

Boaz's body shook. "I can't. I couldn't save them. I let her die. I wasn't strong enough. They needed me to be stronger." His eyes watered.

Fayruz whispered, "She ascended to the Stars, and she knows you did everything to save her." She began tearing strips from her green cape. Carefully, she dressed the wounds on his hands.

"They need me. I cannot break. I cannot break," Boaz repeated over and over.

"I won't let you break. You don't need to break; you need to feel. Then let the feeling pass."

"Why? Why are you-"

"It's like you said, we need you. I-I need you."

Boaz's eyes rolled back in his head as he passed out.

CHAPTER 17

When Boaz opened his eyes, he was in a small bed surrounded by dirt, grass, and sand. He had dark green fabric wrapped around his hands. Bringing his hand near his face, he could identify a faint floral smell. He closed his eyes for a long time. He remembered everything.

As he sat up, he could hear bustling activity from outside the room. He slid the fabric away from the wounds.

Everything has healed.

His body was tired, but he was no longer in physical pain. He was disappointed he got so close to a breaking point, especially in front of an enemy.

When did I start thinking of them as the enemy? Agni and Neptune are enemies.

The sound of the door opening put him on edge.

"It's just me, Fayruz. I'm glad to see you are doing better."

"Thank you."

"I'm sorry about Zuriel. I am not going to make excuses for her behavior. Her abuse was uncalled for. She got paranoid about you talking about meeting with the governors, and thought you were setting a trap. I told her that we could decide what to do after I returned. But you were telling the truth, and I am so sorry."

But I lied.

"Please say something."

"Thanks for helping me, but I should probably get going."

"Boaz, please," she blocked the door with her body.

"Fayruz, I appreciate what you've done, but it's best for the both of us if I go."

"You don't get to say what's best for me!"

Boaz took a step back and sat back down on the bed. Fayruz relaxed before sitting beside him. He felt uneasy until he noticed her hands trembling in her lap. Boaz reached out and gently held her hands.

"Everything has gotten out of hand. I wanted to believe everything that Zuriel said. I wanted to believe that you were going to destroy us. But when I saw the governors talking to you, I felt something I never felt before. It was almost as if I had permission to dream about peace. I never felt that before, like we have a right to peace. I always felt like I had to fight and take it from others to have it myself."

She sighed, "Then I heard you yelling, and when I broke through, I saw my sister as a monster for the first time. The paranoia, the obsession, it's eating up everything that is good about her. I felt your pain. I felt her fear. I felt all of it, and it overwhelmed me. I don't want it to divide our sisterhood. But I'm scared now. Scared that one day I'll have to put an end to her. I'd rather die first."

Boaz squeezed her hands, "No one else is dying because of this. I won't let that happen."

She turned to face him, lightly squeezing his hands, "Tell me about them."

"Who?"

"Oaklee and Aqila."

Boaz gulped, "When I was small, I had a friend. Her name was Oaklee. She was a little older than me. I learned a lot of techniques that advanced my ability from her. Our little village had this story about an underground town that took children from 'cursed' families. The town was destroyed by a Fireheart and Windmaster, who managed to escape. Oaklee thought that we could flee to that town and be spared from war. We skipped school one day to look for the town. Oaklee slipped into quicksand once we got down there. It was dark, and we could not see anything. I tried my best to save her, but I was very young, and I didn't have the skill to save her. She died. I could never shake the feeling of guilt. I'm a Legend, and I couldn't save her."

"I'm so sorry."

"Aqila is my best friend. She's a Windmaster. She got poisoned leaving my house. After she was poisoned, she was kidnapped. She was found shortly after. But the whole situation made me worried that I'd be too late or incapable of helping her. It reminded me of Oaklee. So, when Zuriel was talking about kidnapping the late governor's daughter, it sent me into a bad spiral. I'm sorry you had to see that."

"No, there's nothing to apologize to me for. You were strong. I don't know anyone who could have endured what you did. The Landkeepers and Metalkeepers have been giving you a hard time. But I'm in your corner. I'm willing to do what it takes to end this war."

Their eyes met, Boaz asked, "Can I ask a favor?"

Fayruz nodded.

"Let Zuriel know that the governors want to meet tomorrow morning. If she feels unsafe, the meeting can be held right outside. She can take it or leave it."

"I'll let her know. And if she doesn't show, I'll come."

Boaz stood, "That would be huge! If Zuriel could come, that would be best. But any support from the Metalkeepers is appreciated."

Fayruz smiled, "I know it may not seem like it, but you two are more alike than you may think. Zuriel has also experienced much pain. We've lost everyone in our family, and she has sacrificed a lot for the Metalkeepers. If you believe in the ceasefire, I can get her to be agreeable for a day. Besides, after what she's done, she owes you one, I won't let her forget that."

Boaz nodded, "I should be on my way. I'll be here in the morning, whether it's you or Zuriel. I'll be here ready for us to work together to achieve peace."

He headed for the door when he heard Fayruz call his name.

"Yes?"

She slowly walked towards him as she spoke, "I just want you to know that I'm willing to fight for peace. That I am not afraid. That I am capable of defending myself. That I am reliable. That I will have your back. And if I should die, I will believe in you still as I draw that last breath. No matter what happens, you will not break, I won't let you."

Boaz's mouth went dry as her words imprinted on his brain. Face to face, they stood. He swallowed her in his embrace as he whispered in her ear, "You will not die; I won't let you."

CHAPTER 18

"I hate having to wear this ridiculous hood. It's not like I have something to hide!"

"Zuriel, we are trying to keep the meeting peaceful. We don't want your presence to attract unnecessary attention," Boaz groaned at her complaining. He had given her a dark green hooded cloak to disguise her as she slipped from the compound. She wouldn't go far from her home, protecting her home base at all costs. Zuriel was clearly agitated. He almost wished that Fayruz had come instead. At least she would have been agreeable. He couldn't help but smile when he thought of her.

I have to stay focused.

A wave earned his attention, and Quillon could be seen in the distance.

"Stay here," Boaz commanded Zuriel quietly as he walked away to meet with Quillon.

"They are on their way," Quillon said. "I'm praying to the Universe that this goes well for us."

Boaz recalled his turbulent morning. He kicked Magnar's door down and dragged him from his house as he informed him of the meeting with Zuriel. He told him that the Landkeepers were ready to have him removed from his position if he was unwilling to make peace. That, of course, was not the case, but Magnar believed it.

Othniel was not hard to convince. He was rather open-minded to the idea of talking to Zuriel. He took his time getting ready for the meeting. Boaz spoke to Quillon, who expressed discomfort with standing in for his father. However, he was willing to show his support by assisting in getting the other governors to the meeting spot on time.

"Thanks for your help," Boaz replied. Quillon left in the direction he came. After returning to Zuriel's side, "They are on their way here for the meeting. How do you feel?"

"I'll know once we have the meeting," she calmly stated.

Two figures could be seen in the distance. Boaz's heart started racing. He was nervous, silently praying that both parties would communicate in peace. He realized that the situation was so tense that it wouldn't take much for it to escalate. Taking a deep breath, Boaz committed to staying positive.

Othniel and Magnar reached the sunder line and bowed their heads to Boaz and Zuriel, to which the pair returned the greeting.

"Did we have to meet at such a controversial area," Magnar groaned.

"I felt unsafe going far from this very spot," Zuriel calmly replied.

"I wonder why," Magnar hissed under his breath.

"It is a pleasure to be here finally trying to negotiate, Zuriel," Othniel spoke over Magnar.

"Likewise, governor, aren't we going to wait for the last governor to arrive?" Zuriel began looking around.

"Unfortunately, he passed a few months ago," Othniel replied.

"He was murdered," Magnar corrected.

"I apologize. I was unaware. I am sorry for your loss," she bowed her head.

Boaz cleared his throat, "We are here to negotiate appropriate terms for a ceasefire. I am here to see that everyone has the opportunity to voice their thoughts, and we work to ensure that the final decision will be fair for everyone. Governors, what do you believe is an appropriate term for a ceasefire keeping the best interest of the Metalkeepers?"

"The Landkeepers need immediate access to the resources behind the Metalkeeper compound. The river, particularly the next substantial river, runs between the far edge of our desert territory and Kindle. Sometimes, we exhaust the river, which is not our intention. But that has created conflict and skirmishes with Kindle, who has just enough water to divide among everyone," Magnar requested.

"I agree, fighting each other in this war has been taxing, but a possible war with the Firehearts, Theyra as a whole, would take a devastating blow. We still have not fully recovered from the war with the Windmasters. In our terms, we should incorporate teaching moments moving forward. We have differences with those who wield metal, and we should try to learn more about them and their needs. We should incorporate blended schools with teachers with and without metal proficiency. So the youth can better understand each other and work together," Othniel added.

Boaz asked, "Are these the terms of the people, governors?"

"We can address terms after hearing from Zuriel," Magnar answered.

"Alright, Zuriel, what are your thoughts on the request for the Metalkeepers?"

"Thank you, Boaz. Firstly, we should stop beating around the bush. We are different and embrace what makes us unique. I have considered the Metalkeepers' needs. We need independence from the Landkeepers. We would like a portion of Theyra to call our own that is not void of resources. It need not be large, as we are the minority. If we could get assistance with crops and livestock for a few years, we could stabilize, and our kind will not be a burden or bother for you ever again."

"What? Have you gone mad? Why would we allow that? We are straight out of a civil war. We don't have enough resources to separate. We will need all hands on deck to rebuild," Magnar was shocked at her proposal.

"Do you really think our problems will disappear over a signed piece of paper? Problems will still exist, then we will be back at it again, arguing and fighting. If we give each other space and a chance to rebuild according to our needs, working together won't be so stressful going forward," Zuriel explained.

"But Zuriel, we don't have what you are asking for. We would need access to the main river for at least a year to produce crops for you. Your terms aren't horrible. We just can't meet them right now. We are struggling already," Othniel explained.

"Let's take it easy, now. What parts of the request of both parties can be met immediately? Then we could work on a timeline for the rest," Boaz suggested.

"Don't be a child, Boaz! You can't put a timeline on long-deserved independence. The Metalkeepers need independence," Zuriel snapped.

Othniel spoke, "Zuriel, independence is fine if it can be achieved. You haven't mastered the land. You are raiding our farming because you lack the skill to manage the land yourselves. Therefore, at this time, you won't be successful on your own. If you need us to provide the crops, we can't meet the demand and won't be able to meet it for a year until we have access to the main river."

"Othniel, that's not the only problem! We must do something about the border with Kindle!"

"Well, if the terms can't be met, then we can't have a ceasefire," Zuriel tossed the cloak off.

"Zuriel, don't be inflexible," Boaz called to her.

"You know this is funny. When my people didn't have resources, we were forced to figure it out. So, we took what was needed to thrive. So why don't the Landkeepers figure it out?" Zuriel crossed her arms across her chest.

"That will only perpetuate war. I know you want independence, and you deserve it. Yes, I admit that your people deserve to have their own state. But if you take on a responsibility you aren't ready for, you will run into untold problems that your people will blame you for," Othniel warned her.

Zuriel laughed, "My people, blame me? Please, they could never blame me! The older Metalkeepers were killed off, and I taught them how to defend themselves. And I fight every day for them, this compound I designed and built with my own hands. They would never blame me."

"A leader has to take responsibility for the good and the bad, Zuriel. Othniel is right. Let's try to make things work another way," Boaz extended a hand to Zuriel. She swatted his hand away.

"Legend, I won't go back to my people with terms that won't work for them!" She marched away back to where she came, kicking the cloak as it lay on the ground.

Magnar growled, "Stubborn woman, come back here like a real leader!"

Zuriel clenched her fists, "I'll show you a real leader!" A metal strip flew at Magnar. It wasn't sharp or aimed to kill. But it was enough to rile Magnar up. He aimed rock covered in lava deathly close to her face.

Boaz stepped between them, "Stop, this isn't what we agreed to!"

"That doesn't matter," Zuriel and Magnar shouted in unison. Othniel shook his head in disappointment as he began to walk away.

Zuriel and Magnar knocked Boaz out of the way and began hurling their respective elements at each other. Laying on the ground again, Boaz had had enough! Zuriel and Magnar were fighting, and now the crowd was drawing in. Both were powerful in their own right. He had to stop them. The Metalkeepers were beginning to back Zuriel, the Landkeepers behind Magnar.

Fayruz came rushing out, puzzled as to the conflict she was seeing.

I promised her I'd end this.

Boaz's eyes wouldn't part from Othniel. He really wanted peace and was willing to put his own ideas aside for it. If Boaz let this stand, he'd be letting Othniel down. Not just him but every Landkeeper who believed in the Universe and the Legends. He would be letting his friends down. He would leave his people vulnerable to being destroyed by Agni and Neptune. This had to stop right here, right now.

Zuriel and Magnar, in mid-battle, Boaz separated them with a large mass of rock. Planting his feet firmly, he felt the heat from the core in the middle of the Earth. He summoned a massive wave of lava, making Magnar's gifts look like candlelight in the sun. Zuriel took cover from the heat of the lava, knowing it to be detrimental to her and her people. Magnar and the Landkeepers looked in awe at Boaz, but he wasn't done. Boaz generated a massive sandstorm that surged from the desert, making the

Landkeepers run. They scurried, not wanting to be buried alive.

Finally, the sunder line was quiet. They all fell back. Boaz hated the expression on everyone's faces. For the first time, they saw him as a Legend. "This is over! Right here, right now! Look at us. We don't deserve to call ourselves a Nation if we can't do better than this. I didn't want to do this, but you've left no other choice," Boaz called out to them.

The very earth from up under their feet began to rumble. The ground was splitting. The Metalkeepers and Landkeepers were trying to brace themselves to no avail. The only one left standing was Boaz. Using all of his strength, he changed the lay of the land. The river behind the Metalkeeper compound was separated, forming several rivers. The compound fell. The line was dissipated. The worn-down buildings were knocked down. This lasted for several minutes before a wave of quiet could be acknowledged.

Looking around, destruction was the main event. Nothing looked as it once was. Everyone was silenced and visibly shaken by what had just happened except for

Fayruz, who looked at him in awe. All eyes were on Boaz for an explanation.

"I know what you're all thinking. Why did I do this? Because there was no other way. We are a nation of Landkeepers and Metalkeepers. Our history together has been a rough one. But that changes today! Land or Metal, we have the same fathers and mothers. We shared the same ancestors. We look alike and talk alike. But we have both wronged each other.

Oppressing the Metalkeepers because we don't understand them is wrong. Hoarding resources is wrong. Killing each other over the land that we share is wrong. And regardless of the reason, it will always be wrong! So, let's begin at the beginning! We are all wrong, but we can change this. The main river has been split into multiple rivers. The Metalkeepers will get a separate territory to call home. The pocket of land that borders Kindle near our great library with its own river will belong to whatever Metalkeeper wants to reside there. Landkeepers have every right to access that area, too. But nothing is to be taken or altered without Metalkeeper approval."

"Zuriel will name the area and will govern over it. In turn, she and the Metalkeepers are fully responsible for improving and maintaining relations with Kindle. The rest of the land continues to operate as it was, and Metalkeepers are free to occupy this space. This strip where the sunder line and the compound once were will be developed for schools and businesses for everyone. Now that the river has been split, we have more flexibility in using the land. Theyra is home for all of us. We have so much to learn from each other. The Metalkeepers can help us advance with technology, and we can help them maintain the land. But we won't be successful without each other. Whatever comes next, we will have to face it together."

Boaz felt uncomfortable with the silence. "I second the motion. If the Legend says this will bring peace, then we'll do it," Quillon shouted.

"I agree with Boaz! This is a fresh start for Landkeepers and Metalkeepers alike," Fayruz shouted.

Mumbling could be heard from the Landkeepers. Magnar sighed, "Landkeepers! The Legend has spoken. We will comply with our orders as we work towards peace with the Metalkeepers. Development of the new schools will begin tomorrow, and I will meet with the builders this evening."

"Metalkeepers, we will pack our things. Start heading to the land out west tomorrow. We will confer on the name of our new land and propose it to the Legend tomorrow," Zuriel commanded.

Everyone began to disperse. Boaz was tired and plopped to the ground only to be offered a hand-up by someone he wasn't expecting.

"It's good to see you again."

The tall shadow and raspy voice could belong to none other. "I-I, I'm so sorry I didn't tell you," Boaz couldn't look up.

"Bo-," she embraced him.

"Aqila, I'm sorry I kept this from you."

She pulled away, "What do you mean? You have nothing to be sorry for. All things are revealed in due time. I was on my way to the great library when I saw and heard all of the ruckus. So you're the one who knew?"

"Yeah, I am. I hope you know I had to let you discover your identity alone."

"I know, Boaz, I know. I was just thinking about how Basir and Ila's friendship surpassed so many lifetimes, and here we are."

"You're my best friend, Aqila."

"And you are mine," the pair embrace each other again. "You didn't need to go on an elaborate life-changing journey to find us. We all came into your life at the right time."

Boaz was taken aback. It was almost as if she had read his mind. He smiled at her, "What do you think of my handiwork?"

"Beautiful chaos, if there ever was such a thing," she laughed. "Do you think the Landkeepers will adjust well? This is a great deal of change for them."

"They'll get used to it. It was hard trying to decide what would be best for everyone. The truth was both sides were wrong. Landkeepers oppressed the Metalkeepers, and in turn, they hoarded resources from the Landkeepers, throwing the Nation into a warring bloodbath."

"So, it's officially Landkeepers and Metalkeepers?"

"Yeah, it is official. I wanted everyone to see that we are one people. But now I realize it is important to embrace the beauty in our differences and respect them. What are you heading to the great library for?"

"I need to do some digging into the previous Legends."

"You know that we have records in our library . . . that would save you time."

"I'm not after historical records. We know the history already."

"Well, it's true. Are you sure you don't want me to come with you? That massive library on the Kindle-Theyra border can be confusing. Most information is based on astronomy, and there are a lot of birth records and prophecies and stuff like that."

"I'm fully aware, and that is exactly what I'm after," Aqila calmly replied.

"Alright, it seems like you know what you're looking for. I need to help where I can here to ensure things go smoothly. I saw Tiber over the past couple of days and heard she was switching formulas."

"Yes, that was successful. She's off to Pyroc with Cove to deliver Kavi's antidote if Agni already has enough to level Sheraga's army."

"Tiber to Pyroc? Why not send Jai? You know how Sheraga can be."

"Jai is dealing with some other affairs, but he will go to Pyroc eventually."

"I'm gone for a few weeks, and things have gone haywire like that?"

"That's the state of the world now, isn't it," Aqila sarcastically replied.

"Are we onto anything new?"

"I'm onto something, but I need to research at the library to confirm some gray areas of my visions. You know I hate to give misinformation, so for right now, that's all I have."

"I understand. I'll be here trying to help the transition. If I see or suspect anything, I will let you know. If Agni has his sights on Pyroc, where's Neptune?"

"I don't know. You have to be careful, Bo. Since Agni and Neptune are allies, you're on their target list now, especially since everyone in Theyra knows about you now."

"I'll be careful, Aqila. I have a full handle on my element. If they try something, I believe I'm the most prepared of the four of us. I've always known I was a Legend, and I've had the most time to master my abilities."

"That makes sense, but still be careful," Aqila looked up to the sky as a shadowy figure hovered above. Talon quickly landed, allowing her only seconds to mount before lifting into the sky.

"Aqila, you be careful out there!"

"I will," she shouted as she continued westward on Talon. Boaz was confident in her ability to protect herself, but sometimes, her visions were problematic when they impaired her senses. He hoped that she would be cautious. Either way, Boaz decided to meet her after the transition was in motion in Theyra.

CHAPTER 19

Arin knocked on the door with the signature heartbeat rhythm. As the door began to open, they both gently pushed themselves inside. The moment Jai closed the door, he and Arin were being embraced.

"It's so good to see you again," Yuuna beamed.

"Thanks, Yuuna. It's been a while," Arin smiled.

"Jai, Arin, I'm glad to see you again," Arrow called out to them.

Jai and Arrow shook hands before Jai asked, "It's just you and Yuuna here?"

"Yes, everyone else is out," Arrow answered.

"We ran into Sitara when we were in Upper Ember."

Arrow's ears perked, but Yuuna's eyes narrowed. "How was she?" Arrow asked.

"She seemed to be on a mission; she let us know about the attacks. She urged us not to come back right away." Arin explained.

Jai noticed Yuuna rolling her eyes.

"I can't stay here long. I have to go to Pyroc. Arrow, Yuuna, are things any better? Have the attacks stopped?" Jai asked.

"The attacks stopped a few days after Aqila came by, but we have also moved to our most isolated location."

"Yuuna?" Jai called her.

"Yes?"

"Seems like something is bothering you."

Yuuna shook her head, "I know no one wants to hear this, but I just don't have a good feeling about Sitara. Especially after she didn't stay to help us fight Agni before. We risked our lives trying to help her, and it doesn't feel right. Her daughter died, and her son has left the organization that her husband gave his life to uphold. I just don't feel a genuine investment from her."

"Yuuna, please." Arrow groaned. "We have enough going on without that divisive attitude. No one needs that. Dysis just left; we must keep a unified front as best possible."

"Dysis left," Arin was shocked, "she was such a valuable asset!"

"She wasn't happy here anymore, Arin. Calida and Cahya were her closest friends. Cahya wrote to us about the Phoenix Riders and he's teaching that specialized ability to other Firehearts. Dysis wanted to help him, and it would have been selfish to stop her." Arrow explained.

"The truth is equally important as peace. Sitara wasn't even secured when we fought at the border, meaning that if she had tried, she would have been free! She didn't come back for us, Arrow. We helped her, and she left us. She didn't fight with us.

Arrow turned her to face him, "Yuuna, you know that is one fiery hell of an accusation."

She slapped his hands away, "Regardless, it makes sense! You've always had a cozy place next to Calida! Trust me when I tell you this, Sitara is never too far behind Agni!"

"What do you mean never far behind Agni? I get that you are upset about what happened when we fought Agni! So am I! We are on the same team. I don't believe she'd help us for all these years to betray us. Calida and Cahya are her children. Dehateh was her husband." Arrow stated.

"I'm done! I need to get some air," she shouldered past Jai and Arin.

"I'm going after her, just to make sure she's okay," Arin whispered before trailing behind her.

"Do you think it could be Sitara?" Arrow asked Jai. A sullen expression washed over him.

"I know you loved Calida, but she would have wanted you to find the truth, even if it means that her mother is on the wrong side of the equation. We both know that."

"I know, it's just hard to believe. Why would she betray us?"

"Agni might have offered her something, a position, anything. We just have to keep following the truth. But right now, we have no evidence. And as you stated, Sitara has always been on your side in the past. She also told me and Arin about the attacks. We would not have known anything if it wasn't for her. Yuuna seems stressed and she's worried about you. Go easy on her next time."

"I can't believe I hurt her. She's always been there for me, even before the Flamethrowers. Everything I do hurts her, and I hate it because I care for her."

"She cares about you and just wants to help. All you can do now is trust her. I know I don't know a lot, but I know people. Ultimately, we all want the same thing, to be happy with the people we love. If you live a life only trusting yourself, you'll be a very miserable person." A moment of silence passed between them. "Well, Arin and I have to go to Pyroc."

"Send my brother my regards. Let me know if I can help with anything."

"Zay and Alena could meet with you and Arin in Pyroc later this week. They may be helpful, and besides, Zay is getting tired of seeing forest all the time."

"I don't have a problem with it, and to be honest, I think Arin and Alena have some reconciling to do," Jai whispered.

The door swung open as Arin and Yuuna returned. "Well, Arin, we have to go now. Yuuna, Arrow, you two have been most helpful," Jai started dragging Arin out the door.

She clung to the frame, "We'll be back as soon as we can!" The door was closed behind them. "What was that all about?"

Jai smiled, "What? We have to get to Pyroc. Remember?"

Arin groaned as she followed Jai away from the Flamethrower's cabin.

***

Arrow sighed once he closed the door behind Arin and Jai, "Can we talk for a bit?"

"It doesn't matter," Yuuna whispered.

"Yuuna don't say-"

"You don't trust me, so nothing I have to say matters. I need to finish the assignments for the week-"

Arrow embraced her, "I'm so sorry. I've hurt you so much."

She looked up at him, "We have work to do," Yuuna mustered a smile.

***

"He said what!" Arin was yelling as they mounted their horses.

"Why are you yelling?"

"Jai, why did you say yes? Zay and Alena don't need to meet us! What exactly will they be doing other than getting in our way? Are they even aware of what we've been tasked with doing? We can handle this by ourselves! Aqila thought we could!"

"I didn't think you would be against it," Jai mumbled. He smirked, watching her struggle to untangle the reins due to her frustration. Jai undid the knots while she huffed about. "I don't understand why you are so fired up about your sister assisting us," he tried to hide a smile.

Arin pulled her horse in front of his, "You're a horrible liar. I know you want us to make amends. I was just enjoying this time. It's been nice to get out and help you on these missions." She looked away from him.

Jai placed his hand on hers, "Hey, that's never going to change. Arin, I trust you with my life. I mean it."

She smiled, "Thanks, well, let's get going."

"You're welcome! You were all worked up, can't untie the reins-"

Arin shouldered him, nearly knocking him off the horse. "What was that?"

Jai put his hands up, "Nothing, I forgot what I was saying!" He rode off ahead of her as she whined his name.

CHAPTER 20

Tiber and Cove were both wiping sweat from their faces. The sweltering heat from the volcanoes surrounding Pyroc was nearly unbearable for the Waterbearers. Tiber could tell Mika was tired, "Cove, we have to stop for a minute."

Cove looked majestic, riding a massive tiger. Another tiger of equal size followed behind them, carrying sacks of the antidote across her back. "Alright, we can't stay here long, or the heat will get to us. Medusa, we'll stop here, girl." The tiger he was riding came to a complete halt. As he dismounted, Cove walked to the second tiger, "Easy, Kora, we're going to take a break." He gave Kora water from the water pouch on her back. The cat lapped out of the bag feverishly.

"This heat is almost unbearable for them. It's hard to watch," Tiber sighed as Mika lay on her side, panting heavily.

"Another couple of hours, and we'll be through the worst of it."

"Do you think Sheraga will accept it? Why didn't Kavi just deliver it himself?"

"Sheraga can be a little testy to work with. That's why I'm here. Kavi couldn't leave Kashmala. The man is working double time to make sure enough of the antidote is produced for all of our allies. He makes it himself to ensure the quality is sound."

"I see. We didn't talk much on the way here. How have things been?"

"Busy and tiring as usual," Cove made intense eye contact with Tiber.

She glanced away, "I'm sorry for leaving the way I did."

Cove scratched his head, "I understand why you did it, I really do. I just know you need support to succeed, and I want to support you."

"I know! And you have. I didn't want Neptune to attack your tribe because I was there. That's why I left."

"I wish you wouldn't take things so personally. Neptune is a problem for all of the Waterbearer tribes. He could show up at any of our tribes just because he wants to enforce his will. That's how he is. I thought that you wanted to go home and be with your people. Then, when I reached out to your tribe, they told me you never returned."

"Well, what can I say? We're here now. Let's not stay too long, or we'll be baked."

"You're right," they both scaled their respective cats. "You never told me that you had a cat."

Cove laughed, "Well, Medusa is a ferocious cat, and she doesn't have a gentle nature like Mika. I let her roam the jungle. She always comes when I call her. I must keep Kora busy, or she'll play the whole time. I thought you would have heard about them already."

"Not at all."

"Tiber, don't be nervous. Sheraga will pick you apart if he thinks you're intimidated by him. He's a DragonLord, and that's his nature to exploit weaknesses."

"I'm trying. I'm just anxious that we don't know where Neptune is, and it's always in the back of my mind."

"And?"

"I guess I still haven't come to terms with everything that's happened. It still bothers me. Neptune killed my father, and the attack at the festival just feels like it's all my fault."

"All those things that happened result from what you didn't know. You didn't know about Neptune back then. You didn't know to believe in the Universe to evoke its protection. But now, things are different. You know about Neptune, and you're a believer in the Universe. You're a Legend! The past had some dark days, but the future can be better."

Tiber sighed as they began to move past the fiery volcanoes. Cove grabbed her hands, "At the end of the day, worrying never solved any problems. If Neptune shows up, he's in for a fight. We'll be okay, trust me."

Tiber placed one of her hands over his, "I trust you."

"Alright, now let's make some time! Medusa!" He patted the tiger's neck, and she quickly picked up the pace, followed by Kora.

"Come on, Mika!" Tiber and her panther quickly moved to keep up with Cove. Besides the heat, Pyroc was a breathtaking place. The volcanoes and the lush greenery surrounded them. It was a sight to behold. She caught a glimpse of the palace and could tell it was glamorous in the distance. The air almost smelt like ashes and spice. The village to the east looked lovely as she and Cove hurried to the palace. As they passed the Pyroceans, they garnered much attention. Their clothes and cats stood out dramatically among the Fireheart commoners. Tiber tried not to focus on their gazes and paid close attention to where Cove was leading her.

It didn't take long for them to reach the palace . . . sort of. The beautiful white marble grandeur was barricaded by Pyrocean soldiers who were displeased to see members of the Waterbearer tribes.

Tiber was in awe at their uniformity. The only difference between the men and women soldiers was the variance of their breastplates.

"State your business," a Pyrocean soldier barked at them.

Cove raised his right hand, a typical symbol of peace throughout all Nations, "I come in peace. My name is

Chief Cove of the Jungle Tribe, and we are here to deliver a product to DragonLord Sheraga."

"Amber, have accommodations for such been authorized," the soldier asked without looking back.

"No, sir. No appointments to the DragonLord have been authorized for today," a female voice replied from the line of soldiers.

The man glared at Cove, "You do not have clearance. You may leave. Come back once your authorization has been passed."

"I can't do that. The safety of Pyroc is at risk," Cove persisted.

The soldier took a step toward Cove. Medusa roared and aggressively launched toward the Pyrocean, who dodged the attack without even flinching.

All soldiers instantly turned their weapons upon them. Tiber gulped. She was nervous and unsure if she should speak up or if that would make things worse for Cove.

"Easy Medusa, please understand. She picked up your aggression and responded with aggression. Please forgive me. No harm was intended." Cove rubbed Medusa's head to calm her down.

"If you don't leave, she'll be picking you up from the ground. Do I make myself clear?" This was getting bad. Neither Cove nor the soldier was backing down.

"Pyre, call them back," a smooth yet thunderous voice called behind Tiber.

"Yes, sir! DragonGuard, ease!" Pyre and all the Pyroceans made a single file line, withdrawing their weapons.

All Tiber could see was a gold silk robe with a red dragon emblem and long, free-flowing, blood-red hair. When he made eye contact with her, his gaze was so intense she felt the urge to look away. She had never seen eyes so ferocious yet beautiful.

"Who are you?"

"DragonLord Sheraga, I'm Chief Cove of the-"

"Jungle Tribe, interesting. Who is she," he pointed to Tiber, "Is she your woman?"

Tiber felt like she could pass out. Maybe she should tell him that she's a Legend.

"My companion and I are here on business."

"You should get clearance from me first. You do know that, right? I mean, since you are a chief, right?" There was an edge of aggression in Sheraga's voice and a threatening look in his eyes as he walked toward him. Cove was as calm as ever, never losing eye contact with the DragonLord.

"I knew you'd be difficult," a tall man's deep voice interrupted. He walked past Tiber and toward the DragonLord. Sheraga's army was immediately at attention.

Sheraga laughed to his heart's content and briskly approached the tall, gray-eyed man. Based on his appearance, Tiber could tell that he was a Windmaster. "It is a rarity to see you come out of your hole, baby brother. Now, when should I be expecting an invitation to this all-important wedding? My wife and I intend to be in grand fashion for the event," Sheraga looked over his shoulder, "Dragons, ease!"

"Aqila and I felt the need to reschedule due to current world affairs," the tall man replied. There was a nonchalant air about him.

Tiber's mouth dropped. This Windmaster was none other than Kavi!

"You need to marry that girl, brother!"

"Trust me, nothing is more pressing in my mind than officially making her my wife. Now, I'd like an audience. It's quite a pressing matter of national safety. It is regarding the letter I sent before the Waterbearer's arrival, and I thought you were expecting them."

Sheraga rolled his amber eyes. "Kavi, my brother, if this man is a chief, then he should have reached out to me leader to leader. That's what men do. Do you disagree? Either way! Meet me in the war room since we have much to discuss." Sheraga jogged up the marble stairs of the palace.

Kavi walked over to Cove, his long, stone-gray hair was in a messy ponytail. "Cove, you didn't send notice to Sheraga?"

"No, I thought you did," Cove looked bewildered.

"I did, on behalf of what I was sending. But Sheraga isn't wrong. As a chief, you should have told him that you were coming. However, I didn't spell that out in my letter to you. I shouldn't have assumed that you knew. I will take responsibility. I will also advocate for you and Tiber to join the meeting with Sheraga. He can be a little intense, but he's a great leader. I'll be back," Kavi turned on his heels and proceeded to the palace.

Cove looked at Tiber, "I'm sorry about that, Tiber."

"It's okay, Cove. This is all really new and nerve-wracking for both of us. Do you think Sheraga will let us through?"

"I don't know."

"His gaze was so intense I had to look away. Did you see the way he handles his army? That's what makes Pyroc a force to be reckoned with."

"I know. I just wonder why Kavi is here . . . I thought he was too busy to make the trip. Why couldn't he bring the antidote himself if he wasn't?"

"I don't know. Maybe he wanted to talk to Sheraga about something important."

Several minutes passed before a soldier exited the palace and said something to Pyre. After raising a blood-red eyebrow and throwing Cove and Tiber some questioning looks, Pyre walked towards the Waterbearers, "You will be escorted to the war room. The DragonLord will have an audience with you. We must secure your cats outside with the rest of the animals."

Cove and Tiber dismounted and urged the cats to follow Pyre. Amber rushed to Pyre's side and whispered something. Pyre nodded, and she approached Kora to remove the carefully packaged antidote bottles. Her fellow soldiers assisted her in transporting the liquid into the palace. Mika looked back at Tiber, eyes almost pleading to accompany her. Tiber just blew her beloved cat a kiss and nodded to her to follow Pyre.

CHAPTER 21

Talon landed with Aqila on the border of Kindle and Theyra. Leaping off her dasher's back, her feet landed on the hot desert sand. She put a hand over her eyes to shield her from the sun's blinding rays. She walked on the sandy terrain for a short while before looking around. This library contained some of the oldest records in the world. It was a universal landmark. Most people cannot understand anything written, as everything is organized by astronomical events. Fortunately for this Seer, Zeroun taught her well. Finding what she was after should be relatively easy.

After a short walk, sand steps led underground. "Alright, Talon. I'll be back. Hunt if you need to since it may be a while."

The owl squawked loudly, "Shh, it's alright," she whispered, "The only people down here are old sages looking to expand their wisdom. I'll be alright." Aqila kissed Talon's head gently before rushing down the steps.

Aqila had been here several times before with her beloved mentor. Her heart pounded as she resisted the urge to run through the halls and grab everything. Her thirst for knowledge became insatiable. Memories of her younger years with Zeroun flooded her mind. Upon arriving at the bottom of the steps, an eerie silence existed. This library was always quiet, but never this quiet. Aqila paid that no mind as the scent of the ancient pages nearly brought her to her knees. She parted her lips, almost able to taste the ink in the pages. She felt comforted to be surrounded by so many books. Knowing precisely what section to go to, she took her time, running her long fingers gently along the spines of the books as she passed them.

It did not take her long to arrive at the epicenter of her research. "What will I need? Historical records, birth records, and Legend history should be a good start," she said. She sat on the dusty floor with semi-sufficient lighting as she opened a book.

"I guess I should look at birth records first." She flipped through the birth records of the Firehearts history from five hundred years ago.

Cyra – daughter of Cyrus and Solina
Born during a solar eclipse – golden
eyed child (Fireheart Legend)
Cyra deceased, cause old age (80)

Soleil and Selene – daughters of Cyra
and Aenon (Waterbearer Legend)
Selene deceased, cause fall from
snowy mountain (14)
Soleil deceased, cause lightning strike
during a major storm (33)

Notes Soleil and Selene are born of a
Fireheart mother and Waterbearer
father
The twins have dark brown eyes and
tested as Giftless.

Elior and Lucien – sons of Soleil and Siraj

General Lucien of the Dragon Guard
Served in the guard for 30 years
Lucien deceased, cause infection of old war injury (81)

Elior deceased, cause lightning strike (34)

Taner and Ravi of Lucien and Alina

Ravi leader of the Kindle Nomads for 40 years
Ravi deceased, cause old age (103)

Taner deceased, cause lightning strike (24)

Aelia and Aurora – twin daughters of Elior and Kalinda

Aurora deceased, cause lightning strike (22)

Aelia deceased, cause childbirth (28)

Unnamed baby girl – daughter of Aelia and Rai
Baby girl deceased, cause lung failure (12 hours)

Notes Any further reference to Aelia's daughter will be done so by referring to her as Aelia II

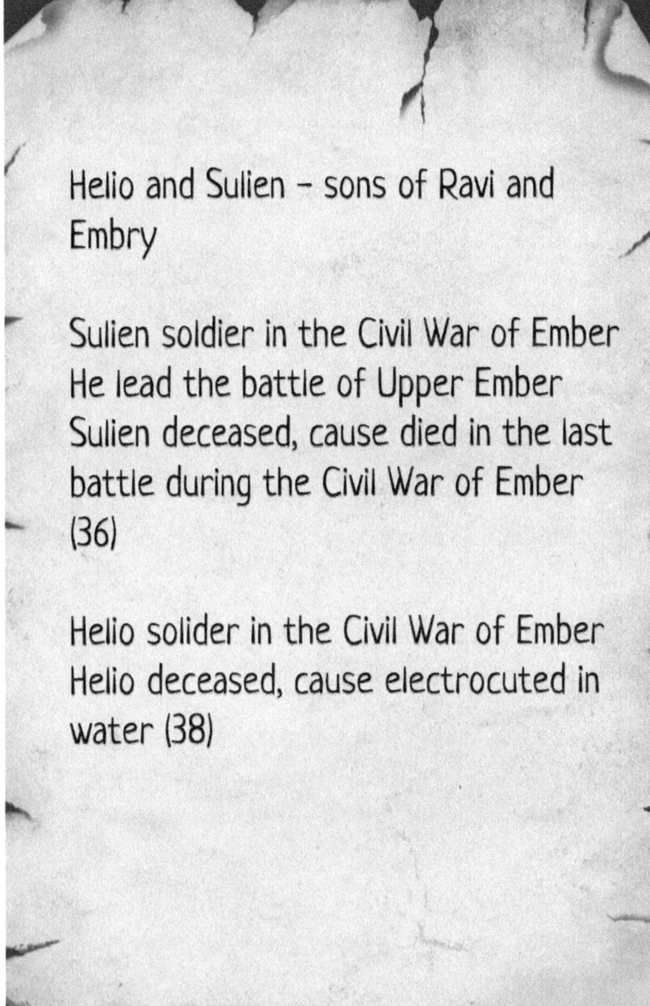

Helio and Sulien – sons of Ravi and
Embry

Sulien soldier in the Civil War of Ember
He lead the battle of Upper Ember
Sulien deceased, cause died in the last
battle during the Civil War of Ember
(36)

Helio solider in the Civil War of Ember
Helio deceased, cause electrocuted in
water (38)

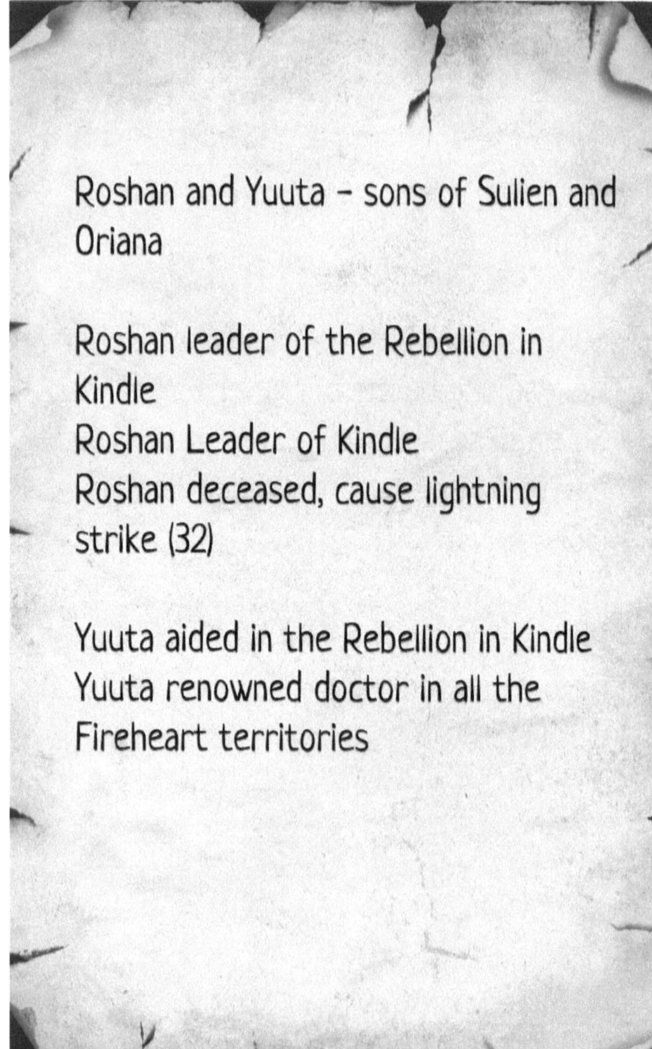

Roshan and Yuuta – sons of Sulien and Oriana

Roshan leader of the Rebellion in Kindle
Roshan Leader of Kindle
Roshan deceased, cause lightning strike (32)

Yuuta aided in the Rebellion in Kindle
Yuuta renowned doctor in all the Fireheart territories

Tora – son of Roshan and Azar

Tora Leader of Kindle

Unnamed baby boy – son of Yuuta and Nuri

Notes Nuri died from hemorrhaging after childbirth. Attempts were made to reach Yuuta who was in a state of deep grief due to the passing of his wife. We will update the records accordingly

Notes 10 years have passed and we have lost contact with Yuuta

Notes 20 years have passed and we have not had contact with Yuuta

The last entry was recent.

The shade of the ink was much darker, and it smudged as she wiped her fingers back and forth. This child was not recorded.

But why? This child was a boy. Probably close in age to Tora. What happened to Yuuta?

She felt pressure in her head and immediately put the book down. She couldn't afford to have a vision when she had to go through Aenon's bloodline first. Aqila returned the Fireheart records to the shelf and chose Waterbearer records.

Aenon – son of Caspian and Coral
Aenon was born during a lunar eclipse
(Waterbearer Legend)
Aenon deceased, cause ice dagger to
the heart (50)

Leomar – son of Caspian and Coral
Leomar deceased, cause mauled by
orca (42)

Soleil and Selene – daughters of Cyra
and Aenon (Waterbearer Legend)
Selene deceased, cause fall from
snowy mountain (14)
Soleil deceased, cause lightning strike
during a major storm (33)

Notes Soleil and Selene are born of a Fireheart mother and Waterbearer father

The twins have dark brown eyes and tested as Giftless. Soleil's lineage continues in Fireheart records

Janara – daughter of Aenon and Avala

Avala deceased, cause childbirth (39)
Janara deceased, cause childbirth (22)

Darya – daughter of Leomar
Darya deceased, cause wounds from war with Pyroceans (45)

Jaci – daughter of Janara and Himesh
Jaci deceased, cause childbirth (26)

Baran – son of Jaci and Tiberian
Chief Baran (19)
Chief Baran deceased, cause hunting
accident mauled by snow leopard (60)

Tuhin – son of Chief Baran and Nivia
Nivia deceased, cause childbirth (30)
Chief Tuhin (22)

Jocasta – daughter of Chief Tuhin and
Rasa
Rasa deceased, cause childbirth (33)
Chief Tuhin deceased, cause sickness
of the lungs (50)
Jocasta deceased, cause childbirth (32)

Mahak – son of Jocasta and Zale
Yas – son of Danu and Zale

Danu deceased, cause childbirth (39)
Zale deceased, cause disease of the heart (50)

Councilman Mahak (22)

Muraco – son of Mahak and Laila
Laila deceased, cause childbirth (24)

Nahal – son of Mahak and Noelani
Noelani deceased, cause childbirth (32)

Aqila closed the book. She clutched her chest. Such a sad fate for the Tribe of Snow and Ice.

Zale had two children? Mahak never said that he had a brother. Does he know? The record doesn't show that Yas ever married or had children.

Aqila put the books back and decided to take a break. She had been in the library for several hours. She sighed, "Well, that was a start!" Suddenly, it dawned on her. None of the sages had greeted her nor offered their assistance. Usually, they would be here and try to explain one's findings to the best of their knowledge.

Let me see if I can check out a book. Someone has to be here.

Aqila returned to the shelf and decided to check out *The Legend History* from the past five hundred years. Her head was throbbing to the point her vision was starting to blur.

"Wise sages!" She called out, but no one answered. "I wanted to check out a book. Sages? It's Aqila the Seer!" She was met with a continued silence as the pressure in her head was becoming unbearable. She felt an urgency to get outside. As she rushed for the exit, she could hear Emet.

You can't leave yet.

"What do you mean?" Her mind's eye was summoning her to the back of the library. Images started coming to her in flashes. But she just kept seeing Tora and Jai alternating. It was becoming dizzying. Then she saw Aenon and Cyra, and they appeared to be arguing. Aqila knew better than to resist a vision. She felt a familiar presence in her mind, Zeroun. She called out to him from her mind's eye, "Zeroun, I can feel you!"

"I called you twice before my pupil. The pressure you feel is a summoning. It always comes from a Seer of the past, and it feels different for every Seer. This is new to you, Aqila. Slow your thoughts when you feel pressure and your breathing just slightly. Then you will be able to hear the events of the vision. My dearest pupil, you're doing very well."

Aqila slowed her thoughts and her breath as she felt herself summoned to a room in the back of the library. It was, as Zeroun said, and she could hear Cyra and Aenon arguing.

"What do you mean, what are we going to do? They're our children, and we must love them and raise them!"

"Cyra! Are you blind? They're giftless! How will they navigate the world, being our children with no gift from the Universe?"

"Aenon, let's stop yelling. It's not going to get us anywhere. Deep in our hearts, we knew that this was a possibility. They didn't ask to be born. We shouldn't be unjust to them. They're our children, and we must be better for them."

"This was a mistake, Cyra. I'm sorry I put you through this. I shouldn't have-"

"Aenon, don't quit-"

"We can't win. The Universe has shown us that our relationship, marriage, and family are wrong. We can't keep going like this, and we must yield."

"Just because things aren't easy doesn't mean we must quit."

"You just don't let up. Nothing good is going to come from this. Our children are going to suffer for no other reason than the fact that we are their parents! They will never be normal or accepted. They'll be outcasts because of us."

"I know you were outcast by your people for a long time. I know this bothers you and pains you. But that doesn't change the fact that they are our responsibility."

"Cyra, we can't keep on like this. We can't stay married. I have to go. The Universe is angry with us; we've angered the Heavens. We have to bend a knee now. We have to submit."

"How could you just leave me with them?"

"Cyra, please. I love you so much. Don't you see, I did this to you. I've brought you to the gate of hell. I'm not a man if I drag you and them through it. I'm going back home to my tribe. Let me know if you need anything, and I will send it." With one last longing look, he left her.

Cyra cried, holding her two infant children, "All I needed was you, Aenon. Curse the Heavens, who rob hearts of their owners," she sobbed. Tears fell on the faces of her twin girls until they, like their mother, cried too.

Aenon heard her cries and curses. He fought back the tears, "My heart doesn't want to leave your side. But I fear the Universe's wrath upon us more than I fear your fury. Why didn't I listen to Basir? He tried to save me from this. Universe, forgive me. Heal her heart."

Aqila reached the door and opened it. She gasped when she saw the sages. "They're dead!"

"If you don't want to be next, I suggest you make no sudden moves," a man's voice from behind her.

She slowly turned around, "Who are you?" Her silver eyes met cerulean ones.

"I'm Neptune, or were you expecting someone else?"

"Let her go. She's an oversized Windmaster. We have other things that are more important on our agenda," a masked man appeared from behind Aqila. Her heart nearly leaped from her chest. How did she not notice his presence?

"What do we have here," Neptune snatched the book from Aqila. "Legend History, this edition was from the past five hundred years. The only one who would be interested in that would be a little Legend. Isn't that so?" Neptune grabbed Aqila's chin. She was only slightly taller than him.

"Let her go. She's a Seer, that's all. We don't want to make a ruckus with the Windmasters," the masked man pulled Aqila from Neptune's grasp.

"Agni, you'll regret it. She was with the Waterbearer Legend back in the Beach tribe. She's a little too close to this situation, and she also knows Jai. She also was strong enough to override our little secret concoction. Weren't you Aqila?"

"I'm a Seer and a Storm. Let me walk peacefully," Aqila demanded.

"Interesting you mention peace, Aqila. Peace is something that can't be attained with the current state of affairs. We have created our own peace and destroyed anything that stands in the way of it. Now, as a Seer, your little mind can phantom all sorts of things, can't it? And you've been here reading some fascinating material about Legends and birth records. You're on their side. If I let you go, you'll still be an enemy. Unless you can use your sight and tell us where they are." Agni's words were slow and deliberate.

Neptune smiled, "You tell us, and we let you walk, pretty lady. It's your choice."

"Alright, I'm a new Seer. If you touch my hands, you can see what I see," she opened her palms flat. Agni walked around to face her, and they both placed a hand on her palms. Aqila took a breath and closed her eyes.

She swiftly did a wind flip, pulling them towards her and spiraling into the air to flip Agni and Neptune. She created a wind sphere to shield her from water and fire attacks. Using accelerated speed, she made for the stairs. But Neptune used water to turn the sand into mud. They would be trapped!

Neptune used ice on the left of her bubble, and Agni used fire on her right. They were trying to breach the wind sphere. She could feel their strength. She hovered over the library ceiling. If she could create a blast strong enough to knock them back, the explosion could break her through the sand. The pressure was beginning to breach the sphere. Aqila hovered higher and higher until she used her strength to blast the sphere open. Agni and Neptune were knocked backward and slammed into the library walls. Aqila dashed onto Talon's back, and they flew high into the air.

Suddenly, she felt herself being snatched backward. Neptune created a water chain that pulled her right from Talon's back mid-air. She landed abruptly on the desert sand. Aqila sputtered out a mouthful of sand. Agni hurled a fury of lightning at Aqila. Quickly, she was on her toes, spiraling out of the way. Lightning shouldn't be too harmful to a Fireheart, but it could prove deadly for everyone else. She couldn't summon too much wind. That would only make Agni stronger. Even if she deprived his flames of oxygen, he would only resort to lightning.

I can take on Neptune, but Agni is a problem.

"My my, I thought we had an arrangement," Agni chuckled as Aqila stood several feet away.

"You're both murderers. Why would I side with you?" Aqila noticed a flashing shadow in the sky.

"Gifted girl, you have no clue what suffering is. You've spent your life surrounded by peace. How blessed you are, but some of us had to struggle to survive," Agni spoke as he slowly walked closer to her.

Aqila continued stepping backward.

"We are bringing equality and peace to the world. This way, we will stop the suffering and make everyone stronger together," Neptune edged water tendrils towards Aqila's feet.

"You can't bring peace through sins! Murdering people is a sin! What did those sages do to you to deserve death? You're not bringing equality; you just want to climb the ladder and rule!"

"Our birthrights have been stolen from us," Neptune's water tendrils wrapped around Aqila's legs, squeezing her until she could barely feel them.

"What birthright, Neptune? The only descendants of Avala or Aenon in the Waterbearer tribes are Mahak, Muraco, and Nahal."

"That's a lie. The records were altered. That's why the sages had to die. They were in this plot to rob me, and I'm Jocasta's son!"

Aqila glared at Neptune, "You're not Jocasta's son! Mahak is her son! If you were so powerful, why did you have to retreat from a fight with a young Legend Neptune, or should I call you . . ."

"Yas," she heard Emet's voice as a faint whisper.

"Yas!"

"So the girl really is a Seer," Agni laughed, " I thought you'd decide to be more helpful, but it seems like you are just as dangerous to society as those Legends. Tell me, Aqila, you wear such a pretty little hairpin. Are you married? If not, it's so shameful that your fiance has to lose such a pretty face," he blasted a stream of fire at her face.

Concentrating with all her might, she deoxygenated the air before her. His flames couldn't get close enough to her face. Then, using the same technique, she freed herself from Neptune, rendering his tendrils useless. Aqila knocked the wind out of Neptune with a wind swipe aimed strategically at his torso.

Suddenly, Agni fell to his knees. He was unconscious. A figure flipped into the air and landed on Neptune with their knees, also knocking him out. The person flew past Aqila and dragged her to Talon.

"Aqila, go. They won't be out for long; leave-" Haneul's deep gray eyes went wide. His body shook violently in front of Aqila.

She looked up and saw Agni piercing her friend's body with lightning. Haneul collapsed, and she caught him, "Haneul!"

"Aqila, don't let them win," he began to twitch in her arms.

Agni brushed the sand from his clothes, "I really hate traitors. They should die a miserable death. Now it's your turn."

She saw the angle of his wrist. He was going to strike a lightning attack at her. The peace that usually occupied her mind's eye was replaced with anger and heartbreak. Her hands were on Haneul's still chest; he was no more. Her knees were drenched with his blood. The lightning went through his back, seizing his life's breath and stilling his heart. She no longer knew peace.

She gently lifted Haneul onto Talon's back as the lightning approached her. Fury was her shield. She felt the hit. It felt like a dagger wound. But it did not harm her. She looked back to see the confusion in Agni's eyes, "You better pray to the Universe that you never see me again. Because if I do, I will kill you." She mounted Talon, and they took to the sky. Agni tried repeatedly to attack her with lightning strikes; they all failed.

A slight sensation of terror filled him because he didn't know why. He tended to Neptune's wounds; he had a few broken ribs from Haneul, but he was confident the Waterbearer would be fine. Agni adjusted his face mask and laughed. It finally dawned on him, "Aqila, you aren't a Seer at all, are you? Just a very well-read Legend." He laughed as he dragged Neptune inside the library.

CHAPTER 22

Tiber was trying to focus on what Sheraga and Kavi were debating, but she was fascinated by the DragonLord's war room. The floor was covered in a rug that showed the world, each Nation depicted by its respective colors. The conversation was interrupted by Liora's entrance, "Sheraga, Jai is here with three Flamethrowers," she smiled at Sheraga before gently bowing her head.

Sheraga smiled back before winking at her suggestively. Kavi cleared his throat. Sheraga shrugged, "That's what happens when you get a wife, baby brother. Their presence fills the air with love and roman-"

"Alright! I get it. How will we continue this discussion?"

"The only way to continue, invite them in, of course."

As soon as the words left his lips, Tiber watched as two men and two women entered the war room. She was taken aback to see Jai. His eyes were the most beautiful shade that she had ever seen. He smiled and nodded to her and Cove when he looked in her direction.

"His eyes are so gentle," she whispered to Cove.

Jai walked toward Tiber and extended his hand, "Nice to meet you. You must be Tiber. Aqila's told me a lot about you." He turned to Sheraga, "I'm sorry about coming unannounced."

"Whatever, you're not the only one to disrupt my plans for the day," Sheraga rolled his amber eyes. "Well, anyways, Kavi, please continue. I was actually interested in what you were saying."

Kavi pinched the bridge of his nose as if he was growing slightly annoyed, "I refuse to stand here and rationalize my findings again. I'll keep this brief. I have a spy in Neptune's camp. He reported to me yesterday the identity of Neptune. His name is Yas, and he comes from-"

"The Snow Tribe!" Tiber blurted.

"True, now refrain from interrupting me," Kavi gestured towards Tiber. "He took Mahak's alias as Neptune and began committing crimes under the same alias. It was actually an interesting process. If anyone was to follow the trail, it would lead you to Mahak, not Yas. Aqila is verifying some information on Mahak. We can't make a move until we know that Mahak told us the truth. If our information is correct, we can move in and apprehend Yas for his crimes. His offenses include the murder of two chiefs, attempted murder, theft of international property, and the list goes on. Time is of the essence; Neptune will start recruiting to recover his forces since most of his old ragtag group was killed."

"His old group was killed," Jai asked, "How did that happen?"

"It's quite simple. They captured Aqila and poisoned her, I found out and retaliated. My intention wasn't to kill anyone. However, poison does have the capacity to be deadly. I must admit a few of them did die by my swordsmanship."

The room became silent upon hearing that Kavi had taken on Neptune's forces.

"Well, we have to treat this situation like war. Our very lives are being threatened. In that case, Kavi's actions were perfectly legal. Capturing Aqila, a Seer, is the equivalent of capturing me or a chief. It is an offense worthy of being struck down. Now, we continue. This has cut Neptune's numbers, which is a plus for us. What about Agni?" Sheraga asked.

Kavi signed, "I don't know. The Windmaster's efforts have been concentrated on Neptune since the Waterbearers share borderlines with us."

"We've had a run-in with Agni when you and Boaz saved us from the border between Upper and Lower Ember. But we haven't uncovered any motives," Jai spoke.

"Well, if it is the motive you're looking for, Agni promised us a united Ember where we wouldn't have to suffer the miseries of life. In Lower Ember, everyone is impoverished. After the Civil War, our lands were damaged, so we couldn't grow food for ourselves. To not starve, we had to heavily rely on Upper Ember, the victor of the war, for food. The prices they charged us were ridiculously high, so Lower Ember is in debt. Until the land is restored to a healthy condition, we will always be in a deficit. But the families in Lower Ember can't afford the price of food. As a result, we steal it," Zay explained. "I used to work for Agni. When I completed my mission, I could eat well. If I failed, I starved. It was like that for many of us. We did what we had to so we could survive."

"Why didn't you get foreign aid as an alternative? The rest of the Nations don't have food shortages," Kavi spoke.

"We don't have a leader to speak on our behalf like the other Nations. Waterbearer tribes have Chiefs, Kindle has Tora, Pyroc has Sheraga, Windmasters have rulers and council people, and Theyra has governors. We don't have anyone. That's why Agni is so appealing to the people of Ember, and listening to him talk makes you believe he can solve your problems."

"I see," Sheraga sighed. Suddenly, Amber came into the war room.

"Humble apologies, DragonLord! A situation is taking place outside. A large bird is hovering overhead. I will resume my post if you don't have orders to relay, sir!"

"Resume post! Inform the lead Dragon to engage in offensive maneuvers. I'm on my way," Sheraga's eyes looked bloodthirsty. For a moment, it seemed his exposed skin had the slight outline of dragon scales. He looked around at everyone, "Let's go!"

Everyone followed Sheraga outside of the palace. Tiber's eyes focused on the giant bird in the sky, which seemed so familiar.

"That's Aqila," Kavi called out to Sheraga.

"Dragons, stand down," Sheraga ordered, and his army promptly relaxed their weapons.

Aqila landed ungracefully, which seemed unusual to Tiber. Talon's feathery legs trembled slightly at the landing before he collapsed, tossing Aqila violently aside. There appeared to be a body fastened to Talon, but she couldn't be sure of the position.

Kavi and Sheraga ran to Aqila. Tiber sensed something off. She looked to Cove, who was eyeing her, "She's injured," they said in unison before running to Aqila.

"Kavi, she's hurt," Cove called out.

"Aqila! Are you okay?" Tiber dropped to her knees.

Her eyes were red from crying, "Haneul's dead! It's all my fault. I didn't protect him," she wailed. Kavi slowly descended to his knees and tried to embrace her, but she pushed him away. Tiber looked at her back; black bruises were visible through her tattered tunic. She hadn't seen anything like that before.

Tiber gasped, "Your back! She's really hurt!" Cove opened one of his water pouches and started applying cool water to the wound.

"I'll get her inside," Kavi said as he gently wiped the tears from her face.

Tiber's heart broke as she watched Kavi pull Aqila to her feet and support her body weight. Her clothes were dirty and tattered, her knees were soaked in blood, and she was bruised. Aqila could barely walk. Kavi carefully picked her up as her body still shook with sobs. Liora was waiting to usher them inside as he approached the top of the steps.

Jai was utterly frozen and speechless. Who could have done something like that to her? Sheraga walked over to him, "Take your party inside." He turned to the DragonGuard, "Harsha, oversee the careful transport of the owl. He's severely bruised. That's why he collapsed. Pyre, instruct squadrons two and three on the offensive maneuver strategy four. I want squadron one to fan out, oversee the villages, and report abnormal findings. DragonGuard is on the offensive. Uninvited guests get one warning. For any resistance, I authorize a kill order."

The Flamethrowers and Tiber followed Sheraga back inside the palace.

"DragonLord, Aqila is in a guest room with Kavi and Cove," Liora spoke as she closed the palace doors.

Sheraga smiled, "I'm going to the war room. When you have time, check our inventory."

Liora nodded as Sheraga beckoned for everyone to follow him. Tiber couldn't really focus on anything but Aqila. She didn't notice that she was stopped at the entrance of the war room by Sheraga's body.

"Aqila's in the second room to the left. You're a Waterbearer. You might be able to assist."

"I'll do my best!" Tiber hurried down the hallway. Jai approached Sheraga from behind.

"I think we should be concerned that someone was able to hurt Aqila like that," Jai pulled Sheraga aside. There was so much buzzing inside the war room, and everyone was concerned about Aqila.

"Looks like she had a run-in with a Fireheart with lightning proficiency. That's where those bruises came from. I'm trying to figure out why she's not dead, like her friend."

Hearing Sheraga's words, everyone grew silent.

"Well, we're glad she's not dead, right?" Alena was perplexed.

"Of course, don't misunderstand me. If we, Firehearts, get hit by lightning, it would just bruise our skin. It wouldn't kill us unless the attacker had an unusual affinity for it, but that doesn't happen. I think . . . anyway, for other Nations, lightning is deadly. That Windmaster was shot in the back with a lightning strike; it shot straight through his skin, causing the wound to bleed. He was hit near the heart, so when the lightning penetrated his body, it shocked his heart. He probably had a heart attack, which did him in. Aqila is not a Fireheart, but those bruises came from lightning. Her bird was obviously hit, too. The surges would have killed an animal. Something else must have happened that allowed her to survive. I'm thankful but curious."

Jai almost told Sheraga that Aqila was a Legend, but he remembered that he had to keep that under wraps. "I hope she recovers soon," he whispered. Jai was also curious about Tiber and hoped to catch up with her soon.

In the hall, Cove and Tiber had exited the room. "Will she be okay?"

Cove nodded, "I think she'll be fine. I can't imagine what could have bruised her like that."

"The bruises on her legs looked almost like her circulation was cut off. I can understand why she doesn't want to talk about it. Let's go heal up Talon. He looked so miserable," she pulled Cove's hand as they went in the direction opposite of the war room.

Aqila was sitting up on the bed. Her fingers would skim the silky smooth red and gold bedspread every now and then. Kavi was sitting on the edge of the bed facing her, but she could not bring herself to look into his eyes. The silence was eating her alive, but the weight of Haneul's death felt like she was tied to an anchor and cast into the sea.

Kavi sighed, "Aqila, I can't take this. Talk to me, please. This silence is killing me. Please," he pleaded with her.

His voice was so gentle she could feel his love for her drip from every word, but she still couldn't bring herself to speak to him, to look at him. Her heart was heavy. She saw his hand inch closer to hers, and she smiled.

"We can stay like this all night or talk to each other. It's up to you. Either way, I'm not going anywhere," he whispered.

Facing her fears, she glanced up at him. Kavi slid closer and gently embraced her, "Does it still hurt?"

"Not as much," she whispered, eyes glassy as she laid her head on his chest.

"Can I ask what happened?"

"Neptune and Agni. I was in that library where the sages operate in Theyra. I noticed something off when I got there. None of the sages were out and about. I thought they may have been in a study session, so I didn't think anything of it. I read through the books I wanted and came across some interesting information. I undercovered Neptune's identity and have some strong leads for Agni. But then it hit me, I had been there for nearly at least an hour, and there were no sages. It didn't feel right, so I tried to check out a book. Then, my mind's eye kept pulling my attention to the back of the library where the sages would study. When I opened the door-" she started to sob. Kavi kissed her hair and ran his hand gently across her back.

She sniffled, "The sages were dead, all eight of them. I noticed Neptune first and then Agni. I had the Legend History book, the last edition, so Neptune started inquiring if I was a Legend. Agni blew him off until Neptune told him I knew Tiber and Jai. I told them that I was a Seer and a Storm."

"They wanted me to have a vision of Jai and Tiber's whereabouts in exchange for my life. I played along and tried to make an escape. We fought for a bit. I couldn't break through the ceiling to escape since Neptune turned the sand to mud to hinder me. I ran and climbed on Talon. Neptune used water chains to pull me off Talon in mid-flight. I noticed something flash above me. Then Agni and Neptune started talking about stolen birthrights when I told them I wouldn't side with them because they're murderers. They argued their point. Neptune had squeezing tendrils that nearly made my legs explode, and Agni was hurling fire at my face. I deoxygenated to keep them off of me. Then Haneul came and knocked them both out, or so we thought. He helped me get to Talon, and I was about to fly off before-"

"Agni killed him," Kavi finished her sentence.

"He shot him with lightning! His eyes were so shocked. It went straight through his back. I broke his fall. Haneul, he-he told me don't let them win. I was so angry when Haneul stopped breathing," she wiped her eyes. "When I saw Agni aiming another strike at me. I just reflexively did the first technique that came to mind, continuous wind. I wrapped our bodies in the continuous wind. As Agni kept striking, it felt like daggers on my back. I wrapped Talon, too, until we could get out of his range. I didn't know that he had lightning. I thought that Firehearts couldn't wield both. I knew I could handle Neptune by deoxygenating. Still, fire uses oxygen as fuel, but I was trying to be careful because winds only fan flames. Agni was strong with fire alone. I thought I was doing the best thing. But Haneul paid for my mistakes with his life," she sobbed into Kavi's chest.

Haneul was a great friend of Kavi's. It pained him to know that he was gone. A single tear fell from his eyes. Before his grief could wash over him, he sighed and thought to himself before speaking. "Aqila, you did the best you could. Neither of you knew that Agni could use lightning. Haneul would agree, and we both know that. We just know that we have to win. That was his final wish for us, to be victorious. So we have to do just that."

"I'm sorry, Kavi. I know he was your friend-"

"Aqila, I'm not mad at you, love. You didn't kill him. Agni did! It hurts, yes. The weight of his death hasn't really hit me yet. But, right now, I just feel blessed and thankful that I still have you. I can't imagine losing you." He wiped her eyes.

"We still have Haneul, too, and his spirit will be in our victory. I still get worried about not being able to see things like this coming, and then I beat myself up about it."

"Why?"

"Because I feel like everyone expects me to be able to prevent things like this. Then I feel stupid for not being able to see enough," she admits.

"People who think that way just don't understand how it works. You shouldn't worry yourself over the opinions of uninformed people. We will succeed and win for Haneul."

Aqila took a deep breath, feeling safe in Kavi's embrace. "You're right, Kavi. You've always been my strength and my comfort. We must focus on our mission—for Haneul and everyone who relies on us."

Kavi smiles warmly, holding her close, and after a moment, he takes a deep breath. "We will avenge him. We will put an end to Agni and Neptune. So, what did we learn about them? Do you think Mahak was telling the truth?"

"Yes, he was. He's the son of Jocasta, and Neptune's real name is Yas."

"Yes, I know, and Tiber knows him. She seemed shocked to hear it, though."

"Neptune is really worked up over this whole birthright thing. It is like he really believes that he is Jocasta's son. Maybe some of the birth records were tampered with. It seemed to be the case for Cyra's family."

"That's almost not even possible. A doctor submits the records, and the sages catalog them. There's always a backup copy in the sages' archives, and the family keeps a copy of the birth record as well," Kavi explained.

"Great Heavens, you're right! Why didn't I think of that? He was a doctor!"

"Who?"

"Okay, just bear with me! Cyra and Aenon had twins, and one of them died, leaving Soleil. She marries and has two sons, Lucien and Elior. Lucien's family is well noted throughout history, all the way to Tora. Yes, Tora is a descendant of Cyra. A renowned doctor, Yuuta, is also mentioned. He and his wife were famous doctors. From what I've heard and read, he could do it all: make medicine, perform surgery and pediatrics, and even deliver babies. Through the years, there were many articles written where his work was given high accolades." Aqila pauses.

"There was something strange. Yuuta and his wife had a baby with no name in the birth record, only the date and time of birth. Then, it said that Nuri died of childbirth. But the thing that's weird is that most writings regarding Nuri note that she became very sick after the birth of her first child but continued the advancement of medicine until she died from a late miscarriage. I remember reading about that. It was around the time Yuuta was working to heal the DragonLady. Nuri was still contributing to the advancement of medicine. So she couldn't have died, at least not then. She had that child around the time Tora was born, and Tora is older than me."

"So the doctor didn't put a name down. That's strange. Tora is Cyra's descendant. But his parents are dead. We could have asked Tora's father if the records were accurate until that one instance."

"Wait, I had a vision about a man that looked like Tora and a man that looked like Jai. It seemed as if there was a long-time rift between them. It may have something to do with this."

"We've been trying to understand why Agni and Neptune are doing what they're doing. I think we hit it on the head with Neptune. What if he really believes he's Jocasta's son?"

"Then we have to ask what he had to gain by being her son? Aenon is not the most popular Legend, especially in the Snow and Ice Tribe." Aqila pondered.

"But, as a descendant of a Legend, that may come with some perks." Kavi suggested.

"Maybe Tiber would know," Aqila reflected.

"I want to play around with an idea that may lead us to this missing baby or who altered the birth record. Let's say Yuuta altered the birth record. He was a doctor. Why would he not deliver his own child? Let's say Yuuta left the baby's name blank and turned that in. The sages would have tried to contact him to validate the records, so he would have avoided them. But why? Was something wrong with the baby? Was someone after the baby? Did someone take the baby? We don't know."

"From the records, the sages did attempt to contact Yuuta with no success. Either way, the child is now an adult, maybe a year older than me. That probably means they don't know their parents," Aqila wondered.

"Funny. We both know a Fireheart who has that problem," Kavi raised his eyebrow.

"Who? Jai? Kavi, he has amnesia. And he recently met his father." Aqila was taken aback.

"You must follow all the leads in an investigation. I'm not blaming or saying anything other than it wouldn't hurt to probe the matter."

"I think we should see if we can ask Tora about his family," Aqila suggested.

"I agree. I can go see him if you'd like," Kavi offered.

"Sure, and I'll ask Jai about his father. Kavi-um . . . Well-"

"What is it?"

"Shouldn't we take Haneul back to Wyndhm to ensure he has a proper burial? I mean, his body is already stiff. I think we should take him back first."

"I'll take him back and make sure he's buried with honor. I also need to relieve our spies of their duties. Any Windmaster near Neptune's forces will be retaliated against now."

"Shouldn't I go with you to explain what happened?"

"No, I'll take care of things on the home front. I'll talk to Sheraga, and then I'll be off," he kissed her forehead. "Try and get some rest."

"I'll try," Aqila got under the covers and sighed as Kavi flashed his charming smile before leaving the room.

As Kavi left Aqila so she could get some rest, he was immediately met by Sheraga as he closed the door behind him.

"How's she doing?"

"The Waterbearers worked their magic. Her wounds are looking better, but I want her to rest here tonight if that's alright with you."

"Anything for old friends. Who did it?" Sheraga asked as the pair headed down the steps.

"Agni and Neptune," Kavi replied. "They killed all of the sages at the library and attacked Aqila as she was leaving."

"What! Thank Heavens, she's lucky to be alive."

"I know. I need to bury Haneul before too much time passes. Do you have a quick way of reaching Tora?"

"I do, but he's not in Kindle. He went to Upper Ember against my recommendations," Sheraga huffed as they walked outside. "He was furious when he left, though. I tried to ask what it was about, but he was too fired up to give me any information."

"I really needed to see his family birth records. I guess I'll have to wait. He may be back by the time I return from Wyndhm. Do you know of a renowned doctor by the name of Yuuta?"

"Yeah, I do. He came to see my mother before she passed. My father followed his recommendations, adding another year to her life. For that, I'm thankful."

"Know what he looks like?"

Sheraga grimaced, "It's been a while, baby brother. He kind of looks like Tora, especially in the eyes, but obviously older. Now, don't quote me on that. I can ask my father about it. He was in contact with him more than I was."

"Please do," Kavi replied thoughtfully.

"What's up? You wouldn't be asking me that for no reason."

"Aqila got a few leads at the library. Our information on Neptune is accurate. However, we need to secure Mahak's location. Aqila told me Neptune argued that he was Jocasta's son, not Mahak."

"If I recall, not that anything which doesn't involve war can keep my attention too long; Aenon is the only thing that family has going for them. But his reputation was scary, to say the least. So, what does he have to gain in wanting to be connected?"

"That's what Aqila and I are curious about. Maybe the Waterbearers can find out," Kavi suggested.

"That's a good idea. I'll send them back. And Kavi, I know Haneul was your good friend, and I'm truly sorry for your loss," Sheraga said and patted Kavi on the back.

"Thank you," the pair reached Sterling. Cove and Tiber had covered Haneul's face with a covering just as they arrived.

"I'm sorry for your loss Kavi. Tiber and I cleaned and repositioned him. He's pretty much ready for burial," Cove explained.

"Thank you, Cove," Kavi waited for Tiber to finish securing Haneul onto his dasher before he mounted. "Sheraga, try to get that information from your father as soon as possible. I'll be in touch," Kavi nodded to the DragonLord before taking to the sky.

Sheraga turned to Cove and Tiber, "Chief, we'll need you to go to the Snow Tribe. Alert them to Neptune's identity. All of our information has been confirmed. However, Mahak could be in danger due to our revelation, especially since Aqila was attacked by Agni and Neptune."

Tiber's mouth dropped, "She's lucky to be alive!"

Sheraga nodded at her statement.

"Shouldn't I go with Cove? That's my tribe anyways." Tiber asked.

"My question is, who are you? What are you doing here? It's glaringly obvious to me now that you're not the Chief's wife," Sheraga stepped towards Tiber.

Cove stood in front of her and looked Sheraga in the eyes, "Just leave her be. She's here because I want her to be here."

"This isn't the time or place for a romantic date, Chief. I'm really starting to question your judgment," Sheraga hissed.

Tiber had enough. "Stop it!" She pushed them apart. "Just stop! I'm here because Aqila asked me to come! I'm a Legend, okay! And this mess with Neptune is my fault, and I'm trying to clean it up! You have your answer. Are you happy?"

"Tiber, why?" Cove asked.

Tiber was frustrated and angry. She couldn't face them. She fled inside the palace as fast as she could.

"What an interesting turn of events," Sheraga snickered.

Cove grabbed Sheraga by the neck of his robe, "Look, I don't know what game you're playing, but it needs to stop."

Sheraga effortlessly freed himself from Cove's grasp as if pulling himself away from a child, "Please, don't try to play tough guy with me. It doesn't suit you. I knew she was a Legend the second I made eye contact with her. The energy and life force of the ancient dragons run through my veins. I'm not your average Fireheart. I pray that you eventually see that what just happened was necessary."

"Making people uncomfortable should never be necessary!"

"As a Waterbearer, this may be hard for you to hear, but don't be emotional. I get it; you really like her. But she's a Legend and light years behind Jai and Aqila in terms of skill. She needs to embrace who she is to be confident in her role. But if she's always hiding, she will always be afraid of not being enough."

"All of the Legends are hiding technically. Agni and Neptune are out to get them! She can't just run around telling everyone she's a Legend!"

"Chief, there's a big difference between hiding from the world and hiding from yourself. Jai and Aqila have come to terms with who and what they are. Tiber hasn't. She's hiding from herself. She's unsure of herself. She has so much power deep inside, but her fears hold her back. And if you love her, you shouldn't nurse her fears. You should push her to be their best self and reach her potential if you love her. But then again, that means you'd have to stop being unsure of what you feel and what you want. Either way, you can stay here tonight but be on your way first thing in the morning," Sheraga took his time as he approached the palace.

Cove swallowed hard. As much as he hated to admit it, Sheraga was right. He needed to make a hard decision. He truly cared for Tiber, but she was a Legend, and he didn't want to be the one that kept her from her destiny.

***

Tiber's vision was distorted by tears. She opened a door, fell to her knees, and sobbed.

"Tiber, what's wrong?"

"A-Aqila? I'm sorry, it's nothing. I know you were trying to rest," Tiber quickly wiped her eyes.

"Nonsense! I appreciate Kavi's sentiments, but I can't rest with so much on my mind," she kicked the covers to the bottom of the bed. "What happened?"

"I feel so useless! Cove and Sheraga started arguing because of me. I told Sheraga I'm a Legend just so he would get off Cove's back. I didn't want them to keep arguing."

"Well, Sheraga probably knew that anyway," Aqila replied.

"What!"

"He's the DragonLord. He can sense things like that. Knowing him, he sensed your power and decided to probe you for information. Remember that if the situation was flipped and you had that kind of power, you'd probably do the same thing. In your own way, of course."

"I guess," Tiber murmured.

"Don't feel bad. This is you, and you must own what the Universe made you. Being a Legend will always be an uncomfortable reality until you fully accept it."

"It is just still a huge adjustment. I was just starting to get the hang of believing in the Universe. Why did it choose me of all of the Waterbearers to choose from? What makes me worthy? Especially after everything I've done."

"That's the past, you can't change it, but you can control what you do right now. I know it's hard, but it must be done."

"I know you understand. It must have been hard to be there and watch your friend die. I just don't know how you keep moving forward."

"Haneul's death truly grieved me. At first, I wasn't sure if I could live with myself. But, I did my best with the information that I had. Haneul wanted me to keep going. Even though he's not with me physically, his spirit will be intertwined with the victory."

"I have to get more confident if I'm going to be of any help. I feel a lot better now. I should talk to Cove. He seemed a little disappointed that I didn't stick to the plan about not revealing my identity as a Legend."

"Well, he probably just wanted to protect you. However, it's not like you will go to the grave with that secret. We just don't want to give Neptune and Agni any more ammunition. Trust me, you should definitely talk things out with him. Besides, since I can't rest, I should prepare to take my leave."

"You're leaving?"

"First thing in the morning, yes. I have to. The sages are dead. I have to tell Boaz there's still a lot of tension between our people. I don't want them to think that I killed them."

Tiber offered a knowing nod to her friend as she slipped out of the room, gently shutting the door behind her. With a soft sigh, Tiber turned around and found herself face-to-face with Cove.

Tiber jumped in surprise, "I didn't know you were right there!"

"I figured that you would talk to Aqila. She's the only person you know here besides me," he explained.

"Cove, I-"

"It's okay Tiber. I'm going back to your tribe," Cove started.

"Okay, I'll get ready-"

"Tiber, you should stay here. It's better that I go back alone."

"You don't want me to go with you," she whispered.

Cove clutched her shoulders, "No! It is not like that at all! I just realized that I'm holding you back. My instinct is to protect you and defend you because I care. But you're a Legend. You don't need me. You need the chance to grow and get comfortable with who you are, and I haven't been helping you there."

"You're wrong, Cove. You've helped me a lot. I'd probably be dead if it wasn't for you. I've been a Legend my whole life, but I needed you to protect and defend me. You helped me grow my faith in the Universe. I know I'm behind, but I just claimed my faith, and so many things will be new to me. I always feel unworthy, but knowing you're in my corner keeps me going." They embraced each other.

"Well, I still have to go. Sheraga sent me on a mission," Cove smiled at her.

"A mission?"

"Yeah, to find out why Neptune wants to be Jocasta's son."

"As in, what does he have to gain? Everything! To be the descendant of a queen and a Legend is a high position in the tribe. But Mahak is Jocasta's son. And she only lived long enough to have one child due to the curse. Let me come with you! I can help you with this!"

Cove sighed, "On one condition, you have to own being a Legend from here on out."

"I promise!"

Cove smiled, "Okay, we'll go in the morning."

CHAPTER 23

It was early in the morning as Jai lay awake in the guestroom of the DragonLord's palace. Zay was sleeping peacefully in another bed across the room. In the quiet of the night, Jai could hear the low rumble of the volcano and the hushed sounds of Zay's breathing. Jai couldn't sleep. He kept thinking about Aqila and wondering about Tiber. He had so many unanswered questions. It was enough to drive him mad.

He sat up, his leg hanging from the side of the bed. He ran his fingers through his hair before slipping out to try to find Aqila. He tiptoed through the hallways of the palace. It was easy to get lost during the day, not to mention when the sun hadn't risen. He opened his hand, and a light shone from his palm. "That's better," he whispered to himself.

After about ten minutes of wandering around, he entered a familiar hallway and door. He slowly opened it. To his surprise, Aqila was already awake and had company.

"You do know that it is common courtesy to knock on a woman's door before entering," Aqila raised an eyebrow. She had a dim lamp on, and Tiber sat at the foot of the bed.

Jai closed his palm and sighed, "You're right. I thought you were asleep, sorry."

"It's fine," Aqila rolled her eyes. "What's wrong?"

"I couldn't sleep. Nice to see you again, Tiber."

"Same to you," Tiber smiled.

"What's keeping you up?" Aqila asked.

"You. You were a complete wreck when you got here. I am sorry about the loss of your friend."

"Thank you, Jai. I ran into Agni and Neptune in Theyra, and Agni killed Haneul," Aqila swallowed hard.

"Do we know what we'll do at this point?" Jai asked.

"I have to go back to Theyra. Agni and Neptune killed the sages at the library. I had to leave for my safety. I don't want them to think that I killed them."

"Yeah, especially since things have been rocky between the Landkeepers and Windmasters since the war," Jai groaned.

"I'm returning to my tribe since we have Neptune's true identity."

"Really? Who is Neptune?"

"He's a senior member of my tribe obsessed with being a descendant of Aenon."

"Do we know who Agni is then?"

"No, still no confirmed leads about his identity yet," Aqila answered.

"Well, Aqila, I don't think you should go off alone now. Agni and Neptune probably have guessed that you're a Legend. It is even more dangerous for you now. The Flamethrowers can go with you! It's just Arin, Alena, Zay, and myself."

"It depends on Talon's health. He can ride with three people comfortably. If he carries four, he will need to rest more frequently. After the incident with Agni, he probably will be up to carrying two people. So how will everyone else get there?"

"They'll ride horses. Talon will arrive first, but we won't be far behind."

"Okay, well, Tiber, can you and Cove meet us in Theyra once you're done?"

"That shouldn't be a problem."

"I should let you two know that the last Legend will be waiting for us." Aqila smiled.

Jai's golden eyes went wide, "You know who the last Legend is?"

"Yes, it's Boaz! That makes everything easier. He's already on our side."

"Do Agni and Neptune know about him?" Tiber asked.

"No, I'm mostly positive they don't," Aqila replied.

"That's good," Jai exhaled.

"Tiber, release Nahal from the ice when you return to your tribe. See what he has to do with all of this and how much he knows."

"Ice? Um okay. What do you think we will find?" Tiber asked.

"I don't know. It seemed deeply personal in Neptune's reason to ally with Agni. Agni is running things, and Neptune sees a benefit in teaming with him. He insisted that he was Jocasta's son, even though the records said otherwise. I have to get to Theyra, and Tiber is needed back at her tribe. Hopefully, we can get more answers before all nations start fighting each other."

"I'm going to sleep before Cove, and I head off. The next time we'll meet is in Theyra. I know Boaz is doing a good job over there." Tiber yawned and stretched as she headed for the door.

"What was up with Boaz?" Jai asked Aqila.

"He officially ended the civil war in Theyra."

Jai's mouth dropped, "He's something! He ended a war all by himself. Man, that's incredible. Well, I guess he wanted to help his people establish unity before things got too crazy with Agni and Neptune. I respect that. Did you know that he was a Legend?"

"No, I didn't. But, I can't think of a better Landkeeper than him."

"I wonder why they felt like they needed to kill the sages? I mean, they are peaceful people. Why kill them?"

"If they validated the records, and Agni and Neptune didn't want to hear that, it could have easily escalated to a lethal fight." A thought suddenly came to her, "Jai, do you know a man in his fifties, tall with black hair that's beginning to gray? He's in excellent physical shape with brown eyes."

Jai hung his head, "I do. His name is Arka, and he probably wants my head. He works for Agni, and Zay worked for him at some point when he was on their side."

"He works for Agni? That's strange. He went to Tora looking for you. Tora didn't say that there was any bad intent. It seems unusual that he would go to him to inquire about you. Come to think of it, based on the timeline, Tora must have left not long after we did. Something's definitely going on."

"You think Tora's in on this?"

"No, of course not. Whatever it is has something to do with those records and may have something to do with Agni. Tora may not realize the potential dangers he faces; he is also a descendant of Cyra. I hope he's careful."

"Let's pray he's not in danger," Jai sighed. "The sun is coming up. I'm going to start getting ready and let the Flamethrowers know the plans for today." Jai headed for the door. When she heard the door shut, Aqila flung herself backward into the pillows. She wanted to ask Jai about his family, but she couldn't organically get the conversation started. She didn't want Jai to suspect anything.

She was immediately claimed by sight.

***

"Who is it?"

"I need help, please," a man called out. He was at Tora's house.

Tora opened the door, "How can I help you, sir?"

"Have you seen or heard from Jai? It's urgent!"

Tora hesitated, "No, sir. To be quite honest, I don't know who you're talking about."

"You are Tora, right?"

"Yes, sir, I'm the leader of Kindle."

"You look just like him," the man whispered. He backed up slowly and shook his head before hurrying away.

"Sir, I didn't catch your name! You dropped something!"

Tora saw a paper on the ground and picked it up. When he looked up again, he didn't see the man. He shrugged his shoulders. "What's that smell? Oh! My food is burning!" He closed the door quickly, the piece of paper clutched in his hand.

***

Aqila shook her head slightly, "That must have happened shortly before Haneul and I arrived. Tora looked like who? He does look a bit like Jai. Could there be someone else? Why was he scared? Why did he leave so abruptly?"

She got out of bed and began preparing for her journey back to Theyra. Nearly an hour after the vision, Aqila was outside checking on Talon. Her dasher appeared to be in almost excellent health.

"Good morning, Aqila," Arin and Alena called in unison.

"Good morning. How are you?"

"I'm well. It's a relief to see you are doing better," Alena hugged her.

"Good morning, ladies. I brought three horses. I'm not sure who's getting a horse. It's four of us, but Jai only wanted three horses," Zay greeted them.

"Jai's riding with me on Talon."

Arin looked shocked, while Alena and Zay were surprised but less so. Jai ran over to them, "Morning! Aqila, is Talon good to go?"

"Yeah, you're good to ride?"

"Hell yeah," Jai said as he mounted quickly on Talon's back. Alena and Zay were already on their horses.

Aqila mounted Talon and took the reins, "We're going to Theyra. I know a shortcut that should get us there by tonight. Arin, come on."

Arin carefully mounted the last horse as Talon took to the sky.

"Is she okay?" Aqila asked Jai.

"I don't know why she wouldn't be."

Aqila shrugged her shoulders as she ushered Talon toward Theyra. She looked down and saw Zay leading the twins in the same direction. "Zay is really good with directions," she said.

"Yeah, he's good at a lot of things. It's funny. He reminds me a lot of Arka. Well, the good days with Arka, I should say."

"Speaking of Arka, he didn't go to Tora hunting you down. He was genuinely worried about you, and it appeared as if he may have wanted to give you something. But he was uneasy with Tora for some reason."

"You had a vision?"

"I did, and it is good to confirm that Arka did not have bad intentions in looking for you."

"I mean, that's great, but that still doesn't explain anything."

"I almost forgot to tell you! I met my family!"

"Really! I know how bad you wanted that! How was it?"

"I was nervous, but everything went really well. Kavi came with me since we are preparing to get married, and he wanted to ask my parents for permission. My parents were amazing, and I have a brother named Athens. We got along so well. My parents have been so happy to return to the fold of their old lives. My father, Cirocco, was the former WindGuardian, and my mother, Brisa, was a teacher specializing in literature. They were good friends of Akash and Sufa. It's been nice seeing them so happy."

"I'm glad you met them. I was so close to meeting my father again. But Agni had to make that difficult. The first time meeting him, it felt so natural. The way he was looking at me, it was like he understood me. I felt like I didn't need to explain myself. I was free. I pray that after this is all over, we can have a chance to talk about things and reconnect."

"I hope so, too! What's your father's name?"

"His name is Yuuta."

Aqila's hands almost dropped the reins.

A lot of people have the same name.

"Why do you ask?"

"I was just curious. I mean, you did cancel on me to go on this pursuit," she looked back and smiled.

Jai laughed, "Yeah, you're right. It's just so crazy. We have a motive for Neptune. But what could be Agni's?"

"Until we know who he really is, we won't know."

"Are you nervous about telling the Landkeepers what happened?"

"Not really, I wish I was going under better circumstances, but I know what happened. I can't force them to believe me, but I'm still obligated to tell them the truth."

"Things will also be easier with Boaz on your side. Who's going to run the library now? Doesn't it have something like important historical texts?"

"Yes, I would like to discuss it with Bo when we get there. Jai, I can't help but notice that Arin seemed a little down. Is everything okay?"

"I think so. I told Zay to get three horses, and I thought it was obvious that we would ride together. We're Legends, and we haven't had a chance to catch up on some things."

"Yes, but they don't know that I'm a Legend. They think I'm just a Seer. She seemed surprised that you chose to ride with me over them."

"I don't think it's a big deal. Alena and Zay aren't bothered," Jai brushed her off.

"Yeah, because it is obvious they really like each other," Aqila said.

Jai coughed, "Wait, what? Nah, they're just friends."

"Okay, Jai, if you say so," Aqila rolled her eyes, "you should talk to her when we get to Theyra."

"I'll check on her when we land."

Metal - an offspring of Land, miracles, flecks, and ores embedded into rock.

Metal is evolution. We are strong, innovative, and ambitious.

Metal is precise control and unwavering discipline. It requires a stable and organized mind to wield.

It does not favor those who seek ease. It favors the unfortunate.

It loves the self-reliant.

Its keepers were born ready for revolution. Are you ready?

METALKEEPERS

CHAPTER 24

Cove and Tiber were face to face with the snowy mountain she once called home. Tiber sighed.

Turning to see the sullen expression on her face, Cove asked, "You okay?"

Tiber blinked away tears, "I've been running from this for so long. I know I'm not going to see my father when I get to the top of the mountain. He's not going to hold me in his arms anymore," she sobbed.

Cove eased Medusa closer to Mika and Tiber and gently wrapped his arm around her shoulders, "I know it's hard. I know things will be a little different from here on out. But your father wouldn't want you to feel like this. He would want you to love your home and people in his stead. Think about your sister; she hasn't seen you, and she's gone through so much. It would really ease her mind to put her eyes on you."

Tiber pulled away, "She's fine. She has Muraco. He has always cared for Shasa and would never let her down. She might miss me occasionally, but she has her rock. I'm the one who lost mine. Father and I had so many things we wanted to do together," she wiped her eyes, "now he's not here to experience any more milestones with me." She sniffled and sighed, looking at Cove.

She reached out to him, "But I shouldn't be selfish. I should be thankful that I enjoyed the time that we did have because everyone didn't get to know their father. I'm sorry, Cove."

"It's okay, I'm okay. Look, I'm here for you. We have to question Mahak, and we can't fail here."

"I know, let's go," Tiber took a deep breath as they ushered their cats to begin the careful climb up the mountain.

Mika was thrilled to be back in the snow, and Medusa was handling the terrain better than Tiber expected she would. It did not take long for them to scale the mountain. Upon entering the tribe, Tiber was immediately met by battle-ready Chelan. His midnight blue eyes twinkled with recognition.

"Tiber, Cove, it is good to see you. I'll take you to the Chief." Tiber and Cove followed him. As Tiber rode through her tribe, none of her tribe's brothers and sisters recognized her. She was surprised to realize where they were going.

"Muraco is the chief?"

"Yes, that's what the decree said," Chelan smiled, "And things are going pretty well. Once you two finish, I know Sita will want to see you, Tiber."

"I'll visit her, I promise."

Tiber and Cove were ushered into her brother-in-law's home. Immediately upon seeing Shasa, Tiber's eyes watered. Shasa turned. Her eyes went wide, "Tiber, is that you?"

"Shasa!" She embraced her sister, and they cried in each other's arms.

"You have grown into a beautiful young woman. Father would have been so proud. It's healed my aching heart to see you. I've been so worried."

Muraco appeared, "Shasa, are you al-, Tiber? Is that you? Great Spirits!" He rushed to see her. "Aqila cleared your name, sister."

"We never believed that nonsense about you! I just wish you had come to us. We've been so worried," Shasa hugged Tiber again.

Muraco looked at Cove, "You must be the Chief of the Jungle Tribe. It's an honor to formally meet you. Thank you for securing Tiber's return home."

"I'm not exactly here to stay," Tiber sighed.

"What do you mean? This is your home! I know things have been hard, but this is *our* home," Shasa pleaded.

Cove cleared his throat, "We are here on international business. The nemesis, Neptune's identity, has been discovered, and Mahak's life could be in danger."

Tiber took a deep breath, "I was working for Neptune. He promised that he could break the Moon Curse. I thought it could save Shasa, so I agreed. Things got out of hand, and I accidentally poisoned the Seer Aqila. I didn't know that Neptune was plotting to take over all of the Waterbearer tribes. I know I lied when called to account, which was wrong. I snuck out to tell Father the truth, but he was stabbed when I got there. He told me to go before he died. He told me to save the tribe. The pulse of the tribe was hostile towards me, and I fled. I've changed myself. I learned why my father told me to go. He put the decree in Mika's bag. So I had it when I left. I didn't know then. This journey taught me to trust the Universe. I am the Waterbearer legend and know what needs to be done to break the Moon Curse. Cove and I need to question Mahak, and I have to release Nahal."

Muraco sighed, "I will allow you to question my father and release my brother on the condition that you both stay here tonight," he smiled.

"That sounds good to me," Cove replied.

"I would also like to hear what my father and brother say."

Cove nodded, "Of course."

Muraco led the pair to another room in the spacious tent. Mahak's back was turned to them. "Father, Tiber, and the Chief of the Jungle Tribe are here for you." Mahak was meditating on a yak pelt on the floor when they entered.

"Tiber, how you've grown. It's wonderful to see you. Chief Cove, it is an honor."

"Mahak, I am here to clear you. You are not the nemesis, Neptune."

Mahak laughed, "I could have told you that. But, I appreciate all the precautions taken."

"Father, I told you I did this for your safety," Muraco insisted.

Tiber sighed, "Mahak, the Neptune that has committed atrocious crimes is none other than Yas. Aqila, Councilman Kavi, and DragonLord Sheraga traced Neptune's origin."

Mahak let out a long, exasperated sigh as he closed his cerulean eyes as if in great pain. He was clearly hurt to hear that his brother was the enemy. "I knew we had strained relationships, but I never thought things would have taken this turn."

Muraco was at his father's side, "Father, what happened?"

"It is a long, miserable story that started with our father, Zale. He married my mother, Jocasta, and I was born. Mother passed away. After she passed, I was the center of my father's world. He would tell me how my mother wanted to bring light to being a descendant of Aenon. When I was about four, he remarried a kind-hearted woman named Danu. She was so gentle, truly a mother figure. I even grew to call her my mother. She passed when I was six after birthing Yas. Then, father changed a bit. He became a callous man. He loved us both without a shadow of a doubt, but he rigorously pushed us to be influential people in the tribe."

"When Yas was six and I was twelve, we had a rough winter. Father, the lead hunter, would be away for a long time to hunt. He was injured in a hunting accident, lost his eye, and his face became disfigured. I became 'the little man'. He noticed my gifts for trading and negotiating and helped me prepare for a future as the Tribe Council. I encouraged him to focus on Yas, seeing that he had a natural talent for hunting. But my father believed I had a flawless pedigree, as he called it. He always reminded me that the blood of a great queen and a Legend ran in my veins. I noticed Yas getting overlooked, and I tried to step in and be a father figure to him."

"It worked for a long time until a beautiful tribe woman took a particular liking to me. Her name was Noelani. She was a few years older than Yas, but he was completely taken by her. He tried to impress her by doing his best to be the greatest hunter he could be. I was good friends with

Noelani at the time, but never more because I knew my brother's feelings for her. I actually took a fancy to a young seamstress who always put extra effort into my council attire. Her name was Laila. I loved her. I asked for her hand in marriage, she agreed, and we married. After the wedding, we met with the elders and were informed that we were required to produce a child. We knew the result, but Laila greatly desired to be a mother. Those four years were the best of my life. Of course, my first love passed away after Muraco was born."

"Dalit became chief and asked me to be his councilman. In taking that role, I was allowed to remarry. It was difficult helping Dalit run the tribe; we were both young. He got married and lost his wife after the birth of Shasa. All of this was happening to us around the same time. We endured and worked and kept each other's kids. It was exhausting. At that time, Yas and I started growing apart. Noelani and Talia offered to take care of Muraco and Shasa. Since we were busy, we began allowing them to keep our children. Yas was still after Noelani's affection, which she showered upon me. Dalit grew closer to Talia, and I grew closer to Noelani."

"Yas went on a hunting expedition. Six months later, he didn't return with the rest of the tribe brothers. They thought he had died. I grieved for my brother. Noelani soaked up all my pain and enveloped me in her care and love. I married her, and a few months after the wedding, Yas returned. He had several broken bones and was in bad shape. He hated me for marrying Noelani. We had a beautiful five-year marriage, and then she wanted to have a baby. We had Nahal, but sadly, she passed away afterward. Yas blamed me for Noelani's death, and he's hated me since then. He would watch Nahal for me. I guess it was the last piece of Noelani he could hold onto. I never tried to sever Nahal's relationship with Yas. Since Yas was not allowed to have children, he turned the women interested in him down because he wanted to be a father. I gave him access to my beloved children whenever he wanted. He and Nahal grew very close. I am sorry about all of the trouble my brother has caused."

"Why would he want to be Jocasta's son?" Cove asked.

"I was allowed marriage rights because of it. It was easy to advance in life, but things were hard because I'm also Aenon's descendant, which comes with its fair share of scrutiny. But having the great queen's blood is quite advantageous. He always felt robbed of equality because he wasn't Jocasta's son, and my efforts to be a good brother to him weren't enough."

"Descendants of royalty and chiefs and their councilmen are allowed this privilege. We can't allow every tribe brother to have children because we would lose all of our women." Muraco further elaborated.

"But that's not fair. Everyone should have the chance to marry if they have someone they love. The Waterbearer tribes stand for equality, which isn't being practiced here," Cove was appalled.

"We aren't like the other tribes. We would lose all of our women and cease to exist," Mahak reiterated.

"Mahak, father held you in high esteem. He would even tell us that there were many times he felt as if you should have been chief. Did you-"

"No, Tiber, I didn't kill your father. We were best friends. We didn't always see eye to eye on how to keep this tribe going, but that is what made us better. Your father wanted to concentrate the tribe's resources on our hunting endeavors. However, I saw how pitiful we were becoming. At one point, we only had fifty people here. We would go to the festival and come back without spouses. We appeared weak and financially unstable. I wanted to change that. I went to extreme lengths, even putting our friendship on the line. But in the end, it was worth it. Five years later, we were thriving. We had an established trade system with the other tribes, we started new ventures, we could secure spouses, and there was an influx of children.Dalit and I made amends. If Yas killed Dalit, I will kill him. He's *my* brother. *I* should put an end to this long, miserable story. How he turned out is my fault."

"Father, no! How uncle turned out is his own fault. He put distance between us. Whenever you offered him anything—dinner, staying with the family, or an invitation to our wedding—he would turn you down and disappear. This is *my* fault. I should have watched out for my little brother better. Yas took Nahal under his wing. We thought it was love, but he turned your son and *my* brother into a weapon to be used against us," Muraco hung his head in shame.

"Muraco is right. Yas is a man with the free will to choose right or wrong, and he chose his path. The Universe is not holding you responsible for his crimes," Cove agreed.

Muraco and Mahak looked taken aback to hear the mention of the Universe. Tiber sighed, "Yas is wrong, and he chose wrong repeatedly. A major part of the problem is our perspective on the Moon Curse. This 'curse' started with Avala. Aqila the Seer believes that when Avala killed Aenon and failed to repent, the Universe punished her. When the tribe sided with Avala, the entire tribe was afflicted with the same punishment. The only way to reverse the curse is to truly repent to the Universe and offer our faith. I'm just sad that so many of our wonderful tribe sisters had to die before we could see what we needed to do to change."

Mahak and Muraco were silent. "Without the Moon Curse, Mahak and Yas would have shared the same mother, and Yas would not have felt unequally loved by his father. Then, when Mahak married Laila, she would have survived to have multiple children. Noelani would have married someone else, whether it was Yas or not. Having men who aren't allowed to marry doesn't give them the same chance to be considered for marriage, especially if a woman wants to be a mother. Even if Noelani married someone else, Yas would have had a chance to have his own family and be happy." Tiber continued.

"I'm going to release Nahal," Tiber stood up and left.

"Actually, you can't," Sita walked into the tent.

"Sita!"

"Tiber!" The pair embraced.

"I'm so sorry! I had to encase Nahal in forever ice to stop him from joining Neptune. I'll go and release him," Sita explained.

"I'm coming with you!" Tiber and Sita left the tent.

Mahak sighed, "Son, you have nothing to lose by turning your face to the stars. We aren't men if we don't do everything in our power to protect our women."

"Won't we face opposition from inside?"

"Don't be afraid of nay-sayers. But we will turn our faces first and see if we get a different result. If we do, everyone will want to know how you did it. If they are about the brotherhood, they will listen."

"I understand, father. I will talk to Shasa about it," Muraco replied as Tiber and Sita re-entered with the forever ice cracking. Within seconds, she released Nahal. He coughed and spat water from his mouth. Looking around, disoriented, he was trying to catch his breath.

"I'm home?"

"Yes, brother, we are waiting for you to explain yourself for your crimes," Muraco glared at him.

"Muraco! Please," Sita tried to calm him down.

"What crimes?" Nahal spat

"Your alliance with Neptune!" Muraco shouted.

"How did that get to be a crime? The fallen chief aligned with him first!"

"We all know he dissolved his agreement with him, and Fallen Star Dalit was not pleased with those who continued to support Neptune." Muraco continued.

"So I'm a criminal now because I believed Neptune was helping our tribe? I haven't done anything but be a supporter. Yes, I supported Neptune, the only one brave enough to try and solve our pitiful problems. But I also supported the tribe and the fallen chief. Ask uncle! I can't believe you're trying to have a little family meeting and leave him out! You don't understand what that does to him!" He looked at Tiber, "Come on! Speaking of crimes, Tiber killed her father and poisoned the Seer! But I'm the problem! Uncle was right! Where is he? He'll vouch for me!"

Tiber kneeled beside Nahal, "I didn't kill my father. I loved him very much. I lied about poisoning the Seer, and

I repented for that. I snuck out to tell my father the truth. He was stabbed *when I got there*. I tried to help him, but he died in my arms. That's the truth, Nahal. I was trying to tell you, but you wouldn't listen."

"I didn't listen because you *always* lie about things. Nothing is ever how you say it is, so I tend not to trust you. How many missions did we go on that you didn't tell me the whole story? Given the situation, I thought you killed him, even by accident. And still! Why am I a criminal if you're telling the truth? I haven't killed anyone if that's what you're thinking."

"Your crimes are conspiring with Neptune and slander of Tiber and Chelan. Sita told me what you did to him!"

"Where's uncle?"

Mahak sighed, "Your uncle is Neptune, Nahal."

Nahal smiled, "No, he wouldn't keep that from me! Neptune has done so much for this tribe. Why is aligning with him a crime?"

"Done so much like what?" Mahak asked.

"Tiber was there! Neptune told us how the tribe's leadership was struggling, and he came in and helped us secure a trade system and medicine. He turned around the financial affairs of the tribe. We became stable, and he found a way to solve our most pressing problem of the Moon Curse in his journey, but he needed our support to do it."

"Yas didn't do those things, son. I did. Neptune was a name I used to trade with the other Nations so they wouldn't find out that I'm the descendant of Aenon. Yas has used my trade name to force the hand of the other Waterbearer tribes. He killed chiefs and council members to try and take control by force of all tribes."

"Uncle wouldn't lie to me! He loves me. I know Muraco's your favorite, but Uncle Yas loves me. He wants me to do great things and to be somebody. He wouldn't lie to me," Nahal shook his head.

"Favorite? Nahal, I love you and Muraco equally. You're both my sons."

"Really? You always take out more time for him. You support him in whatever he wants. You could care less about what I want to be, but you break your neck to support him. Either that, or you're never around. I don't even think you know me. Only my uncle took time for me. He guided me, something I wished you would do! And he never lied to me. Uncle told me why Muraco was your favorite."

"Brother, that's not true."

Mahak raised his hand. Muraco grew quiet. "Son, according to Yas, why is Muraco my favorite?" Mahak's smooth mahogany hands trembled slightly.

"Because his mother was your true love, and my mother wasn't. Isn't that the truth, Father?"

"Laila was my first true love, yes. But in time, I grew to truly love, appreciate, and care for Noelani. When I married your mother, I loved her," Mahak scooted beside Nahal. Gripping his chin, he made Nahal look him in the eyes, "When I buried your mother, I loved her."

Nahal's eyes watered, "I'm sorry," he hugged his father. Mahak quickly wiped Nahal's eyes and placed a small kiss on his forehead.

Mahak sighed, "Your uncle wasn't allowed to have children, so he didn't marry. He had been in love with your mother for a long time, but she didn't reciprocate his feelings. He was angry with me when Noelani passed but took a special interest in you. He treated you like his son, and I didn't have the heart to rob him of that experience."

"Father, I'm sorry, I really am! I should have trusted you!"

"Nahal, I love you, and I forgive you."

Nahal stood up, "I admit I'm guilty. I supported Neptune, and I slandered Tiber and Chelan. I apologize, Tiber, for not giving you fairness and equality. I apologize to everyone for allowing myself to be misguided in supporting Neptune. Whatever punishment is deemed fit, I deserve it. And Sita, if you wish to disassociate with me and break off our engagement, I completely respect that."

"Nahal," Sita whispered.

Muraco pinched the bridge of his nose, "Go to your tent. I will discuss your punishment later."

Nahal didn't make eye contact with Muraco but slowly turned on his heels and left.

"I'm going after him," Sita spoke.

Muraco stepped in her path.

"Step aside, or you'll be in the ice next . . . permanently," Sita hissed. Never losing eye contact with Sita, Muraco stepped aside as she ran after Nahal.

"Mahak, we need to move you to a secured location. Aqila had a run-in with Neptune and Agni, and we have reason to believe he may attempt to attack you," Cove spoke with urgency.

"Chiefess Marina offered to support us if we needed assistance dealing with Neptune. We can slip father out to her tribe within the hour," Muraco suggested.

"I'm not going to run, I'd rather Marina come here, and we devise a plan instead. Besides, if Yas comes and I'm not here, he will go to her tribe next. After everything we've gone through together, I wouldn't forgive myself if I were the cause of any harm to her or her tribe. I stay here," Mahak asserted.

"Then so do we," Cove looked to Tiber. "I'll get some reinforcements from my tribe and ask for Marina. Tiber, if you're okay here, I'll be back."

Tiber nodded, "I'll be fine."

Cove left the tent, followed by Muraco and Tiber. Muraco turned to Tiber, "So, you're a Legend now? I'm proud of you. You're brave like your father, and he would be proud of you too."

Tiber smiled, "I think he would be."

Muraco went back inside the tent.

Tiber caught Chelan's eye in the distance.

"How did things go?" He asked.

"Nahal had a chance to account for his actions. He was misguided by Neptune like many others have been, including myself. To be completely honest, he's not a bad person. He needs some support with what he's going through right now. I'm going to check on him. I'll catch you later," Tiber explained.

She waved to Chelan before making her way to Nahal's tent. She gulped. Would he be angry with her? "Nahal, permission to enter?"

"Come in," he groaned.

Sita was standing, "I'll take my leave." Tiber and Sita's shoulders brushed lightly as she left the tent.

Nahal was lying on the yak pelt floor of his tent with his eyes closed. "Are you okay?" Tiber asked.

"No, I'm not," he slowly sat up, "how can I be? I love my uncle, but everything he's told me has been a lie. The great Neptune I thought was so spectacular was my father the whole time. My uncle is a liar and a murderer. I feel lost, out of place, and unworthy of anything. I've been so blind."

"Don't feel like that. We're in this together. I followed Neptune and believed in him, as did many of our tribe brothers and sisters. I admit I've done some things to make you distrust me in the past. But we can't change our past. However, we can change what we do now."

"That's easy for you to say, look at you. You're a Legend. You have a place already. You just didn't know it yet. I don't, and after this, I never will."

"Nahal, that's not true. You're a good person, you're intelligent, and -"

"Spare me, please. The brain is all I have going for me. Either way, I'm out of here after I do what Muraco wants. No one wants me here, and no one will miss me if I go. I just killed any chance I had at having a future."

"I'd miss you, Nahal. Before this whole Neptune thing, we were good friends, and I'd like things to go back to the days when we trusted each other."

"You're kidding? You're going to be off doing Legend stuff. Besides, if you marry that Chief, you'll move to his tribe. We won't see much of each other."

"Whoa! Okay, yes, I will have Legend duties, but no one said I'm off to marry anyone yet, you got that!"

They eyed each other for a brief moment before bursting into laughter. "Thanks, Tiber. Well, you should be off before someone says something about an unmarried woman in the same tent as an unmarried man."

"Really? You're my brother-in-law!" Tiber stood up.

"You never know, Tiber, the Changing's got you looking-"

"Nevermind, I'm leaving," she laughed. Before she left, she smirked, "And don't forget how much *Sita* would miss you if you left."

CHAPTER 25

Boaz was exhausted. Fortunately, things were progressing smoothly. The Metalkeepers were a touch behind schedule moving to their new territory. He was hopeful that the move would be complete no later than tomorrow. He thought he heard someone call out to him. It wasn't until a winged creature landed a few feet before him that he realized someone was trying to get his attention.

"Storm?"

"Bo! Where are you staying? I really need to talk to you. It's important!"

"Okay, can you give me a lift?"

"For a short distance, I can," Aqila replied.

"Hey, Boaz," Jai acknowledged him as he slowly mounted Talon.

"Good to see you again, Jai," Boaz answered.

"I've been staying with a Landkeeper family, and it's closer to the heart of Theyra than my own house."

Talon gracefully landed, and the trio hopped off, "Talon, go hunt and meet me back here. But please, take it easy."

The Great Gray squawked and gently flapped his wings, taking to the sky once more.

"Quillon and Armani aren't expecting guests. Knowing Armani, she'll start stressing about how much food she needs to make. Can we talk out here?"

"I ran into Agni and Neptune at the library. They killed all the sages, and Agni killed Haneul."

Boaz's mouth dropped, "Aqila, I'm so sorry. Does Kavi know about this?"

She nodded slowly.

"I have to tell the governors in the morning. They need to know about this. I'm glad you're okay, and this probably means that Agni knows you're a Legend now."

"I know. He and Neptune know about all of us now."

"Except for you, Boaz," Jai chimed in. "I'm glad you're on our side."

"But this means Agni is probably here looking for you," Aqila sighed.

"Where's Tiber?" Boaz asked.

"She went to her tribe, and we found out that Neptune is one of her tribe members," Aqila replied.

Boaz's eyes widened, "But we still have nothing on Agni?"

"No, but at least we have something. If we catch Neptune, we can interrogate him to get information on Agni. I'm going to check and see if the Flamethrowers are in sight."

"A few Flamethrowers came with us," Aqila explained as Jai walked away.

"There's something you're not saying, Storm," Boaz observed her.

"I'm not sure. It could do a lot of damage if I'm wrong."

Boaz touched her arm, "Let's meet at my parent's house, to discuss it. How does that sound?"

"Okay," she sighed.

"Hey, Boaz! You've got guests? Bring them in!" A loud voice bellowed.

"Who's that?" Aqila asked.

"It's Quillon. Let's get everyone settled, and we can slip out afterward."

"Sounds like a plan. I would rather talk to you privately-" Aqila stopped as Jai jogged back over.

"They should be here shortly," Jai huffed.

"Boaz's friend Quillon is letting us stay here tonight." Aqila said.

"Arin has my hood! I'll just wait out here until they arrive."

"Man, go ahead. They know I'm a Legend already. We're all safe here," Boaz insisted.

"Really? I'm going to introduce myself . . . and hopefully use their bathroom," Jai hurried inside.

Boaz cut his eyes at Aqila. "It was a long trip, and we didn't take any breaks," Aqila rubbed the back of her neck.

The pair chuckled, "Are you worried about telling Jai what's going on?" Boaz asked.

"I want a sign that I'm wrong. I don't want to be right about this. If I give Jai misinformation, he would be hurt behind it."

"It's that deep?" Boaz questioned. When Aqila nodded quietly, he sighed. He could completely understand the feeling of being in a tight spot. After standing outside for another ten minutes, the canter of the horses could be heard. The Flamethrowers looked beat as they dismounted their horses. Alena and Zay were walking side by side while Arin trailed behind them.

"Nice to see you again," Boaz called to them, "You all can go inside. You look tired."

"Look tired? Pfft, we are tired. Zay was riding like a crazy man," Alena groaned.

"I got us here, didn't I? Could you do it better?"

"I guess we'll have to find out, won't we," Alena playfully bantered with him.

They slowly walked inside Quillon's house.

Boaz and Aqila gave each other a mischievous glance, "Let's take our chance."

"But Talon's not back."

"Relax, I'll take you across the desert Landkeeper style," he said, pointing to his sand raft.

Jai had just walked out of the bathroom inside Quillon's house when he saw the Flamethrowers, "You made it!"

"Like hell we did," Zay walked past him, hurrying to the bathroom.

Alena talked to Armani and Quillon while Arin leaned against a wall alone. Jai walked over to her, "How was the ride?"

"It was okay," she whispered.

"You seem a little tense. Is something bothering you?"

She turned to him and raised her eyebrows, "No, what makes you say that?"

"You seem down and slightly irritated. I'm here if you want to talk," Jai offered.

She sighed, "It was a long, hectic ride. I'm tired and hungry, that's all. Thanks for asking."

Jai grabbed her shoulders and peered into her eyes, "Make sure you eat up and get a good night's sleep, okay?" He smiled at her.

Arin nodded. Jai walked past her to join Alena in talking to Quillon and Armani.

CHAPTER 26

"So, what's all of this about?" Boaz asked Aqila.

"I have a hunch at who Agni's identity is. I still don't have a motive, though. It might have something to do with Jai and something deeply personal to him. If I'm wrong, it would definitely offend him."

"Have you tried to have a vision about it?"

"No, but I'm afraid I may regret it if I wait for the sight before I act."

"With the relationship you've been building with him, don't you think he'd understand where you're coming from?"

"I don't know, I don't want to be the one who divides the Legends."

Boaz laughed, "The irony of it all, you don't want to be the new Basir, even though you technically are."

Aqila nudged Boaz hard on the shoulder, "It's not funny. We know what happened the last time."

"Well, in all fairness, Aenon and Cyra wanted to marry and merge their respective Nations, and Basir only told them the truth."

"The truth about something deeply personal to both of them! In this case, I might be wrong. I don't have enough evidence!"

"Did Basir have hardcore evidence? No, he couldn't have. The Nations have never merged together before. He was going off the belief that if the Universe made us separate Nations, there was a good reason for it. He stood by that choice, and when Cyra and Aenon saw their errors, they had a person to return to. I know this is different, but only two things will happen: Jai will hear you out, or he won't. Too many people are dying to not try. Like you said, Agni could be here looking for me right now. Isn't that a reason to try?"

"I guess you're right. Kavi made a good point about following all leads in an investigation."

"And unlike with the last Legends, when one brings up a concern, we will all listen to their reasoning."

"Thanks, Boaz," Aqila hugged her best friend.

"Alright, let's head back," Boaz stood up and extended a hand to Aqila.

Back at Quillon's house, the Flamethrowers had finished eating. "Quillon, where's Boaz?" Armani asked.

"Well, I saw him outside with a really tall girl, I thought they were talking, but I'll go check."

"Thanks. I would hate for their food to get cold," Armani replied, covering the leftover food. "If everyone is finished, I can show you to the guest bedroom, and I have already laid out some blankets."

"Thank you, Armani," Jai stretched and headed to the guest bedroom. Zay followed Jai while Alena and Arin helped Armani with the dishes.

"Thank you for helping. I appreciate it." Armani beamed at them.

"No, thank you. This is my first time experiencing Landkeeper hospitality, and It has been quite enjoyable," Alena smiled.

"We can just stack the dishes since I want to make sure Boaz and his friend eat as well," Armani replied as she started stacking plates.

Afterward, Arin and Alena began heading to the guest bedroom. Before they could enter, Alena grabbed Arin's hand, "What's wrong?"

"Nothing. I don't know why everyone keeps asking me that." Arin rolled her eyes.

"Because you seem upset. If I've done something, I wish you'd tell me."

Arin sighed, "Oh, like when you threw me off the trail on our last mission together? That was reckless, and I was worried about you. Then you went about like nothing happened."

"So? You went off with Jai without saying anything to me because you were mad? Are you crazy? You didn't think I was worried about you? I was supposed to be tailing Zay, and I put you in the same location I was just in case something happened. I didn't even know you were leaving!"

"I was fulfilling my duty to help Jai. I wanted to support him on the personal journey he was on."

"Oh, like the rest of us aren't helping? That's your problem. You think everything is your problem to fix. You get so personal about everything."

"I thought we were closer than this. I knew you felt bad about what happened to Zay, but you two are inseparable now. I guess I should have seen it coming," Arin shouldered past Alena and went outside. She noticed Quillon walking toward the house with Boaz as she left. She passed by them while they were talking.

"Want to talk about it," a raspy feminine voice called her.

"I'm done talking, Aqila," She huffed and plopped on the sandy terrain.

Aqila sighed and sat beside her, "You know the Flamethrowers really care about you, right?"

"I care about them too, but no one ever sees it that way! I try my best for everyone. I want them to know that I'm invested in them and willing to do what it takes to support them. I hate that about myself. I hate that I feel so passionate about people. I wish I could make it stop. I wish I could stop caring so much; then maybe it wouldn't hurt like this."

"I know for a fact Jai really appreciates everything you've done for him."

"I really care about him, but I don't think he notices how much he means to me," she whispered.

"I don't think he's in a place to understand what you feel. He's gone through a lot, Arin. Despite that, he is trying his best to be a good Legend. He has much on his mind, but I know he cares about you too."

"I'm just starting to feel a bit out of place. It's not just about Jai; I also feel the pain of growing apart from my sister. I'm happy she's so happy with Zay. He's a good person. He exceeded my expectations. I just hate that we aren't as close anymore. I guess I did need to talk about how I was feeling. It's not that I didn't want to, but I felt uncomfortable."

"It's normal; maybe talk to Jai about this when you feel strong enough."

"I won't anytime soon. Like you said, he's busy. The world is going through much, and I don't want to be a distraction."

"Well, my lips are sealed. It is not my place to tell."

"Thanks, I'm going to try and get some sleep now," Arin stood up and walked inside the house.

Aqila noticed that Talon had returned from hunting, and she decided that she would sleep on her dasher instead of inside. It was a beautiful night. She was tired from the journey. Her mind was reeling with possible explanations for Agni's identity. They had to find him before he could find them.

She laid on Talon's back in a comfortable reclined position when she felt him shudder his feathers. Upon looking up, she saw a messenger bird. She observed the metal talon covering, etched with a dragon scale design.

Sheraga!

The bird landed, and Aqila retrieved the message. Her hands trembled. She reread the contents a second time. Taking a pen from her bag, she hastily wrote a reply, struggling to write straight in the dark. Making haste, she sent the bird off.

"Bo!" She yelled, violently pushing the front door open. Boaz was calmly talking to Quillon and Armani, and they were surprised to see Aqila so frantic.

"What's wrong?" Boaz jumped to his feet.

"It happened. Pyroc was attacked! Sheraga said it happened a couple hours after we left."

"Are they okay?" Boaz asked.

"They're fine for the most part. Pyroc didn't have a lot of casualties. The antidote worked!"

"So?"

"They were expecting *us* to be there! At least Jai and myself! How did they know that we would be there? I understand Agni taking a guess about me being there, but he shouldn't have known about Jai!"

"How do you know that Agni was looking for you and Jai?"

"Agni told Sheraga to surrender us, or they would attack. Sheraga pretended he was securing the palace so Agni would believe we were still there. But the worst thing is he said that he was positive that Agni is a -"

"What's going on?" Jai groaned and stretched. "All I could hear was yelling."

"I'm sorry, Jai. You've had a long day. Try and get some sleep." Aqila replied awkwardly.

"My day hasn't been any longer than yours, Aqila. Is something up?"

"Yeah, Agni almost had you!" Quillon bellowed. Armani gently touched his arm to settle him down a bit.

"Agni! When? Where?"

"Agni attacked Sheraga shortly after we left. Agni was looking for us specifically." Aqila explained

"Wait, I can see why he would have thought you were there. He saw the direction you flew off in. But how did he know that I was there?"

"That's the other thing. Sheraga said that Agni is not a man but a woman," Aqila groaned.

"What!" Everyone shouted in unison.

Jai shook his head, "Do you mean to say that a woman wiped the floor with me back at the border? No, I don't believe it. It can't be. Is Sheraga sure?"

Aqila folded her arms and tilted her head. "He's the DragonLord! Of course, he's sure! He would know a woman from a man. Besides, he said his DragonGuard recognized a woman too."

"I mean, Agni always has that mask on, so the voice is distorted. Something is crazy off with that. Like, we nearly came face to face with Agni. Did you think you were fighting a woman?" Jai asked.

Aqila touched her chin as she began to pace. "I can't really say. I guess it's possible? Neptune is, for sure, a man. Agni had a smaller frame than Neptune, but a woman? But this is a confirmed lead. Sheraga's a DragonLord with advanced heat sensing and the DragonGuard with the most powerful fire abilities. Could they all be wrong? What's the likelihood of that?"

"I hear what you're saying, but something feels wrong about that. I can't shake that feeling," Jai sighed.

Aqila tossed her head back, "It gets worse. Agni realized that the tranquilizer didn't work. Sheraga fears Agni is already on his way here to question the Metalkeepers."

Boaz clenched his fists. "No! They haven't moved yet. They just finished closing their compound. The Metalkeepers are left exposed. I can't let Agni attack them."

"Boaz man, you're acting like they can't hold their own," Quillon spoke.

"Not against fire. Fire will melt metal. And they have metal flecks in their clothes, which is why they can command their Element so easily. They always have it on them. Zuriel might be the only one who could handle herself, but even she wouldn't be safe for long."

"Neptune's probably headed to Tiber's tribe, and Agni is on the way here. We can work with that," Aqila nodded.

Everyone looked perplexed. "How in fiery hell can we work with that? They both have armies," Jai shouted.

"No, they both had armies," Aqila calmly replied. "Neptune's main role was to support Agni, which gave him time to pursue his true motives of wreaking havoc in the Waterbearer Tribes. He capitalized on Mahak's venture in Theyra, giving him a gateway to have whatever he wanted manufactured to support Agni. Neptune doesn't know that his tribe knows what he has done, so he's already defeated. The Windmasters that were his 'allies' were all spies sent by my fiance. Neptune doesn't have any forces anymore. He's headed to recruit more people from his tribe now, but he's in for a surprise. As for Agni, would Sheraga battle anyone and let them retreat with an entire army? No, he wouldn't. If Agni had to retreat, she was wiped out for the moment. She would probably get her reinforcements as she passes through Ember on her way here. But we can pull this off! Three Legends, Landkeepers, and Metalkeepers, there's no reason we can't win!"

"I hear what you're saying, but my people aren't ready for war. The Landkeepers especially. The Metalkeepers are battle-ready, but there are only a couple hundred of them, including children," Boaz explained.

"Zay won't like this, but we could send him to get the Flamethrowers, which would help. He's the best rider out of all of us, and he could make it there and back the fastest," Jai suggested.

"We're going to need all the help we can get. I'll ask Kavi to alert the WindGuard. It would be helpful if we could find Cahya, but we don't have time. We'll have to work with Legends, Flamethrowers, and the WindGuard."

Quillon stood up. "I have a few Landkeepers who can help. I can help, too. Like Aqila said, if we gather everyone we can, we could win this thing!"

"Then we're going to need a plan. We should get started tonight," Aqila suggested, looking at Boaz and Jai.

"Well, we'll leave you to it. If you need anything, just let one of us know. We'll be in our rooms." Armani spoke.

The trio was thankful for Armani's hospitality. The brother and sister duo left the Legends to devise a plan.

"Okay, so what do we want to do first?" Aqila asked.

"We should lead Agni somewhere specific. That way, we can do our best to ensure that innocent people will be out of harm's way."

Boaz liked Jai's idea, "Maybe we could lead them to the desert. Not a lot of people live here."

"It might be too harsh, and we need the terrain to serve as an advantage for us too. What about leading Agni and her army to the Metalkeeper's compound? Bo, do you think you can move them out in time?"

"It's pushing it," he groaned to Aqila.

"To be honest, we may have no choice. Agni is probably furious that the tranquilizer didn't work on the Pyroceans, so she'll immediately think it was Metalkeeper's betrayal. Regardless of what we decide, the battle still could be coming straight to the compound." Aqila explained.

"Hey, I think Aqila is onto something. Right now, Agni doesn't know that we are here. She'll come to the compound, but it won't be suspicious if the Metalkeepers leave? That makes them seem guilty, which actually puts them in more danger. We should delay their departure. When Agni arrives, Zuriel will just tell the truth," Jai suggested.

Boaz caught on quickly, "The truth is that 'Neptune' wanted her to change the formula, and that would throw Agni off completely."

"The thought of Neptune betraying her will also invoke panic, which helps our case," Aqila added.

Jai continued, "After Agni confronts Zuriel, she will be looking for Boaz, the Legend who managed to stop a civil war."

"Yes, but she wouldn't go looking for Boaz as Agni. She must have a disguise of some sort."

"Exactly, Aqila," Jai exclaimed.

"But what to do with her army? If she brings a ton of soldiers, that complicates things," Boaz pondered.

"Like Aqila said, Agni will have to have a disguise. She wouldn't just bring an army into Theyra. Zuriel would get suspicious."

"That could be the Flamethrowers assignment. They could watch the border for Fireheart civilians coming into Theyra, and Boaz and Quillon's allies could watch the compound. If we could keep the village desolate to a degree and create a hub around the Metalkeeper compound. When Agni switches up, she will stay in the radius of the compound," Aqila explained.

"What will the Windmasters do?" Jai asked.

"They can't just come into Theyra. Tensions are too high from the war. We should save the Windmasters for if and when the battle begins," Boaz warned.

"I agree with Boaz. If we come from the east, we could create a sandstorm to bubble the Firehearts. They will think that my people are inside the bubble and go on the offense, resulting in them attacking each other."

"Where will the Windmaster be?" Jai raised an eyebrow.

"With the desert not far from our border, we could create the storm on the outskirts before the terrain changes."

"It sounds like we have the makings of a solid plan. Jai, if you can wake Zay and send him off, that will buy us a little time. I mean, Agni is probably on her way as we speak," Boaz suggested.

"He won't be happy, but I'll go wake him up," Jai groaned as he walked away.

"I can send a message to Kavi to have him send the WindGuard to us. Can Quillon rally your allies so he and Zay can leave together? We need as much time as possible."

"Yeah, I'll go and ask." As Boaz left to get Quillon. Aqila went outside to get a few of her things. She needed to write a message to Kavi. She was confident that if all of them could unite and do their part, they could successfully rid their lands of Agni and Neptune.

CHAPTER 27

She was so worried that the plan would fall through, but she didn't voice her fears. Instead, she picked at her fingers until she felt a stinging sensation.

"Calm down, look at you! You've picked the skin on your fingers until it's bleeding. Tiber, relax. We'll be okay. Everyone knows what to do." Cove patted her shoulder, hoping she would calm down.

"I know you're right. I just can't help being nervous!"

"Hey, look at me," he turned her face towards him, "we've got a good plan, and we're just going to stick to it."

She slowly nodded. Cove was right. Everything was in position. He had alerted the other tribes, and for the first time in many years, there was solidarity among them. The

Tribe of Snow and Ice moved about as usual. Anything else would alert Neptune to their intentions. Tiber and Cove were hiding in a room in Mahak's tent.

Muraco was pacing back and forth, clearly nervous. He sighed when Chelan entered the tent. "He's here. Should I send him in?"

"Yes, just be careful. Is everyone in position?"

"Everyone is in position," Chelan nodded.

As he left, Muraco spoke, "He's on his way here. Stay quiet until it's time."

Instinctively, Tiber and Cove crouched lower on the floor.

About five minutes passed before Yas entered the tent. He looked to see Mahak gagged with a cloth and kneeling with his arms tied behind his back. "Muraco, what's going on?"

"Uncle, some unfortunate events have transpired. The decree has been found. My father stole it and killed Chief Dalit. The succession decree has named me chief of the tribe. My father is to be executed for treason. I delayed until you returned. And the worst part is that he is Neptune. Can you believe it, uncle? My father, your brother, murdered another chief, and nearly destroyed the

Beach Tribe under the guise of conducting business for our well-being. It's shameful. He froze Nahal in ice when trying to escape his influence."

"He attacked Nahal? Where is he?" Yas looked around for Nahal.

"I've moved him into the room right there," Muraco pointed to his right.

Yas sighed, "Muraco, I should have done more. I suspected Mahak was dealing in something treacherous, calling it business ventures. I just didn't have enough evidence to connect the dots. But son, as a chief, you shouldn't be the one to stain your hands with his wretched blood. Allow me to execute him. I will do it tonight and quickly. But I'd like to see Nahal first. I want to see if I can do anything to help him."

"Uncle, you've been a lifesaver.I can't believe I listened to all Father's crazed notions about you."

"Mahak has been a great deceiver and master manipulator his whole life. But you shouldn't refer to him as your father. Look at him. He doesn't deserve for you to call him father."

"You're right, uncle. I can't show sympathy to a traitor. Please, execute Mahak tonight, and then our tribe will be free of his stain." Muraco patted Yas's broad shoulder and left the tent.

Yas waited a few minutes, then peeked through the fabric flap to ensure Muraco was gone. He scoffed at Mahak, before pulling the cloth from his mouth..

"You look pathetic, brother," Yas laughed.

He opened the flap to the room with Nahal encased in ice. " I almost thought he was a genius." Yas shook his head in disappointment at seeing Nahal immobile.

"Your mouth isn't tied shut, so speak. What did you tell Nahal? You obviously said something to drop his guard."

Mahak sighed, "I told him the truth, Yas. He didn't want to believe it. I discovered that he had stolen the decree, so I trapped him in the ice. I don't care if the tribe thinks I'm guilty. I wanted to protect Nahal."

Yas crouched beside Mahak, "You know, it's been a while since we've had a heart-to-heart. Just me and you. You're so stupid. I hate you, the ground you walk on, and the air you breathe. You being the council of the Chief was a great convenience. It gave me access to everything you loved, so I could take it from you, just like what you did to me. Be grateful that Muraco was so pressed to please you. I would have turned him against you, too, just like I did with Nahal. It was quite easy. He reminded me so much of myself, the younger brother, hungry for my father's attention. Everything that has happened is your fault. Your friendship with Dalit got him killed, your alliance with the Jungle Tribe Chief got him killed, and your alliance with Marina *almost* got her killed. I will kill you. I vowed over Noelani's grave that I would kill you."

"Yas, you're sick. You need help from these delusions. That woman wasn't in love with you."

"Yes, she was! She was! You stole her from me! You stole her attention like you stole Father's attention and the attention of the tribe! I deserved everything you had!"

"Yes, you did deserve everything I had. Yas, I urged Father to give you his time. I saw what you needed, what you wanted, and I have always loved and supported you."

"You're such a stupid brother. Why would he give me his time? You were his pride and honor. I was never anything more than a hunter. You, the descendant of a great queen, are blessed to get anything you could have ever wanted. And now, I'm going to kill you. I'll kill all the pain and inequality. No one should get a hand out because they have royal blood."

"You're right, but before you kill me, I must tell you that I didn't get a handout. Father was hard on me like he was on you. He didn't accept anything that wasn't his will. Had it been my way, I would have run away with Marina when I was just a boy. But Father wouldn't have it. I didn't have a say in a lot of things, Yas. I gave up a lot of things that I wanted in the name of honoring a family name. After learning his iron fist the hard way, I tried to make things easier for you. I bought you a freedom that I could never have."

"I didn't ask Dalit to be his council. I was satisfied knowing that we were friends. I worked hard to turn the tribe around in ways that hadn't been done before. It was work and sleepless nights. Having to be a single parent didn't make anything any easier. I loved Laila, but she wanted to have a family. Losing her was incredibly difficult for me. As for Noelani, I advocated for you all the time! But remember yourself as a young man, too shy to do anything other than give her gifts and run away. Yas, if you dared to walk up to her and tell her how you felt, things may have been different. She may have been completely overtaken by you. You went on a hunting mission and didn't come back! Everyone thought you had died! I thought you died. I thought I lost the last of my family except for my baby son! So yes we grew close, and I thought you would have wanted her to be cared for. So, I married her and grew to love her. I have always loved you, but it's clear that you never loved me. Don't paint me with the brush you painted Father with. I didn't turn my back on you." Mahak explained.

"That doesn't change the hate I have for you. You took what I love, and I took what you love. Simple. You're dying today anyway, so it really doesn't matter."

Tiber and Cove saw the pelt being pulled from the tent. "It does matter, Yas. You've lied and murdered for years, and it's over now." The pelt came entirely off. Yas saw the entire tribe huddled around the tent, and everyone was murmuring.

"Tribe, please, don't humor me. Are you really going to listen to the girl who killed her father?"

"I didn't kill him. He was stabbed when I found him! You killed him!"

Cove grabbed her shoulders and shielded her with his body, "Yas, it's over! You killed Chief Dalit, my father Chief of the Jungle Tribe, and destroyed Chiefess Marina's tribe."

"Lies, I've fought for great unity among the tribes. I fought to stop the Jungle and Beach tribes from exploiting us!" Yas frantically yelled.

"That's not true," Marina stepped forward, "my tribe has never taken advantage of another tribe!"

"Is that your final answer, Marina?" Ice surrounded Yas's feet. Suddenly, the tribe brothers and sisters were covered by ice. None of them could move. Tiber heard the faint sound of ice cracking. When she peered into the room where Nahal was, she did not see him. Suddenly, the icy mountain began to split. The tent was completely isolated.

"Yas, stop," Tiber shouted, straining to keep the ice together, but Yas was too strong. Mahak freed his hands and tackled his brother.

"Why can't they melt the ice?" Cove asked.

"Proficiency is only as good as the user. Only a handful of the tribe members even use their Element. Yas is strong even for me. Cove, help me keep it together. They'll die if we don't," she panted. With hands outstretched, both tried to melt the ice that was splitting the mountain. The ice was so sharp it dug into the skin, causing several tribe members to have deep cuts.

"Tiber, we can't just melt this. You have to try and push the mountain together. Melting the ice won't be enough."

"Where's Nahal?" Tiber asked, breaking a sweat. She was scared. She was supposed to save the tribe, not get them all killed.

In a fury of snow, ice, and water, Mahak and Yas fought ferociously. Tiber wanted to direct her attention to them, but she had to stay focused. Mahak would have to hold his own.

"What in icy hell are you doing?" Nahal yelled.

Cove turned on his heels and grabbed Nahal's parka violently, "Who's side are you on?"

Nahal pushed Cove aside, "Tiber, stop! What you are doing is going to get them killed! Look at me and mimic what I do."

"Why should we trust you, Nahal?" Tiber's hands trembled.

"Because there won't be a Snow Tribe if you don't." He stretched out his hands and raised a giant ice block on either side of the severed mountain, "We have to push it back together. You push from the left, I from the right."

With all their strength, they both exerted themselves to push the mountain together. As severed parts moved closer together, the divided ice began to crack under pressure.

"Tiber, push harder before we're worn out. Cove, slowly start melting the ice that's separating us. Don't do it too fast. We're gonna have to freeze it again once it becomes thin sheets." The trio worked together, and Yas' work was becoming undone.

When Tiber was about to freeze over the thin sheets, where the mountain was obviously cracked, she saw a flash in her peripheral. She heard Cove call her name. She saw Nahal, Yas, and nothing at all. Her body collapsed.

Tiber's eyes fluttered. A powerful sensation was taking over her body. She felt herself being in the clutches of something warm. Opening her eyes, she slowly sat up. Her hand immediately went to her neck, where a warm liquid was running down the left side of her body. It was blood. She saw Cove crumpled beneath her, his face bloody. Yas was battling Nahal and Mahak. She stood up despite feeling lifeless. Every droplet of water surrounding her seemed to call her name. Her dark blue eyes began to glow. She curled her fingers and commanded every droplet to serve her. Tiber pressed her hands together until the water solidified into a trident.

Mahak was clutching his chest near his heart and was staggering. Then, his body froze, and he collapsed.

Nahal was angry, "You killed him! You murderer!" Tiber's heart felt his pain. She threw the trident with incredible accuracy, and the sharp shards of ice cut deep into Yas's right side with an impact that knocked him onto his knees. Tiber began to cocoon him in water, and the water went from clear to red instantly. Nahal danced elaborate wisps of water in front of Yas's face, "Tiber let him go. You don't have to die for this."

Feeling herself stagger and falling to her knees, she watched as Nahal created a hypnotizing mist in front of Yas's face. She heard the cries of her tribe, helpless to do anything other than watch them bleed. Women and children fell unconscious as blood pooled around their feet.

I'm supposed to be a Legend.

"Noelani, Noelani, I'm here. Don't leave me," Yas looked about frantically as if he was delusional.

Reaching into his pocket, Nahal pulled out a syringe, "You don't deserve to even say her name," as he plunged it into Yas' neck. Nahal stepped back and watched as Yas collapsed to the ground. With his demise imminent, the ice no longer had any strength. Marina was the first to free herself from the icy encasement and ran to Mahak screaming for him to stay with her.

With one sweeping hand motion, Nahal released the rest of the tribe. Muraco and Shasa hurried over to Mahak. Everyone ran past Nahal as if he didn't exist. Sita and Chelan ran to Tiber and Cove. Tiber was still lying on her side, her eyes glassy, as if in a trance.

Nahal walked over to Sita and Chelan, "Sita, tend to Cove. You aren't strong enough to help Tiber with her wounds."

Sita wiped her eyes before rushing off to help Cove.

Nahal kneeled beside Tiber, leading a luminous ball of water toward her neck. She was stabbed with an icicle, and she was bleeding profusely. Nahal worked to repair the damaged vessels and keep her alive.

"I'm sorry, Tiber, I really am. This is all my fault. I almost destroyed everything that meant something to me. No amount of good I do can ever atone for what I've done. Once I heal you, I'll leave the tribe in peace."

Tiber's wound on her neck began to close, and her eyes rolled back in her head. She felt like she was dreaming. She heard every word Nahal spoke. The stars filled the sky of her dream world. It was night, and she was all alone. As she called out into the empty space, only her echo answered. She sighed. The pressure nagged at her heart, and her mind was gone. Although it was a lonely night, it was peaceful. A kind of peace that Tiber didn't know could ever exist. A newfound light came into her dreams. When she looked up, she could see the moon. Tiber couldn't pull her eyes away from it. She could see a pair of navy blue eyes that looked similar to hers. Then she heard the soft cries of a baby. She heard whispers.

"It's a girl," a woman smiled with tears.

"Thank you, Marina," her father whispered.

"Dalit, she's - the tribe won't accept her," the woman gasped.

"Whether you believe in the Universe or not. The lunar eclipse has peaked. The baby girl is a Legend," Marina confirmed.

"Talia, don't worry. I'll tell everyone tomorrow that the baby was born. We just have to keep her quiet."

Talia gasped heavily, "Just - let me hold her, just once," tears filled her eyes.

Marina gave Talia the baby gently. Talia smiled and began to cry. "You hear me, I wish- I could stay with you, but

I can't," she huffed. "You were born to do great things. You'll heal us. You'll fix us. I don't know how, but I believe in you. My little Tiber. Dalit- take her."

Dalit clutched the baby, "Talia, I'm so-"

"No, I'm happy to be her mom - even though I won't live long enough to see her grow up. I know she's safe with you. Dalit, protect her... protect her for us." Talia went limp. Her navy eyes were open, tears still lingering from them.

With a baby in one hand, he gently closed Talia's eyes. "I'll protect her with my life, Talia. I promise."

When she looked away from the moon, Tiber cried and wailed. "Universe, forgive us, we repent. I repent! Just forgive us, spare us, please! We can't take this pain anymore." She wiped her eyes time and time again. The moon began to fade, then the stars.

Her navy eyes flashed open, and Tiber sat up straight. Her hand immediately went to her neck. It was healed. She could feel a faint scar. Tiber sat up motionless. When she looked around, she was in her own tent. She stood up, feeling fine. If she didn't remember fighting Neptune, she would not have believed it had already happened. Hastily pulling the flap back of her tent, it was early morning.

Yesterday was over! Did they win? What happened? The tribe was eerily quiet.

As she stepped outside her tent, she noticed Nahal sitting there.

"Nahal, what happened?"

"I'm glad you're okay," he said absent-mindedly.

She kneeled beside him, "I'm okay, thanks to you. You saved me."

"No, I almost got everyone killed. I created a breach in the tribe. I supported an enemy against my own people. I broke the basic tribe pillar of equality and unyielding fairness. I festered hate in my heart for my father and my brother. I lied, I manipulated, and I hurt people. Ensuring that you didn't expire early was the least I could do."

"Nahal, you were deceived. Yas was plotting to use you to usurp your father since you were a baby! You've made some heartless choices, but we're all in the wrong here. This didn't start with you. The Moon Curse has pushed us to do some horrible things. The idea of someone coming to save us is what we bought into. You are no more wrong for that than I am."

"I really messed up, Tiber. You don't understand. You have a place in society. You're a Legend. I don't have a place here. I ruined the one I wanted to make for myself. Everyone hates me. And I deserve that."

"I don't hate you. I've always admired you, and I liked that you were different. I used to lie on you a lot when we were young, but I was just jealous." Tiber admitted.

"Of me?"

"Yeah, you could do it all. You're a good hunter, healer, and fighter; your handle on your Element has always been insanely good. You can command people's attention and make them listen. It's been hard on all of us, not having the balance of being raised by two parents. And when the one parent you have is crazy busy, it only makes it harder. I guess I'm trying to say I forgive you, Nahal," she embraced him, "You're my brother, and I love you. Now, you just have to find it in you to forgive yourself. You're worth it. Did you see what you did? You put the mountain back together. I didn't know how. You killed Yas, and freed the tribe from his grip. He was so powerful but you were stronger, Nahal. Then you saved me, your healing abilities were stronger than Sita's. You are worth it."

"Thanks, Tiber, I don't feel like I deserve this, but I will work on myself until I do."

"How's your dad?"

"I don't know. Muraco won't let me see him. Most of everyone doesn't want me around."

"I want you around. I hope that means something," Tiber sighed and stood up.

Nahal smiled, "It does, thank you."

Tiber walked off in the direction of Muraco's tent. Inside, Muraco was pacing back and forth in the front room.

"Tiber, you're up!" He embraced her, "It's good to see that you're okay after everything that happened."

Tiber pulled away, "Everything is still a little foggy from yesterday. What exactly happened after I got injured?"

"You got stabbed in the neck by an icicle from Yas. Cove caught you, and he . . ."

"He what?"

"Yas hit him with an ice dagger. I'm sorry, Tiber." Muraco touched her shoulder.

"Is he okay?" Tiber's eyes widened.

"Sita's doing her best. Nahal killed Yas with that paralyzing stuff." He sighed, "It's over Tiber. We can't thank you enough. You didn't have to come back, but we're glad you did."

"I did have to come back. My tribe is my everything! How's your dad?"

"Marina had some antidote for that paralyzing liquid. She said she received it a couple of days ago from the Windmasters. She had to use it on my father since Yas poisoned him during their fight."

"What about Nahal? Are you going to talk to him?"

"I'm still angry with him. I can't look at him the same right now. All of this could have been avoided."

Tiber balled her fists at her side, "How can you say that? He saved the tribe! Not me, him! I didn't know what to do when the mountain split. What I thought was best probably would have killed you all. Nahal knew what to do, and he pushed himself to his limits. I can't let you stand there and shun him like that. Besides, if you want to punish him for working with Neptune, *Yas*, you have to punish me and everyone else in the tribe who was in on it. The truth is only Nahal truly had what it took to defeat Yas. He's truly gifted. That man is a prodigy. As his brother, he really needs your support right now. He's repented for what he's done. Let him close that chapter of his life and move forward. He deserves to have a tribe to call home. Anything else is not equality and unyielding fairness. And if you can't do that, Muraco, I have no problems admitting that maybe Father was mistaken when he chose you to be chief."

Tiber's navy blue eyes met his cerulean ones confidently before she hurried from the tent to Sita's lair.

"Sita!"

"Shh, please keep it down," she hushed before embracing her. "How are you feeling?"

"I feel fine. Nahal saved my life. How's Cove?"

Sita sighed heavily, "He'll survive, but life will be different for him from here on out."

"What do you mean?"

"He was hit with an ice dagger when he caught you. Besides wounding the right side of his face, it injured his eye. I've done what I could. The few times he woke up, he complained he couldn't see out of his right eye. I fear he may permanently lose sight in that eye. I'm sorry, Tiber. I really did my best."

"Can I see him?"

"He's resting-"

"I just want to put my eyes on him."

"Okay, follow me," Sita led her to where Cove was resting. Tiber's lips trembled when she saw him. The right side of his face was neatly stitched from forehead to cheekbone, passing over his right eye. His face was swollen from the injury. Tiber kneeled beside him as tears streamed down her face. Her hands were shaking. "I'm so sorry, Cove," she whispered.

Sita pulled Tiber to her feet. "Hold onto hope Tiber. It is not over. I'll call you when he wakes up." Tiber wiped her face as she left the medicine lair. She was met by her sister at the entrance.

"Can we talk for a bit?" Shasa asked.

Tiber nodded. The pair walked silently as they moved from the tribe hub to a secluded area. It had a majestic view of the small mountain chain that made Avala.

When they stopped, their dark blue eyes met, and the sisters embraced each other. "I'm so glad you're okay. I love you so much, Tiber. My heart stops whenever you're away from me."

"I love you too, Shasa," Tiber sobbed.

The pair sighed as they let each other go. They both sat in the snow, taking in the view. Shasa touched her growing baby bump before turning to Tiber. "Father told me you were a Legend when I was very young. I didn't understand what it meant then, but I saw how protective he was of you. It made me realize that I had to do the same. After I told you about the baby, I felt us growing apart. I didn't know what it was, but I felt like I failed you. Maybe if I had done more, you wouldn't have felt like Neptune was a way out."

"Shasa, I turned to Neptune because I believed he could free us of the Moon Curse. You've been a mother figure to me in addition to being a sister, and the thought of losing you was too great to bear."

"You understand that Muraco and I have to have a child."

"I know, but I understand what Father's last words to me meant. He told me to save the tribe. It wasn't about Neptune, and it was about the Moon Curse. In the end, Nahal saved us from Neptune. But I know why we have the Moon Curse and how to get rid of it."

Shasa's eyes lit up, "You do?"

"Yes. Nahal isn't the reason for Neptune; we all are. Even if Yas went off the deep end, we followed because we thought he could save us. But we were the problem the whole time. It started with Avala. She killed Aenon. She wanted to kill Cyra for destroying the tribe's home. But Aenon took the blow for her. Avala didn't repent for what she did. She tried to justify it through her anger. But that made life hell for all of us. We threw our faith away after Avala, and then instead of using the Curse to turn back, we used it to continue turning away. The Universe wanted us to learn and repent, but we brought this on ourselves. Without the Curse, none of this would have happened."

"I don't know how the tribe will feel about this, but if it is a chance to be relieved of the Curse, I think we should try. I'm so proud of you. I have your back, and I believe in you. Don't ever forget that."

"I won't."

CHAPTER 28

Aqila's eyes shot open, glowing. She rubbed them as they returned to their normal silver color. Looking towards the morning sun, she shook her head slightly before dangling her long legs off Talon's back. She sighed a long sigh before standing. She headed towards Quillon's house. She gently knocked on the door, and Armani welcomed her.

"Good morning, Aqila. Did you sleep well?"

"I did, thanks for asking. Did Boaz leave already?"

"Yes, I think he went to see the governors. Quillon left, too, as did the Flamethrowers. Jai is still here. I don't think he was ready to leave with everyone."

"Did someone call me?" Jai emerged from the hallway.

"To take as long as you do to get ready. You can never seem to do anything about that messy mop on your head," Aqila rolled her eyes.

"Never met someone who wakes up taking shots," Jai groaned. "What's wrong?"

"Let's ride," Aqila replied as she walked out the front door.

"Real charming, Aqila," Jai huffed and ran after her.

Aqila was moving swiftly as she mounted Talon, "Come on!"

"What's wrong," Jai asked as he followed her. The bird took to the sky immediately after Jai climbed on, causing him to hastily grab Aqila.

"What in fiery hell! I hope you don't wake up like this every day!"

"Neptune is dead," she stated flatly.

"How do you know - don't answer that! Wait, isn't that a good thing?"

"I don't know, Jai. Killing Neptune wasn't a part of the plan. We needed to question him to reveal Agni's identity."

"Maybe Tiber was in danger, and it couldn't be avoided."

"Tiber was in danger, but she didn't kill him. Nahal did."

Jai was shocked, "Then what happened?"

"I don't know. The realization surprised me, and I woke up. I don't know what state that tribe is in, but we have to focus our attention here. I agree that something is off about Agni. In reflecting on my encounters, I too believed Agni was a man."

"Yeah, but Sheraga said Agni is a woman."

"What if we are all right," Aqila murmured.

"What? That's actually impossible."

"No, it's not impossible! Neptune is Mahak, and Neptune was also Yas. Mahak used it as a business alias. Yas used it to hide his crimes. Is it impossible for Agni to use the same tactic? Woman Agni may be on her way, but man Agni may already be here. Man Agni may already know where we are and what we are planning."

"But we still aren't sure," Jai reminded.

"Jai, I'd rather be on the move and be wrong than sit around and be right. If wrong, we have nothing to worry about. But if right, Armani could be in danger. We can't forget that this terrain is not hospitable to our gifts. I need to drop you off near the border to await the

Flamethrowers. That is the best climate for you. And I need as much air time as possible."

Aqila had a deep, unsettled feeling. She couldn't place what it was. Something was coming. She could feel the uneasiness in her bones. Her hands wouldn't stop trembling on the reins. She wanted to check on Tiber, but she knew leaving Theyra would jeopardize that plan. She prayed to the Universe that she was okay. Tiber was stained with blood in her vision. She just hoped that she was alright. Aqila couldn't imagine what happened that made Nahal kill Neptune. They rode for an hour before she dropped Jai off at the border of Lower Ember and Theyra.

Talon landed smoothly, and Jai waved to his Windmaster friend as she rode off. Jai cautiously walked toward the border. Zay and the twins left immediately after the three Legends had discussed the plan. They should be back soon, Jai silently prayed. He was feeling a little uneasy about a few things. For some reason, it seemed like Aqila was holding something back. He wanted to ask her about it this morning, but her vision took precedence. Maybe he imagined things. Or perhaps it was the stress of everything going on. It was starting to take a toll on everyone. Zay was irritated to have to ride back; the twins had been arguing nonstop, and Aqila was beyond antsy. He, too, was tired. Tired of running, tired of hiding.

Jai ran his hands through his messy hair, fingertips being caught in knot after knot in a feeble attempt to groom himself. He noticed how well-kept the Landkeepers were. Quillon and Armani's home was cozy and organized to a fault. Armani seemed to have a specific routine. Despite all of her housework, she looked like a proper lady. Walking through this town of Theyra was something he had never seen before. The town resembled an ancient city of old ruins. Many buildings were semi-destroyed, and the ground was heavily stained with blood in several places. The metallic aura of blood tinged the air. It made inhaling nearly unbearable. Jai coughed and gagged as he walked about.

How do they deal with this?

Jai tried to find an inner calm to ease the somersaults in his stomach when he felt the presence of another. He thought for a moment. If he needed to attack, he wanted to be as close to Ember as possible. Jai quickened his pace. Whoever followed him was so close that Jai could hear their footsteps behind him. The second Jai's foot hit the official border of Ember, he turned, hurling his fire-laced fist.

His assault was caught midair by someone he never expected to see.

"Why in flaming hell were you nearly running from me?"

"You're insane, right? Normal friends and acquaintances announce themselves," Jai hissed, slightly furious.

"Are you insane? I wanted as little of that disgusting taste in my mouth as possible. Besides, since I'm a normal acquaintance, I wouldn't have wanted to put you in direct danger."

"What are you talking about, Cahya?"

"You have to get out of here. I don't have time to explain!" Cahya pushed Jai deeper into Ember.

"I'm waiting for the Flamethrowers. Let's just talk!"

The canter of horses was heard and felt, then a fiery arrow just narrowly missed Cahya as it nicked his nose.

"Jai!" Arrow hurried to the Legend's side.

"Cahya?" Arrow dropped his bow as he rushed to Cahya's side.

"I'm going to assume shooting at me wasn't intentional! What are you doing? You have to get out of here!" Cahya shouted as he was surrounded by the Flamethrowers.

"Cahya, we are in the middle of executing a plan. It is important that we do this," Jai explained.

"Shut up! Do you wanna die?"

Yuuna's amber eyes widened. "Cahya, what are -" she was abruptly cut off by the sound of an explosion inside of Theyra.

"Idiots, that's why! You have to leav-"

A violent lightning surge hit all of them. The horses panicked and fled, knocking the Flamethrowers to the ground. They all shook violently. Jai was gasping for breath as he collapsed to his knees. His vision blurred as he saw the Flamethrowers neutralized, writhing in pain. They shook as if experiencing a vicious seizure. The sensation came and went for Jai as he groaned and rolled on his back, trying to catch his breath.

Just as he was about to sit up, Cahya's arm crossed his chest, keeping him down. "Play dead," he whispered slowly.

Jai closed his eyes and let his body relax into a limp.

Footsteps approached, and Jai was prodded in the chest with a heavy object. "I think he's the one. He should be dead, right?"

"Just check, man. If he's not, we can kill him for Agni, spare him the trouble of dealing with this one."

Just as Jai thought he would have to fight for his life, his heart was eased by the scent of fire. When his eyes opened, the two men were pillars of burning flesh consumed by the majestic beak of a fiery phoenix.

Cahya sat up, "Am I worth listening to now?"

Jai stood up and offered Cahya a hand, which was immediately rejected.

Standing on his own, Cahya's intense honey-colored eyes bore holes in Jai's golden gaze, "You have to go. They know you're here. Jai, this is my fight. I don't have time to explain everything but trust me when I say this is *my* fight. Go home and forge your own peace. Be the Legend who lives a long life serving his people. Phoenix fog!" A smoky haze came between Jai and Cahya. When Jai reached for him, Cahya was already gone. "Don't die here, Jai. This isn't your fight!" Cahya's voice echoed.

Confusion was all Jai knew as the smoke slowly cleared and the Flamethrowers began to stir. Arrow staggered to his feet, "What was that? Or I should ask who?"

"Agni knows I'm here," Jai replied angrily.

"How did Cahya know about this?" Arrow asked.

"I don't know, Arrow, but I have to go. Aqila went into the heart of the town, and I have to make sure she's okay."

Arrow and Jai turned their heads upon hearing a horse neigh, "Really? We pull up the rear, and everyone's lying here half-dead," Zay replied, with Arin and Alena following him.

Arin jumped off the horse, "What happened? When she touched Yuuna, she shocked herself and pulled her hand back, "They were shot by lightning?"

"Arin, I need your horse. Alena let Arrow ride. Zay, Arrow, and I have to go. Make sure everyone's okay, then follow our tracks."

Zay nodded. Arrow and Jai hurried into Theyra. "Jai, Zay doesn't have an Element. Isn't this too dangerous for him?"

"No, it is actually perfect. No one will pay attention to him because he doesn't have an Element. But for the record, that man could make a bomb out of sand if he wanted to. I have to find Aqila. Agni is already here."

CHAPTER 29

Aqila took several breaths before withdrawing her protective sphere. Minor cuts covered her arms from Talon, sending her crashing to the ground. The second they landed, it was like she was flung into a raging volcano. She immediately donned the protective sphere. The realization hit her like a ton of bricks. Agni was already here, looking for them.

The explosion was a summoning to draw them out. She was right to leave Quillon's house. She looked at the dead bodies flanking her left and right. Armani wouldn't have survived anything like this. She and Talon were out of place within the scene. Aqila smirked; she would use that to her advantage. Mounting Talon quickly, he flew to his highest point. Aqila rushed to the Metalkeeper compound.

***

Boaz had alerted the governors early that morning to the possibility of a threat. He was walking around the compound, helping Fayruz. He kept pace with the other Landkeepers and Metalkeepers, boxing up their belongings. The most advanced Metalkeepers aided Zuriel in carefully disassembling the compound's exterior structure. As Zuriel worked, someone pulled her away. Boaz noticed the sense of urgency in which she moved and discreetly moved his work in her direction.

He tapped Fayruz's shoulder, "Who's that?"

"I'm not sure." She shrugged her shoulders.

A man was speaking to Zuriel. Boaz's heart started to pound. Despite the dark brown pants and mossy green buttoned shirt, that was not Landkeeper. This man wasn't broad or muscular enough to handle the weight and pressure of an Earth Element. He wondered if Zuriel noticed.

It was as if Fayruz had heard his thoughts, "He's not one of us," she whispered in his ear.

He meant to clutch her arm, but his hand slid. Her hand was cupped inside his. Slowly, their gaze met. "Shh, I'll look into it. Stick to the plan."

Fayruz's lips parted. No words were spoken; she awkwardly bobbed her head up and down.

Boaz gently let her hand go. He continued towards Zuriel, desperately trying to refocus himself from the velvety softness of Fayruz's hand and the warm color of her eyes. He could hear Zuriel in the distance, "I have a deal with Neptune. Whatever he asks for, I'm confident the Metalkeepers can produce."

The man looked up at the sky before responding in a hushed voice. Boaz was confused. Sheraga said Agni was a woman. However, Zuriel was clearly speaking to a man. Boaz grew concerned.

Maybe Sheraga's message was intercepted and altered.

If that was the case. Agni knew the general direction they were staying in to send a messenger bird. He held his breath. Everyone might be in danger at Quillon's house.

He noticed the man continued looking at the sky. Was something up?

"Yes! I've already told you we did make an adjustment to the formula! Per Neptune's orders! One of his agents came to me with specific instructions on what to adjust. We destroyed the old product and immediately began producing the new one he sent. As Neptune's best customer, I wish I could show you the facility. But we are in the process of relocating and are already behind schedule. I had to complete Neptune's products first. Can we continue this discussion later with one of his agents present? They can vouch for me." Zuriel turned to continue working.

"You'll regret turning your back on me!"

As fire extended from the man's fist, everything seemed to go in slow motion. Zuriel seemed to sense the attack and dodge the blow with incredible ease. In an instant, several people dressed as Landkeepers began wielding flames in their hands. Boaz was shocked. They were completely surrounded.

Zuriel's eyes widened to where the Metalkeeper children were, and she darted in their direction. Boaz created a rock wall in an attempt to shield Zuriel as she went to protect the children.

Screams and shrills filled the air. As Zuriel's back was turned towards the instigating man, he raised his hand. Suddenly, he was knocked to the ground. Talon! Aqila hovered from the ground, beating Zuriel to the children.

"Command your soldiers. I'll keep them safe!" Aqila enclosed all of the children in an air sphere before hurrying to Boaz's side.

Boaz stretched the rock wall around the compound in a circular motion, "Zuriel, you have to get everyone out. The heat of the fire will kill you and them."

"We may have to stand our ground!"

"Zur-" Boaz was cut off by Fayruz.

"She won't listen when she's like this. Let her fight. I'll help evacuate." With that, Fayruz took off to gather Landkeepers and Metalkeepers alike.

Aqila used air swipes to keep the overhead assault to a minimum.

"Aqila, keep that up! Zuriel, take your best and make a metal drill-"

"I know what you're thinking, but if we can't keep it cool, it won't work," Zuriel interrupted.

"What won't work?" Aqila asked.

"Sending the citizens underground, the heat won't keep the consistency of the metal," Zuriel explained.

"Try this, make the drill and start the tunnel. After the drill, I will push the wind sphere with the kids in it, which should keep it cool," Aqila suggested.

Zuriel nodded and gathered her soldiers. They formed a massive drill in minutes. The Metalkeepers were strong and graceful as the drill head began to disrupt the smooth surface. After two soldiers followed the drill head underground, Aqila pushed the children in behind them.

"Something's up!" Boaz had broken into a sweat from keeping the rock wall together. "The pressure stopped on the other side. They aren't throwing fire at the wall. Zuriel, go with your people," Boaz said, watching Aqila frantically keep the flames overhead at bay. Unfortunately, the wind was making them spread.

"I'm staying here."

"Look, I don't want to argue-"

"I can use liquid metal. It will create a poisonous reaction on the skin."

Boaz recalled surviving Zuriel's torture and knew she was right.

"Bo, they're planning something. Drop the wall," Aqila shouted.

"What!" Boaz and Zuriel shouted in unison.

"Drop the wall!"

I have to trust her.

Boaz blasted the wall backward, sending rocks of varying sizes in a flying assault. Several Firehearts were knocked unconscious. Dropping the wall was necessary. Now, they could see the horrific sight before them: a golden mask glistening in the sun.

The deep, echoed voice called out, "Nice to meet you again, Aqila. Interesting fate. You know I actually might keep *you* alive after all. I had a good reason to be at the library. I had to find out the identity of the new Legends."

Aqila grit her teeth as Boaz, Zuriel, and herself were in a fighting stance, ready to attack if Agni and his Firehearts came any closer. Suddenly, a burning bird came from the air. A fiery beast landed before them. Someone dismounted.

"Alright! Enough already! Do you want a battle? Fight me!"

Aqila immediately recognized the voice.

Cahya!

"Cahya, stop! You fought Agni before. We have to fight smart," Aqila shouted to him. It was the four of them and over one hundred Fireheart ahead.

"You don't understand. This is my fight, and I have to end this. Don't I, mother?"

Suddenly, another figure appeared behind Agni, and another golden mask was visible until it was removed, revealing a woman's face.

"Cahya, leave. I don't want you to get hurt. This is not your fight. It doesn't involve you."

"Phoenix Fury!" Cahya's fiery bird encased Sitara and Agni. The rest of the Firehearts spurred fire at the four. Aqila protected them in her wind sphere and gusted a violent wind towards the Phoenix, strengthening its flames. The Phoenix retreated. Cahya looked surprised to see Sitara and Agni unfazed.

Sitara shook her head. Her honey eyes formed an expression that laced anger with sadness: "Phoenix Incinerate!"

"Oh hell, take cover-" Cahya shrieked.

Aqila formed a protective sphere around herself, Boaz, and Zuriel. She attempted to cover Cahya, but he moved away from her in an attempt to best the fiery beast his mother summoned. She lost him, and Aqila fell to her knees.

"Aqila, what's wrong?" Boaz embraced his friend.

"I don't know what happened. I feel so drained all of a sudden."

"Aqila can't keep using this technique for these high-power blows. Boaz, she still has the children underground in the protection sphere. We can't keep asking her to shield us like this. We have to use another maneuver," Zuriel suggested.

"I can do the rock wall, but it won't hold as long," Boaz replied.

"It doesn't matter; she has to get into the air."

"That may leave you too vulnerable," Aqila complained.

Zuriel shook her head, "You just focus on getting into the sky. Boaz, you use lava."

"I can't do that with you right here."

"You can and you will!"

Aqila took a deep breath, and in a swirling motion, she used the wind from the sphere to blast a direct attack, hitting Agni and Sitara, knocking them to the ground. The rest of the Fireheart tried to get momentum from wind gusts. However, Aqila had other plans. She lifted herself off the ground in a high-intensity tornado, pushing the Firehearts away from the remains of the compound.

Boaz and Zuriel, using their respective gifts, were able to hold firm. Talon met Aqila in the air, and the Windmaster seemed to take flight towards the sun.

"They are going to charge at us after they gather themselves," Zuriel pulled metal flecks from her uniform. Pressing her hands together, the metal became a fluid ball, and she rolled it on the ground as if she were playing with children. As soon as the liquid substance made contact with the earth, it spread and multiplied. Boaz had never seen anything like that in his life. He stifled a gag, as the air started to taste metallic.

The Firehearts that came in contact with the substance began to scream about the burning sensation. They tried to douse it with flames, but it only quickened the substance, to their dismay.

Boaz used the distraction to his advantage. He split the earth again and summoned forth a wave of spewing lava. This tactic pushed the Firehearts back towards their border even further. "Zuriel, they won't be fazed by the lava for long. They all can manipulate fire."

"I know. We're letting Aqila regroup."

Agni lifted himself into the air on a blazing flame. The moment he did, Cahya charged, using his Phoenix to attack. This pushed his mother back several yards as they both commanded the mass of fiery feathers in an intense battle. As Agni rose, a loud rumbling could be heard in the distance.

"What is that? It's coming from all over," Zuriel groaned.

Boaz smiled, "It's reinforcements."

Jai and the Flamethrowers were charging forward. Quillon and the battle-ready Landkeepers came from the West. A wild wave of water from the East rolled in, revealing Tiber on her sleek panther. Suddenly, the sky became dark. Something massive was in the air, so significant that it blocked out the sun.

Agni lowered back down, "I'm almost impressed, Legends. You've done surprisingly well. But can you bear the touch of the inferno?"

Zuriel dropped to her knees. Boaz caught her, and she began gasping for air. The metal in her uniform was melting on her skin.

"Ahh!" Zuriel screamed.

He created a rock wall to shield them, "Zuriel!"

"I can't get it off!"

"I'll take you underground where it's cooler; you have to stay there," he said, feeling his power surge as he punched a hole in the earth. He allowed her to descend into the hole, and he covered it, leaving enough openings for air.

CHAPTER 30

In the air, Aqila noticed the temperature change.

"We have to make our move, Aqila. Tiber has arrived, and she and the Metalkeepers can't survive this kind of stifling heat," Saar spoke. The WindGuard were all hovering on their dashers in full formation. As a unit, the birds were large enough to block out the sun. The elite team of the best Storms alive feasted off of the hostile atmosphere.

"Kavi was supposed to be here," Aqila whispered to Saar.

"I know, but we can't wait any longer. We need this advantage. He'll be fine. We can't stall anymore."

The silver-eyed Legend sighed before nodding to the Wind Guardian. Saar nodded before letting out an almost feral shrill that was mimicked by all of his Guards. They moved the wind like a deadly thunder clapping from the heavens as they descended upon Theyra. Talons of mighty birds slashed to kill as they fell upon their enemies.

Saar stayed in midair with Aqila. "Skies of Grandeur, you know the purity of our intentions. We sought peace, yet the enemy will only yield to the smell of their own blood. Make us scourge, not in hate or in glory, but to purify the lands that you graciously entrusted to us. Universe, see into my soul and hold me accountable for what you find." Crash was the roar of thunder as Saar awakened his raw power as the WindGuardian.

When Saar dove, hurricane winds followed his dashers' wing flaps. Aqila watched the scenes of death below her, and her fury raged. She inhaled and ushered tornado after tornado to intimately dance around the enemy, scattering them across the land. Aqila flew near Tiber. The Legend was holding her own, but the feverish heat was wearing her down.

"Aqila!" Tiber called her as the mighty pair blocked and dodged before combining wind and water into a surreal attack.

"You okay, Tiber?"

"Yes, Neptune is-"

"I know, I saw. We'll be okay, Tiber," Aqila assured her. "Are there no more Waterbearers?"

"The tribes are in disarray. I didn't trust anyone to follow me into this. I'm sorry."

"We don't need Neptune to admit that Agni is a criminal. Let's do some Legend stuff!"

Tiber smirked and made a defensive ring of water that neutralized the Fireheart attack. She doused the flames before converting water to ice, slashing the throats of Agni's soldiers.

Aqila focused and embraced the surge of power. She robbed her enemies of much-needed oxygen, causing them to fall to their knees. The look in their eyes as they suffocated meant nothing to her. They struggled with quick thrashing movements until they moved no more. She honed the oxygen from the dead Firehearts before her, hurling a pressurized beam that leveled the heart of Theyra as if a bomb had dropped. Tiber and Aqila looked around. Only the Legends stood.

Tiber crashed multiple waves of water magically, exhausting all of the flames Agni's soldiers ignited in Theyra. The water turned most of the ground into mud. Boaz twisted, and in stiff, rigid movements, many of Agni's soldiers were encased in drying mud pillars, only to be finished moments later by an ice shard to the neck.

Standing together as a team, they all took one heavy, deep breath. The subtle moment of peace ended when lightning erupted from the sky like a plague. Aqila used the wind sphere to shield them, but the impact still whipped their skin as they tumbled to the ground.

"Who is that?" Tiber's eyes were wide with fear, knowing that the lightning could kill her in seconds.

"That's Agni," Aqila gasped. Gruesome shouts were coming from above. The WindGuards were falling from the sky with their dashers. "No! The lightning will kill them." She grunted, "I can't keep both spheres much longer!"

Jai looked and saw that the sphere was cracking under the continuous lightning. Aqila's power was being pushed to the limit.

"Jai, she needs to drop the shield. What can you do?" Boaz asked.

Jai inhaled, "Girls, take care of each other. Tiber, try to heal who you can."

Aqila dropped the wind sphere and staggered. Agni saw an opportunity, and the Legends were out in the open. A blinding lightning bolt was headed for them, but Saar blocked it with a massive wind-shield.

"Look, I can't hold this long, but it will refract the lightning when it breaks. Use it to your advantage," Saar groaned before shattering the shield. The light refracted as he said, and the lightning made a luminous beauty.

The Legends scattered. Tiber and Aqila went to help the Flamethrowers and WindGuard.

"Boaz, I have a plan. Agni wants all of us dead. I'll be the bait. If you have to let him beat me up, let it happen. He has to feel confident. He has to keep the mask on. When you can, melt it on his face. Then I'll attack with what I have left in me."

"Jai, that's risky. He's strong! He eluded an attack from four Legends!"

"This is all we have right now." Jai ran out into the open.

CHAPTER 31

Cahya struggled to catch his breath. His phoenix was exhausted. As he inhaled and exhaled, the fiery energy returned to him, and the beast faded away.

"You quit?" His mother asked.

"Murderer," he hissed.

"Cahya, you don't understand. Everything I've done is for a reason."

"Why should I care? You set us up! I blamed myself for not protecting Calida. But the whole time, it was your fault! You sent me that message, but you weren't trapped at all. Calida was right, and I should have left you there! You played me. You played on my love for you. And Agni killed her, and it's your fault!" He spewed flames at her, which Sitara met with her own fire.

"You don't understand! Agni is *not* wrong. This war is the Legends' fault! The Legends did this to all of us! Jai may seem like a great person, but he's an offshoot of Cyra. A weak point in our history! You can't imagine what I had to watch your father suffer in the name of that ridiculous Legend! When Agni told me that Jai was chased to the forest, I knew he would find the Flamethrowers. Look around, son. Why didn't he surrender to spare you from this if he cared about you? Agni just wants the Legends. Agni didn't kill Calida. Jai did. Cahya, you know I love you. Come here, son, my pride and joy." Sitara slowly walked to Cahya. Her arms were outstretched in a loving embrace. Her eyes were no longer hostile but filled with motherly love and admiration for her son.

Cahya's eyes watered as his lips trembled. He couldn't look at her. With his head hung down, he accepted her embrace and rested his head on hers. She patted his back, "I love you so much, Cahya. I can't bear to see you lose your life because of that Legend."

"I missed you, mom. I love you more," he whispered. It was some peaceful and nostalgic being in her embrace.

The warm vanilla scent in her hair reminded him of his sister. Quickly, he burned her from her back until his hands were covered in her blood. She gasped and collapsed. "You might be right about the Legends of old, but you conspired with Agni to justify your selfish desires. Father died an honorable man, and you've marred his legacy. If I die for Jai, I die with honor." Cahya left his mother and ran as fast as he could, tears falling down his face.

A familiar feeling got Aqila's attention as she shielded Tiber from healing the Flamethrowers. "Tiber, be alert. I think someone is here."

"Aqila, behind y-"

The attack was coming before Aqila could move. Before Tiber could complete the sentence, a tall figure killed the attacker.

Aqila smirked, "You're late!"

Charcoal gray eyes looked up from that assault, smirking, "You're welcome."

The man wiped his sword from the blood of the dead man. Tiber immediately knew that it must have been Kavi.

"We must move the injured into the safety zone that Boaz created earlier," Aqila explained. "The Landkeepers are secured closer to Kindle. Can we pull that off?"

"I can do it," Tiber offered. All I need is a carriage for Mika to pull, then I can heal and defend the injured on the way there. I won't need to be guarded against any Waterbearer offense. Neptune is dead, and the tribes are in disarray right now."

"That could work. The WindGuard shouldn't go because Agni will know where the civilians are," Aqila explained.

"My exact thoughts," Kavi replied.

"I still have the children in a protective air sphere underground. The farther they are, the more energy it takes for me to keep them protected."

"The WindGuards that have recovered from their wounds can make a barrier and take over that part for you. Agni still has it hot, which could prove injurious to any Metalkeeper. The WindGuard takes over, then you, Saar, and I have some work to do. We can't let Agni keep this up. Theyra will be completely destroyed, and the Landkeepers won't have a home, which will only create more problems in the long run."

"What about Jai and Boaz? They went after Agni," Aqila inquired.

"If we hurry, they'll be fine. Tora is here, too. He asked for time to make a show."

"Well, I'll be on my way," Tiber said, hurrying off making a makeshift carriage from the rubble.

It was just Kavi and Aqila, "Are you alright? It's not like you to be late." Aqila asked as the pair stealthily moved to gather the WindGuard.

"I know, but it will be worth it. We got a lead that allowed us to crack the case. That's why Tora's here. We have to make time."

Boaz hid in the distance. He watched the fiery battle between Jai and Agni. He had never seen a Fireheart that could command their Element like that. Once a Fireheart chooses a lightning proficiency, they exchange it, no longer allowing them to use fire. This anomaly is the secret to Agni's power, being able to wield both lightning and the flame with complete mastery.

Allowing Jai to take on the challenge wasn't the best idea. He had been hit by lightning at least ten times to the point blood was oozing from his wounds. Blessed by the Universe, he was strong. He kept Agni on his toes. Boaz didn't see an option that allowed him to get close enough to burn the mask. He turned to look behind him as he felt the earth tremble beneath him. It appeared that Windmasters were surrounding the compound. He silently prayed to the Universe that Tiber and Aqila were alright.

Feeling a presence directly behind him, he covered his back with a rock shield.

"Chill, it's me," a familiar voice called out.

"Glad you're alive," Boaz murmured.

"Yeah, I guess," Cahya whispered absent-mindedly.

Boaz felt for him, "I'm sorry about-"

"I don't want to talk about it, and I don't want your apology. How's Jai holding up?"

"I don't think this is the best idea, but he's holding up since he can heal himself to a certain degree."

"He's not going to hold up. Healing takes a lot of energy from him. I'd send a phoenix, but I'm spent. It's a mirror reflection of my physical strength and willpower. I can summon two, one as my strength and the other as my willpower. But I need time before I can summon them again."

Suddenly, Jai fell to his knees. He was utterly beaten. Boaz felt the impact on the ground as he fell. He got this twitchy feeling that almost dared him to move closer. Agni came within feet of Jai. He didn't look like he had been fighting at all.

"You put on a nice act. Will you submit and allow me to do the honor?"

"Tell me why, and I'll willingly let you kill me," Jai panted.

"You don't see it now, but you will only leave a legacy of turmoil in your path. How is it justice that the rest of us have to suffer for the four people's choices? Tell me how it is justice! We are slaves to the aftermath of whatever you choose to do with your life! The only way to achieve true justice and freedom is if the Legends don't exist. Four people born to be more powerful than the rest will always throw the world into a grave imbalance. We, the people, are tired. We have suffered from the choices of the Legends. We don't want or need you. If you aren't wanted or needed, then why not die. Let us be free of you."

"You forget one important thing. I didn't ask for this. I didn't ask to be born. I didn't ask to be a Fireheart. I didn't ask to be a Legend. I was chosen. We were chosen. You can ask why all you want, but we don't know. We are here by the stars' permission. Nothing takes form on this earth without the Universe's blessing. Agni, killing us today will not do anything about the Legends of Tomorrow. Because we didn't choose ourselves. This fate isn't easy, but it's the Universe's will."

Agni prepared a white lightning bolt. Boaz, with his hand covered in lava, hurled at Agni. Jai rolled backward and blinded both Boaz and Agni with incredible light. Boaz's hand nearly missed Agni's face. Meanwhile, the lightning bolt missed Jai and landed on Boaz. Both shouted in agony. Jai rushed to Boaz, who was trembling under the effect of the bolt. He was hit in the side near his stomach, and Jai couldn't heal him while he was twitching. Agni yelled again as a crash of lightning struck him from the back.

Agni ripped off the mask before it could melt his face. He turned to see his attacker. Agni and Jai were both shocked to see Tora standing there. Agni's light brown eyes widened as he saw the young man standing before him. Tora shot another lightning bolt at Agni, which he deflected with a bolt of his own.

Seeing that he was distracted, Jai tried to heal Boaz, whose twitching was seemingly less frequent. Agni and Tora were passing lighting at each other in a dizzying frenzy. Jai thought that something was unusual. Agni seemed more focused on deflecting Tora than attacking him. His concentration split between Boaz's wounds and Tora. Jai noticed that Agni actually wasn't attacking at all. Was this his chance? He looked at Boaz, shocked to a near lifeless state. Boaz took that blow for him, and he would not leave him to die.

Cahya noticed that Jai was distracted by Boaz.

Agni must be tired. Jai's busy. I've got this. Phoenix, don't let me down.

Cahya lunged forward, spewing fire from all directions. Before he could summon his phoenix, a bolt of white lightning met his eyes. It was blinding and powerful. Cahya was moving forward too fast to stop or turn. He couldn't even think before a body passed between him and the lightning bolt. The shock made him feel like his blood was boiling. He yelled in agony before dropping to his knees. Turning to his right, he saw his mother struggling to grip her side.

"She took a hit for me," he whispered.

"Cahya, go!" She screamed.

The sky suddenly darkened, and a loud roll of thunder rang in their ears. It was so loud that one couldn't even hear their own thoughts. Aqila, Saar, and Kavi whizzed by Agni continuously. Agni was surrounded by a flurry of feathers. The series of dives and turns were so well orchestrated that Agni couldn't choose a target.

They were too fast, and the bird's feathers also impaired his vision. Tora sent a wild, golden lightning bolt into the air. It illuminated the sky in place of the sun. The pressure of the air was getting heavier, which made breathing difficult.

The three Windmasters leaped from their dashers in midair and landed on their feet. Saar used wind whips to slash Agni until he had cuts all over his body. Aqila stiffened her fingers and pulled her hands downward. Agni's entire body followed the motion of her hands. Once he was brought to a kneeling position, Kavi encased him in a wind sphere.

Boaz's eyes began to flutter, and he sat up quickly before groaning. Jai shook his head, "Take it easy. You got struck by lightning."

Jai helped Boaz to his feet, supporting his weight as they walked toward Kavi.

"Don't let your guard down. He isn't defeated. His abilities are just neutralized now," Kavi said as he motioned for Saar to come over.

"Saar, take Boaz. He's injured. Everyone else needs to remain here," Kavi ordered. He turned his attention to Jai. "Do you know this man?" The pair walked until Jai could clearly face the man.

"No, no! He's my-"

"No, he's not! He lied to you," Tora interrupted as he got in Jai's face.

Jai couldn't understand what was going on. Why was Tora so angry with him?

Kavi stopped in front of Agni, "You have two options. You either talk or die. If you talk, I will make sure you get a fair trial. You don't talk, and I tell my queen to suck every ounce of oxygen from this wind sphere you need to breathe. And we will all watch you suffocate to death. Then, we'll tell the world our perspective on your crimes."

Agni laughed, "I thought you, Windmasters, were peaceful people."

Kavi laughed, "Kill him."

Aqila curled her fingers, and Agni grabbed his throat. His body trembled as he was visibly trying to gasp for air. Agni twisted and turned inside of the wind sphere. The veins in his neck were enlarged as he struggled.

"Easy, Aqila," Kavi sighed. She let her fingers relax. "See, I'm beyond reasonable. I'm even giving you a second chance. Talk or die!"

Agni sighed, "Yuuta, my name is Yuuta. I wanted to bring an end to the Legends. I wanted to end their reign of chaos upon the people of the earth. You cannot understand, there is a plague on Legends! There is a curse! By the time you see it, it will be too late."

Aqila's body shuddered at his words.

Jai's voice shook, "Why would you want to kill your own son?"

"Because you're not his son!" Tora hissed with rage dripping from every word.

"You're not my son, Jai. You're the son of my brother. Our wives gave birth on the same day. I was excited because the solar eclipse was coming, and there was a possibility that my child could be a Legend. I delivered Tora first. He cried, never opening his eyes. When I delivered you, you blinked, and I knew those were golden eyes. I knew you were the Legend. I was furious that this plague dared visit our bloodline again. With both mothers in great pain, it was quite easy to switch you two. I gave Jai to my wife. I gave Tora to my brother's wife."

"I thought I could raise Jai and ensure Cyra's stain wouldn't be repeated and figure out how to break the curse. But I also wanted my own son. I wanted to raise Tora myself. Roshan didn't like that I always sought to take Tora away from him. I blamed it on him being the leader of Kindle and not having the time for Tora. By three or four years old, Tora looked like my carbon copy, and Jai looked like him. Our wives thought it was so sweet. Roshan had other thoughts. He had gone to the sages and looked at the birth records. He saw Tora's registry and saw that I never registered Jai. I told him that I did and that we could meet and I would show him everything."

"I was supposed to take Jai hunting that day. But Roshan would not be patient. I sent Jai off to wait for me in case things got ugly. I had made two birth records, one of which accurately showed Tora as my son. The other was a fake that said that Jai was my son. I showed Roshan the fake. Roshan was not to be convinced. We argued about old quarrels, recent quarrels, and things that never manifested. Then we came to blows. I was the better Fireheart when it came to using my Element. I didn't even realize that I killed him until he was lying there dead, things just out of control! I made it look like he was trampled by an animal when I broke the news to his wife."

Jai staggered backward, "You killed my father?"

"Unfortunately, I did. Then hate grew in my heart for everything that Roshan and I were. The descendants of those Legends. They marked us with a terrible curse. I have tried for years to break the curse. I wondered how the world could be a better place without the Legends. I didn't want people to end up like Roshan, me, or our family. But I'm not the only one who believes we are better off. We don't need Legends! They have only created hell for us! It's not justice for one person of each nation to decide our fate and be stronger than the rest."

Tora walked forward, "You don't see it. It is people like *you* that make us need Legends. Look at yourself! You can wield fire and lightning without choosing one over the other. And the lightning is white, the kind that can even kill a Fireheart. No one is telling you that you didn't deserve that power! The Universe actually gave you a chance to be better than them! You had a good life as a famous doctor known worldwide. You threw away a good life to be a murderer. You gave me up, your son! Firehearts may not like Legends, but they'll forever hate *you*."

"The curse is not over, you don't understand! It will be too late if you don't listen to me!" Agni was frantic, but his words fell on deaf ears.

"Is he telling the truth, Kavi?" Aqila asked, holding her position.

Kavi nodded, "You've earned a fair trial. Unfortunately, Neptune is dead. He would have gotten a fair trial as well."

Agni's eyes widened, "Yas is dead?"

Kavi kneeled at eye level with Agni, "Yes, his tribe killed him."

Agni lowered his head.

Kavi sighed, "Aqila, Saar, and I will take it from here. Can you handle her?" He asked, pointing to Sitara.

"Yes, I can." Sitara never moved as Aqila approached her, and she encased her in a wind sphere. Sitara looked at Cahya, but he turned away from her.

"Cahya, I did what I thought was best. I pray you can forgive me."

"I'll never forgive you."

"Cahya, if it wasn't for the Legends, your father would still be alive. You can't imagine how hard it was to raise you two on my own in the middle of a war while trying to support a dying vision. The Flamethrowers would have never survived without my financial support. A military group fell to becoming a ragtag group of vigilantes. I heard Agni's pleas for unity and to be a people independent of Legends. And I liked it. I could have kept my family together. Son, I believe in the Universe, but I don't believe that Legends are needed. Their problems become the world's problems and I grew tired of that. Brace yourself, Cahya, for the day when the things that plague them will plague you."

Cahya turned away, shaking his head in dismay. Aqila began to move the sphere in the direction Kavi went.

"I always knew Agni had deadly lightning. You'd be dead if I didn't intercept it. Regardless of what happens, I'll always love you." Sitara whispered. Aqila continued to push Sitara until she was out of sight from the others.

Jai looked to Tora, then to Cahya. And for the first time, he questioned his existence. Then he became aware of Tora and Cahya looking at him. He opened his mouth to speak, but both Firehearts walked away from him. It disturbed him. Tora was family, and Cahya was his brother-in-arms, but one moment changed how they looked at him forever.

Aqila returned, "Are you okay?"

"I don't know. It just hit me how so many people agree with Agni. So many people followed him to this extreme."

"I'm sorry, Jai. I honestly was afraid that this would happen," she whispered.

"What?"

"I had a hunch that Yuuta wasn't who he said he was, but I had no proof. Then when Sheraga said that Agni was a woman, I thought that disproved my concerns."

"Why didn't you say anything?"

"I didn't have any proof. I was going on a hunch. I could have been wrong, which is a serious accusation, especially about someone's parent or loved one."

"And finding out this way was so much better, right?"

"Jai, I didn't know. And when Sheraga said that the leader of those troops was a woman, what reason did I have to press forward with that line of thought?"

"But you didn't say *anything*! When Sheraga said Agni was a woman, you could have told me your suspicions then. I would have let it go upon hearing Sheraga's viewpoint. And you still never said anything when I told you something was off. I trusted you with my life. I'm closer to you than any other Legend, or so I thought."

Aqila hung her head, "I didn't intend to disappoint you. I did what I thought was best, and I didn't want to give you misinformation."

"You kept asking me about him, trying to get information that suited your case. The bottom line is that you should have told me. Goodbye, Aqila-"

"Jai, wait!"

He raised his hand, gently pushing her away as she touched his shoulder, "Don't. I don't want to see you."

A single tear fell from her silver eyes. She felt a familiar presence that she recognized as Emet.

Don't worry, Aqila.

I messed up! I'm the new Basir. I ruined our relationship. I tried so hard to do things in a way that kept us together.

And you did. Jai feels hurt, but there is nothing you can do about it. You must be brave and keep moving forward. Let him heal, so when the world needs you again, you'll all be ready.

Kavi placed a hand on her shoulder, "Don't fret. He'll need some time to adjust. Same with Cahya and Tora. We have work to do to prepare for a trial. Together, the Windmasters will lead the world through this."

He's right. Agni had to be stopped, but he was the leader that Ember believed in. The Waterbearer tribes are in turmoil, and Theyra is all but destroyed. The Windmasters must lead the world to healing and peace.

THE AFTERMATH OF SCATTERED SKIES

Tiber sighed long and hard as she left the palace at Pyroc. A month had passed since the final showdown with Agni and Neptune. In complete justice, the four Nations decided to hold a two-week trial for Yuuta and Sitara. It was the first time all four Nations were united for a common goal. Account after account was heard, tears were shed, old wounds were opened, and it was miserable. She was glad to be on her faithful companion, Mika, heading home.

In the end, Yuuta was sentenced to confinement in the Metalkeeper territory, surrounded by liquid metal that would poison him if he ever tried to escape. He could have unlimited visitors as long as each was approved by either Tora or Zuriel. Yuuta begged to die, but Ruler Akash and DragonLord Sheraga thought that would be an easy way out. He needed to live with the weight of what he had done. Sitara, unfortunately, didn't survive the trial. The wounds she sustained from Yuuta refused to heal correctly, and she rejected Jai's assistance. She died in Cahya's arms after the first day of the trial.

However, some progressive things came from the trial. Theyra announced the end of their long civil war, with Zuriel announcing their territory's name as Tungsten. Arrow resigned from the Flamethrowers to accept an official position in the DragonCourt as Ambassador of Pyroc. Chief Muraco was recognized as the leader of the Tribe of Snow and Ice. Chiefess Marina announced her engagement to Mahak of the Snow Tribe. Governor Othniel announced his resignation as governor to train sages for the ancient library with Boaz as his apprentice. Ruler Akash recognized Aqila as a Legend Seer and revealed the date of her and Kavi's highly anticipated wedding.

It was nice hearing from all of the Nations. Everything went so peacefully that it was decided to hold two international summits yearly in alternating Nations. In even-number years, the Spring Summit will be held in Pyroc, and the Fall Summit will be held in Wyndhm. In odd-number years, the Spring Summit will be held in one of the Waterbearer tribes, and the Fall Summit will be held on the border of Theyra and Tungsten. To this, everyone agreed.

Many thoughts danced in Tiber's mind as she returned to Avala. She prayed that she would arrive in time to witness the birth of the first baby, since changing the Snow Tribe to align with the Universal Order. Her sister's baby! She was nervous and excited all at the same time. She also wanted to see if Cove was making any progress. He hadn't been able to go back home since his eye injury. Although Sita was able to save his eye, he lost sight in his injured eye. Every time she thought about it, she felt guilty. She couldn't stop blaming herself for what had happened.

Tiber was so lost in thought that she did not hear her name being called until a massive bird landed in front of Mika.

"I didn't mean to startle you," Aqila smiled.

"No, I just wasn't paying attention. Are you coming for the birth?"

"Of course, I want to see how everything's been working out." Talon hovered low enough to the ground for Tiber and Aqila to continue a conversation.

"I'm surprised you had time for this. I mean, shouldn't you be preparing for the wedding?"

"The wedding preparations are in a good place. My dress is almost finished. The gems and beads were gifted by Ruler Sufa. My mother is working on my headdress. Kavi is selecting the food for the dinner menu. And we are both working on our vows."

"Will you have bridesmaids?"

"It doesn't really work like that. In Kashmala, the mother of the groom is the honorable lady. She precedes the bride in walking down the aisle, showing her approval of her son's choice. Then the bride walks with her esteemed sister, usually a close friend of the bride, following behind with two doves in an ornate cage."

"I know you're excited. You've wanted this for a long time."

"I know. I've loved Kavi since I was four years old." Aqila signed with happiness.

Tiber giggled, "I hope to meet someone that makes me feel that way."

"What happened with Cove?"

"What makes you ask that?"

"He's really put a lot on the line for you. And it's clear you care about him."

Tiber let out a long, exasperated sigh, "I don't know, Aqila. I don't know if I can give up my tribe and family."

"Why would you have to give them up?"

"In Waterbearer tribes, we can intermarry between tribes, but the woman has to join the husband's tribe. Unless she is a queen or chiefess, like in Marina's case. Mahak is leaving the Snow Tribe to join her tribe. I would have to leave my tribe to marry him. Then there's the part where he lost vision in his eye because of me."

"If the tradition is to join the husband's tribe, what's the problem? That's what your people do."

"You don't understand. You've loved Kavi for a long time. You haven't put him in danger or a bad situation that could change the nature of your relationship."

Aqila burst into laughter, "Because we've loved each other so long, Kavi has seen me at my worst. Trust me, I've done plenty of things that have put him in less than favorable positions. But you learn as you go. If you love each other, you'll keep choosing each other no matter what. If you feel uneasy, you should talk to him. Chances are he feels the same way."

"I should at least talk to Cove. I can't avoid him forever," Tiber sighed as the pair started up the icy mountain that led to the snowy wonder called Avala.

Upon entering Muraco's tent, Tiber heard crying.

A baby? Shasa!

Tiber gathered herself.

Suddenly, Sita hurried from one of the rooms. "You're here! Come on. Are you ready?"

She pulled Tiber by the hand and opened the flap. Sita's curly hair was a bit wild and somewhat wet from what appeared to be sweat. "Go on in!"

Shasa was resting on several pillows. In her arms, she cradled a tiny baby.

"How are you feeling?" Tiber asked.

"Tired and sore, but I'm excited about my son. He's so precious," Shasa replied.

"How long has it been?" Tiber asked.

"Several hours," Shasa replied. "Tiber, you did it! Father would have been so proud of you."

"Thank the Heavens!" Tiber ran as fast as she could until she reached Talon. Aqila was laid back relaxing on her dasher when Tiber started jumping up and down.

"Aqila! It worked! The curse is gone!"

Aqila sat up and was immediately attentive, "Exalted Skies! That's great news. Your tribe will be able to live more comfortably now."

"I couldn't have done it without you. You pushed me to be the person I needed to be to save my people. I'll be forever grateful to you."

"Hey, we both pushed each other in the right direction," Aqila smiled.

"Hey Tiber, Aqila," Nahal approached them. "I heard that Shasa had a successful birth. I just returned from seeing my father off to the Beach tribe. I was actually thinking of going with him."

Aqila raised her gray eyebrows, "You want to leave your tribe?"

"It wouldn't hurt, and I could start over fresh. I've been thinking about it."

"Well, I know you'll make a good choice," Aqila smiled at him.

"Hey, I'm going to check on Cove, be right back," Tiber hurried off, leaving the Windmaster with the Waterbearer.

"Aqila, I'm-"

"I know, Nahal," she whispered.

"I was horrible. You could have died-"

"Stop beating yourself up about it. You apologized already, and you genuinely didn't know what was happening. Your tribe forgave you, and I forgive you."

"Thanks. I'm not sure if they have really forgiven me, though," he leaned on Talon. "I mean, at least my brother. Sometimes I look back on everything, and I don't know how I can have a future here anymore."

"If you want a future anywhere, you must fight for it."

"Thanks."

"It is up to us whether we dance in the light or with shadows. You're choosing the light now. Make that mean something." She patted Talon's head, and he hovered in the sky.

Tiber entered Sita's lair, looking for Cove.

"He left a couple of days ago, Tiber," Sita spoke gently.

"Oh," she looked down at her feet and forced a smile onto her face, "he must have been doing better. That's good."

Sita walked over, "You want to talk about it?"

"Oh, it's nothing. Just didn't think he'd leave without saying anything."

"Tiber, you were at the trial, and Cove has a tribe to run. He didn't mean to hurt your feelings. He really did have to go back home."

"No! I get it," Tiber laughed, "my feelings aren't hurt. I was just surprised, that's all." She shrugged her shoulders and left the medicine lair.

Tiber went to her tent and looked at the mountains in the distance. She sighed long and hard.

What did I really expect? Why do I keep holding on, knowing that I will have to let go?

"Tiber, permission to enter?"

"Come in, Muraco," she replied.

"Aqila just left. She was needed back home. Are you okay?"

"I'm fine!"

Muraco was taken aback by Tiber's tone, "I am sorry. I should have told you about Cove when you got here. His tribe was worried about him, so he went back home."

"Maybe it's for the best," she shrugged, "don't worry about me."

"Shasa and I never want you to leave, but we want you to be happy. If you and Cove decide that you want to get married, we'll be your biggest supporters, along with your new nephew, Kallan."

"Aww, you've named him," Tiber's eyes were glassy.

"Yes, we've finally settled on a name."

She sighed, "I'm not sure I'm ready to leave home. It's my fault Cove lost vision in his eye. I don't think he would choose me. After all that's happened."

"It sounds like you're the one not choosing him. It's okay not to be ready. It is better to admit that now than to hurt someone's heart down the road. I remember my father once telling me that every tribe is our home. Regardless of how the sky scatters us, we will always be one."

Tiber thought about how her mother moved from the Jungle Tribe to the Snow Tribe, hoping to find a husband. Eventually, her mother met her father, they married, and Tiber was born into the world.

I can't imagine how hard it was for you to leave. I just wish you were here to tell me how to do it. I wish you could tell me if Cove is the one. I just feel so conflicted right now, like my tribe still needs me.

"How do you think the tribe will feel to learn about the future international summits?"

"I think they'll like that," Tiber murmured.

"Do you mind doing me a favor?"

"Sure, what is it?"

"I put together a monetary gift for the Jungle Tribe, for Cove assisting us with the Neptune situation. I would deliver it myself, but Nahal and I have a meeting."

"I'll deliver it," Tiber hesitated.

"I really appreciate it. Being chief is hard work. I'm thankful that Nahal and I are mending our relationship, and he's been a huge help. He probably would have run things better in many areas than myself," Muraco sighed.

"It will really pick his spirit up to feel useful."

"When we left for the trial, I thought about how he was running the tribe by himself. He did an excellent job. I've been thinking long and hard about this. I'm going to make him the councilman."

"That's wonderful news! He'll do great! He'll feel better knowing he truly has a place in the tribe."

Muraco handed her a weighted package, "Send Cove warm regards from the tribe."

Tiber nodded, "I will."

She hurried off to the tribe hub to get Mika. She saw Aqila looking eagerly at the sky.

"I thought you left," she said to the Windmaster.

"Forgot to ask if everything is good here! Didn't want to leave you hanging," she replied.

"Yes, I have to run an errand for the chief. Thanks for all of your help and support. I can't wait until the wedding!"

Aqila waved as she and Talon hovered higher into the sky, silent wing flaps propelling them toward Wyndhm. Tiber called Mika and headed down the icy mountain path. She was a little worried about going to the Jungle Tribe. What would they think of her - being responsible for Cove's injury? She had actually made friends there. Would they dislike her for what happened? Would they be upset that no one from their tribe was present at the trial? So many questions whirled through Tiber's mind as she made her way into the lush green jungle.

Upon entering the Jungle Tribe, she reminisced over all that had happened to her. She passed the spot where she went through the Changing. Afterward, the river where she first saw her new self. She smiled as Mika paced through the dense terrain. Then she came to the spot where she fought with Rilian and Kano before being captured in Cove's vines. She recalled fearing for her life as she and Mika were dragged across the jungle floor.

She arrived at the tribe quicker than she expected. Tiber gulped hard, her hands began to tremble. Suddenly, Mika was tackled, and she tumbled to the ground.

Getting in a fighting stance, she quickly picked up the package.

Someone was laughing, "Did you make up your mind?"

"Rilian!" Tiber huffed before running to hug her.

"You disappeared after the festival! Girl, then the way Cove came back, I was worried about you," Rilian embraced her tighter.

"I'm doing okay. Things have just been a little crazy with the world."

Rilian walked with her inside the tribe hub, "Yeah, we heard about a trial happening."

"Yes, it is over, and Agni is locked in confinement. Neptune is dead."

Rilian's mouth dropped, "Well, I pray that we can all heal and find peace. I can let Cove know that you're here."

"You don't have to do that. I'm here just to send this package from our tribe. No need to disturb anyone-"

"Nonsense!" Rilian silenced her as she pulled her by the arm towards Cove's tent.

Tiber thought her heart was going to explode as she drew nearer. Rilian called Cove's name before nearly tossing Tiber past the flap of his tent. She stumbled on the tent floor.

"How many times have I told you to ask for per- . . . Tiber?"

Tiber hurried to stand and brushed her knees off. Her eyes scoured the floor for the package, and she picked it up and handed it to Cove. "This is a thank you from my tribe for your help," she lowered her eyes to avoid his gaze.

"I look that bad, huh?"

She slowly met his teal eyes, the right one with a black patch over it, "No, you're still handsome as always. I'm so sorry."

He embraced her, "What are you sorry for?"

"It is my fault that you can't see out of your eye."

"Hey, stop that! We were in a battle, and I got hit. That's all, okay. The light still hurts my injured eye. That's why I have the patch. I was joking, but I don't want you to be upset about it. I was more worried about you. I couldn't believe that I didn't protect you better." His fingers traced around the outline of the scar on her neck.

"We're both here now. That's what matters. I'm thankful you helped me and believed in me."

He nudged her shoulder, "Of course. How was the trial?"

"Progressive, Agni is confined with the Metalkeepers surrounded by this poisonous liquid metal. The Nations will be having international summits twice a year now."

"Maybe that's what Muraco wanted to tell me about."

"I was surprised that you weren't there when I returned."

Cove sighed, "Kano and Rilian wrote to me. The tribe was uneasy about what happened at the festival. They needed me to return, reassuring them that everything was alright. I didn't want it to appear that I left without speaking to you."

"No-no. You have a tribe you're responsible for. I understand," she said, looking away from him.

"Tiber, I-"

"Please don't. I'm already really conflicted about a lot of things."

"That's why I need to say this," he chuckled. "Tiber, I want you to stay with your tribe." Tiber staggered backward a bit. "It's for the best. I know how much you love your family and tribe. You are working on turning to the Universe and really reestablishing yourselves. They need you. And you need them. I am so proud of you. You've done well, and I know you will continue to be a great Legend."

"Cove, I do really care-"

"I know, so do I. But you have to do what's best for everyone. Besides, your heart is in making sure that you uphold your father's last wish for you. And I know your choice would make him proud."

She flung herself into his arms, "Don't forget me, Cove."

Tiber stepped back, and Cove smiled, "I could never forget the woman who allowed me the chance to avenge my father. Thank you, Tiber. You know I'll be here if you ever need anything or change your mind about things."

She smiled at him before nodding, "I know, Cove. I know." Tiber held his gaze and smiled before leaving his tent. After calling for Mika, she hurried from the Jungle Tribe.

Rilian turned and peeked inside Cove's tent only to see his back turned to her. "You know, I shoved her in here so you could be a charmer and ask her to marry you or something of that nature, not make her run away! Why did you let her go?"

Cove turned to her, "I let her go because I love her. She wasn't ready for me to ask that of her. And it would have been unfair to do so. She's still grieving for her father. She wants to hold onto everything that reminds her of him. I've been there. I know what that feels like. I'm happy to know her, be her friend, support her, and know that she cares about me. And if that's all that ever happens, I'm fine. I love her, so I won't ask anything from her that she isn't willing or ready to give."

THE DEPTHS OF DUSK

Jai was waiting at the old cabin that was the first Flamethrowers headquarters. He had a meeting soon, but he wasn't expecting to be swallowed by nostalgia as he entered the cabin. Memories whirled around in his mind. The first time he met the Flamethrowers was here. And that one day changed the trajectory of his life forever. The map fragments that Calida was reading were still attached to the wall. He missed her. She was a great leader. She had a commanding presence and the know-how to lead a team to victory. A woman of honor and dignity, she was willing to put her life on the line to secure the success of a mission.

He wondered what Calida would have thought about the trial and the future of the Flamethrowers. He reflected on Arrow's announcement to accept the Ambassador of Pyroc. Jai was happy for Arrow. It settled that long burning sensation that Jai knew he had - the longing to return home. In a way, Jai felt somewhat envious of Arrow having a family to go home to. It made him hate himself more, especially after his conversation with Boaz at the trial.

***

"Can I talk to you for a minute?"

"Yeah, Boaz, what's up?"

Boaz sighed, "It's about Aqila. Jai, don't treat her like this. I understand you're hurt, angry, and maybe even confused. But, trust me, Aqila wrestled long and hard with what to do and say. She didn't want to hurt you or be wrong about your family."

"I know you're her best friend, but she should have told me instead of asking me questions and trying to get an answer. She let everything explode in my face! Do you have any idea what that was like? I just wanted peace and closure,

and I'll never have that. And what's worse, other people are attached to this terrible decision she made!"

"Jai, calm down! Don't take your anger out on Aqila. You would still be trying to figure yourself out in Pyroc if Aqila hadn't stepped into your life. I'm not saying her decision was right or wrong, but don't make her the problem!"

"She's not the problem. I know that."

"Jai, you're not the problem either! I know this is hard, but Yuuta had his own problem. He inflicted pain and problems on the world."

"So many Firehearts believed in his message and were willing to die for it," Jai sighed.

"Exactly why we can't afford to be against each other. We don't know what's going to happen following this. We're a team for a reason. We have to keep the unity. Imagine how hard it was for Aqila to be attacked and nearly killed by Tiber only to find out she was a Legend."

Jai took a step back, "I never considered it."

"I was there! She was furious to see Tiber again, but in the end, they made amends. Did it change the fact that they nearly killed each other? No, but we can't let our personal feelings and emotions sever the unity. If our predecessors taught us anything, it was that."

Jai groaned, "I don't hate Aqila. I just wished that she had told me so I could have been prepared. Yes, I was angry, but I was angrier that I was at the center of my people's problem."

"You know what I think? I think it is time the Firehearts get to see a Legend working on their behalf instead of their own agenda. Once the Firehearts see what you're about, they will see that you are different from Cyra."

"I've been thinking about that too. I want Ember to be one again. I have to meet with Tora and Zay, and then I need to make amends with Aqila. But I will be going off on my own mission to heal my people and help them believe in the power of the Universe once again."

"You'll do great, Jai. I know it."

"Thanks, Boaz. I should get Aqila a wedding gift, but I don't know what she would like," Jai murmured.

"Just bring yourself. That would mean the most to her."

***

His thoughts were disturbed when someone walked into the cabin and gently closed the door shut. Gold eyes met hazel ones as Tora walked over and shook Jai's hand. It nearly made Jai tremble to see how much Tora resembled Yuuta.

"Thanks for meeting me, Tora."

"Yeah, we've been needing to talk."

"I'm sorr-"

"No, I didn't come here for you to apologize to me. I was taken aback. Everything I've known my whole life has been a lie. I wanted us to talk since we are technically family. Figured you were just as unaware as I was."

"Yeah, I was unaware and shocked. When I met him, it was like a prayer had been answered. Then, I wanted to know more and find closure."

"Closure, that's a funny thing, huh. I think you found it. Now you know what happened to your father. I know that is not what you wanted, but at least you know what happened."

"And my mother?"

"She passed away many years ago. Her name was Azar, and she was very kind and sweet. You look a lot like her, and you have her temperament."

"I'm sorry that Yuuta wasn't the father you needed him to be. You're a great man and deserved better."

"I vaguely remember him as a doting uncle. My father-well, your father wasn't too fond of him. Then, we stopped seeing him altogether and his wife. Your father was a good man. He was fearless; he led Kindle through some trying times and worked hard for his people."

"Do you remember me?"

"No, I don't, but come on, kids' memories aren't always the best."

"I suppose," Jai whispered.

"So what are we going to do?"

Jai raised a black eyebrow, "What do you mean?"

"Your father was the leader of Kindle. I'll resign so you can-"

"No way! I don't want to be the leader of anything! Being a Legend is a challenge in itself. I have things I need to do and peace to make. Your people love you, and you love them. Lead them."

Tora scoffed, "Yeah until they find out that I'm the son of a murderer. And it doesn't help that I'm his spitting image."

"That only means something if you let it mean something."

"Alright, I'll lead them. Jai, we're the only family we have now. I'll be your brother if you'll accept me."

Jai smiled, "Of course I accept you. To have a family was all I ever wanted for a long time."

"What do you want now?"

"To bring lasting peace to the Firehearts so the next Legend will be accepted with open arms. I don't want them to have to hide like I did. I want them to be free to accept everything that makes them great. I never want a Legend to run from themselves again. They won't be successful at it anyway."

Tora headed to the door, "It will be a lot of work, but you can do it. Your successor will thank you. I'm going back to Kindle now. Don't be a stranger, brother. If you need anything, don't hesitate."

Jai smiled as Tora left, "Thanks, brother," he whispered to himself.

Not long after Tora left, the cabin door was being pushed open again.

"Hey," Zay mumbled.

"Zay," Jai met his gaze and couldn't tell the mood behind Zay's expression.

"So, I guess we're trying to...."

"I just want to know why you hate me so much. You've disliked me for a long time, and I want to walk away with the facts. I want to know I've done my best to heal what I've broken, knowingly or unknowingly. Now that you're the leader of the Flamethrowers, I'd hope to at least be on good terms."

Zay breathed heavily, "It was just my mother and me for a long time. I didn't miss having a father because I was small, and she cared for me. Things were always hard, but I leaned on her for everything I needed. I asked her about my father, and she told me he went to fight in the Civil War. Several parts of Ember had been bombed, and she was expecting me at the time and had to evacuate. Then, she gave birth to me several months later, but she never heard back from him. That entire time, she never knew if he was alive or not. When I was about two, the Civil War ended, and she searched for him. We moved around for a year, town to town, looking for any information on him. She got sick after that year. It wasn't bad at first, but we couldn't afford any kind of medical help, so her condition only worsened. By the time I was eight, she had gone completely blind, and the sickness was ravishing her body."

"She couldn't work, we were behind on rent, so I worked. I was a kid, so work was hard to find. I made just enough to keep us somewhat paid up on rent, but we never had enough for food. So I had to steal. I would steal, get in a fight, and beat the hell out of someone. It was a never-ending cycle. It didn't matter if I told them what I was going through. Sometimes I didn't even eat. I would take the food and cook for my mother," Zay's eyes began to water.

"I couldn't provide for her properly, and she passed away when I was fourteen. I had never felt so angry and alone. I continued to try to scrape by, do odd jobs here, and steal there. I just didn't want to lose my mom's house. Even today, her scent still lingers on the walls. I took on this odd job with Arka one day. He had a son close to my age. Arka kept looking at me. I ignored it at first. Once I finished the job and was paid, he pulled me aside and asked who my mother was. I told him her name was Harsha and that she had passed. Then Arka cried. He told me that I looked like his wife. He told me he had gone to war, and when he came back, everything had been bombed. He looked for her and never found her. I was angry. I looked at you and realized that I had been replaced. Arka told me that he found you passed out near some tunnels and that you didn't remember your family. I told him it seemed like he got his son, and I left. You were so content, and I was angry and hateful. That should have been my mother and me happy and content with Arka."

Jai's mouth dropped, "Zay, why didn't you come and stay with him. I would have understood. I wished for my family my entire life. I wouldn't have-"

"What did it matter? He didn't know me or what I had to suffer. And staying with him wasn't going to bring her back! She needed and longed for him! She prayed that he was alive and that would return to her. He seemed content with his little life, while I spent the last several years blaming myself for not doing enough. So I left."

"Zay, I'm sorry. Do you want to talk about this with Arka?"

"Arka wrote both of us a letter," Zay handed a crushed envelope to Jai.

"Why can't we just talk to him?"

"He's dead, Jai. Agni's soldiers killed him for stealing two birth certificates from Agni's house. He gave it to Tora, and Tora went to Kavi. That's how they discovered who Yuuta, 'Agni', really was. Yuuta kept the original copies of your and Tora's birth certificate. When Tora checked the one he had, it was clearly a forgery. Then he went to Kavi. The rest is history."

Jai dropped his head. Things weren't perfect for him and Arka, but he was the only father he had ever known. He clenched the envelope tightly and took a deep breath before looking Zay straight in the eye, "I understand, Zay. I enjoyed your father, just like someone else enjoyed mine. I understand the anger, the pain, the frustration, and the need for closure. I don't know if it means anything now, but Arka loved you. I should not be asking you for anything, but if you'd accept me as your brother-"

"Jai, I can't accept you as my brother. My life has been hell. I lost my mother and now my father. I'm angry, not at you, but at what our people have become. I appreciate you trying, but you'll never know hell like I do. I can't accept you as my brother, but I'll accept you as my friend. Just forgive me for all that I've done."

"You were just trying to get by. I accept your friendship." Zay nodded as he left the cabin.

Jai looked at the envelope, and his hands shook a bit. He took a deep breath and opened it. It read,

Jai, I fear I may not have much time left, but I wanted to tell you a few things in case I never see you again. First, I'm sorry about the whole Agni thing. Life in Lower Ember was almost impossible without his support. Once I entered his fold, business picked up, and things were looking up. I was just trying to make life a little better for us. I didn't know that you were a Legend. I lost my faith and gift long ago upon returning from the Civil War to find my town destroyed and my family missing. Being close to the heat of the fire reminded me of the good days; therefore, I chose to become a blacksmith. In truth, I'm glad I found you. My wife was expecting a child when I had to leave for war, but providing for you allowed me to truly be a father. Secondly, Zay is my son. My absence in his life has hurt him deeply, and I'm not sure I can recover that relationship. I love you both. Don't blame Zay for Agni. I recommended him for the job, thinking it would improve his life. I didn't know that he would be tasked with hunting a Legend. I would have tried to stop him if I had known. Forgive me, Jai. I love you. Regardless of what you find in your search for your parentage, you will always be a son to me. ~ Arka

A single tear fell on the crumpled paper. Jai's heart hurt. He swallowed hard, trying to get control over this whirlwind of emotion just as the cabin door opened. He immediately turned his back, trying to get himself together.

"Jai!" Hasty footsteps approached him, and Jai just hung his head.

"Jai, what's wrong? Did your meetings not go well? Talk to me, please." Jai kept his back turned and took a few steps, then sighed, knowing that pushing people away wouldn't change anything.

"I'm sorry, Arin, it's been a rough day."

She had a large tray of food wrapped up. "Well, maybe this will help?" she said, offering the tray to him.

"Thanks," he accepted the food. His gaze caught hers, and he could feel her sadness. She lowered her gaze and slowly turned to leave.

"Arin," she stopped, "I don't know if I can eat all this. Can you help me?" She turned and smiled, which warmed Jai's heart. They sat on the floor side by side. Arin began to carefully unwrap the food. Jai couldn't stop looking at her. Her jet-black hair had grown a little longer, her hands were nimble and delicate, and when he caught a glimpse of her honey-colored eyes, it almost took his breath away.

"Ready to eat?"

He nodded, "Thanks for staying."

"I wanted to. I hope everything's okay."

"I know things will get better. I'll make it better."

"Do you mind me asking what happened?"

While they ate, Jai told her everything. He told her about Aqila, Tora, and Zay. Afterward, he let her read the letter from Arka.

"Are you okay? I mean, after all of this?"

"It hurts. But I have the closure I need. My parents lived and died without knowing me, and Arka was the closest thing I had to a father. He loved me equal to his own blood son. It wasn't the closure I wanted. However, I have what I need. That makes my mission mean even more to me."

"Your mission?"

"I made up my mind. I want to help Cahya and rebuild Ember. It's time to let go of what divides us and become one. We are stronger united. The Phoenix Riders have a lot to offer the Firehearts. I want to do something good for my people, so when I die a hundred years from now, and the Firehearts hear of a Golden-eyed Legend they'll smile. That's what I want."

"What about the Flamethrowers? What will we do?"

"What Cyra wanted you to do. You're a part of her legacy that lived. Something that brought honor to her name and the Flamethrowers will remain as she left them for all of her struggles."

Arin nodded, "Kind of crazy that she's your ancestor."

"Actually, it makes sense. That's why this had to be this way. She worked hard to fix her mistakes but needed someone to handle her unfinished business. She tried to fix the world, but it didn't work. She didn't fix her world or her family. They suffered for it, but that ends now with Tora and me."

"I'm proud of you, Jai. I pray the Universe continues to light your path."

They sat in silence, both wanting to say something to the other. They took a deep breath simultaneously. Before turning to each other, both asked, "What?"

Jai started, "You want to come to Ember with me? I know things got crazy the last time-"

"Yes! I don't care about what happened last time. I just want to support you because . . . I love you."

"I've known that for a while. I couldn't give it my full attention then, but Arin, I love you too. Thank you for supporting me. This would have been a hundred times harder without you. We set off tomorrow?"

"Yes, I want to tell Alena I'll be leaving for a while. We've really been working on our communication. And I've accepted how she and Zay feel about each other. We aren't missing Aqila's wedding, right?"

"No! Trust me, we'll be back in time for the wedding."

She stood up and headed for the door, "It's dusk. I should go before it gets too dark. You should try and rest."

"I will, and Arin," Jai called as she left.

"Yes?"

"Thanks for everything."

She beamed with happiness before waving as she headed into the thick of the forest.

A BEAUTIFUL LIGHT

It's not easy walking in the footsteps of greatness. It is like having your entire presence swallowed by the shadows of others. Ever since I was a small child, I knew that I was different. It was often like the stars were speaking to me. My dreams were never my own but like another world under Ila's guidance. It has been two weeks. Now, when I sleep, there's nothing at all.

Boaz never realized how much he leaned on them for guidance. In particular Ila, she was like a second mother to him. She was firm and unyielding but loving all at the same time. Then there was Basir, his wisdom paramount.

Where Ila nurtured him, Basir informed him. Boaz related to them the most. Ila represented his nation, and Basir was the Legend who was immediately touched by the stars with the ability to identify all Legends, sometimes before they realized themselves.

He was not visited often by Cyra or Aenon. While Aenon would urge him to be brave when needed, Cyra never showed herself. She would only speak, and even that was rare. Boaz learned a lot about the last Legends because he had the rare opportunity to get to know them. He was connected by their spiritual unrest. However, now whenever he called them, he was met with silence.

"I hope they don't feel like I don't need them," he murmured, missing their presence.

In his heart, he knew the truth. The unrest of the previous Legends to locate their successor to continue the cycle was over. All the Legends are known now. That part of his journey is complete. Their presence ensured that he did not prematurely tell the other Legends of their identity.

Riding his sand raft home, he prayed, "Great Skies, thank you. I pray that peace has been secured. Thank you for the Legends of today and yesterday. I wish I could have thanked them individually, but I was unaware of how soon they would leave my side. I've learned, and I vow to be more grateful for every blessing. Then, I won't feel any regret for having moved too slowly. I hope you smile on us, Universe. I also pray that our predecessors have been forgiven. I wish to speak all of their names with honor."

Securing his raft behind his house, Boaz's hands trembled. He hadn't seen his family in such a long time and missed them. He wished Aenon could have given him a little courage at this moment. He swallowed hard before going inside.

The delicate aroma of aged pages tickled his nose, nearly making his mouth water. How he had missed home. He smiled, seeing his father trying to log books with his aging eyes.

"I'm home," Boaz said, walking towards him.

"Bo! My son!" His father slammed the book shut and hurried to embrace him.

Boaz closed his eyes, knowing there was a chance he didn't make it home to his family. "What's wrong, son?"

"Aren't you mad at me?"

His father looked bewildered, "Why would I be mad at you?"

"I never told you that I'm a Legend. I was the One Who Knew."

"Bo, your mother and I always recognized that you had a special relationship with the Universe. That was a blessing to us. Legend or not, you're still our son. You've made us proud. And I heard that you are going to be moving soon!"

"The sages were murdered in the ancient library. Governor Othniel is resigning to become a sage and wants to train me as an apprentice."

"The murder is such an unfortunate thing. But blessed stars! I know you will make an excellent sage, my son. Now, what will your mother and I do without you? Batu and Bali are still too young to learn the family business."

"Well, I know someone who would do well and learn quickly. It will give you a little time before working the twins in. Would that help?"

"Bo, that would work wonders," he slapped Boaz's back hard.

"I'll be back this evening, Dad. I have a few errands. I can't wait to see Mom and the twins. I really missed them."

"They missed you too. Stay safe, son."

Boaz nodded to his father before grabbing his sand raft and navigating the sandy desert terrain. He rode on for about half an hour before slowing to a stop.

He steadily approached a familiar house and cleared his throat before knocking on the door. He waited, but there was nothing. He closed his sage eyes and sighed, "I must have been too late."

He turned in the direction he came and dared to look straight into the sun. He smiled desperately, trying to push away that lingering sensation of being too late again. Then he smiled again. "Well, things must be looking up for them. Heavens, I'm thankful for that." Accepting no one would greet him, he slowly headed back to his sand raft.

"Boaz?"

He spun around, "Hey! I was starting to think that I was too late! How have you been?"

"It's been crazy! It's hard to have peace," she giggled. "My brother has gotten popular, I guess."

"Well, being a Governor is an honorable position."

She smiled, "Father would have been thrilled to witness Quillon follow in his footsteps, and mother is so happy. How rude of me, come in, Bo."

Boaz followed her inside, "Well, it's quiet."

Armani sighed, "Too quiet, but I shouldn't complain. I heard that you're going to be a sage."

"Wow, news travels fast. I wanted to tell you myself."

"Well, news travels fast when it pertains to you, the mighty Legend," she lowered her gaze.

"Legend, Sage, or whatever, I'll always be Boaz."

Her olive eyes gently captured his, "I know," she whispered.

"Now that we have established that, I have a favor to ask."

"Ask away."

"Well, now that I have to prepare to move, my parents would need some help with the library since my siblings are still young. Would you -"

"Of course! Why would I want to be stuck in this house? I would love to help your parents out. It's the least I could do for all you've done."

"I must get ready to go, but I'll visit often. I promise," he clutched her hands to his heart before leaving.

She watched his back as he rode his sand raft away. She watched until her eyes could no longer distinguish his figure among the sand and dust. The sun beautifully landed upon Theyra. It had been a long, brutal war for the Landkeepers, but one resilient Landkeeper seemingly brought peace overnight to them. Armani could not remember the last time the sun shined so bright over their land. She felt blessed to have ever crossed his path, "What a beautiful light and this is just the beginning," she whispered to herself.

Boaz rode through the desert until the terrain changed. He was excited to start training to become a sage, a protector of the legacy of all history. Theyra was under development. The place where the Metalkeeper's compound once stood was the beginning of a school. The streets looked cleaner, and new soil covered the blood-stained earth. Boaz inhaled, and the smell of blood was a distant memory. Theyra's new landscaping was coming along.

Thank Glorious Heavens. Now, this looks like a change.

Boaz walked his raft for hours, observing the new developments until he reached the border of Tungsten. The smell of metal claimed his nostrils. A tear slipped from his eye. "Ila, you would have loved to see this place. Your people will never be without a home. I did it for you and all that you have done for me. I pray to the Stars that your soul and spirit can rest now. I miss you, mother of the Metalkeepers."

There were metal sculptures everywhere, and basic landscaping was scattered among the stony terrain. The compound had transformed from a rugged military fortress to a sleek, modern design with smooth edges. In the distance, houses could be seen. Boaz continued walking with his raft and saw the training grounds with metal obstacles.

"Hey, trespasser."

Boaz laughed, "Hey Zuriel, you've outdone yourself with Tungsten. I almost thought I slipped through surveillance."

"Slipped through? Of course not. The guards let me know that you were looking around. Thanks for the accolades, but it was a team effort. What do you think of the factory? Sleek, right!"

"The Metalkeepers have outdone themselves."

"Feel free to look around. It's my turn to guard Yuuta."

"Thank you for your service. You're an incredible leader, Zuriel."

She smiled, the most beautiful smile taking its place with those dangerously gorgeous emerald eyes: "Thank you, Bo. That means a lot coming from you. And thanks for setting us straight; I'm forever grateful." She nodded and walked away.

He heard footsteps behind him and turned around, "Othniel!"

"Boaz, it's good to see you! We'll start our new journey next week. The ancient library repairs are nearly complete."

Even though Othniel was speaking, Boaz's eyes searched for someone else.

"Is something on your mind?"

Boaz's eyes widened, and he scratched his head. "I've received an invitation to Aqila's wedding, but it's for two people. I was considering asking Armani, but for some reason, I couldn't bring myself to do it. I also want to ask Fayruz. It's complicated."

Othniel chuckled, "Once you know the difference between a flower and flame, wind and water, the complication will cease to be."

"What?"

"Let's walk and talk, I have something I want to show you." The pair continued as they walked along the border that separated Theyra from Tungsten. "All women are either a flower or a flame. And men are either the wind or water. A flower is gentle and delicate; a strong wind would utterly destroy it. However, when in contact with the right amounts of water, the flower can grow and flourish. Now, the flame is fierce, a strong wind enhances the flames. On the other hand, flames and water cannot occupy the same space without one destroying the other. So the question is who are *they* and who are *you*?"

Othniel brought Boaz to a fertile spot of land peppered with several young trees.

"What is this?"

"Do you know what this tree is?" Othniel asked. "Look at the leaves." Othniel plucked a leaf and handed it to Boaz.

His eyes watered, "It's an Oak."

When the mighty oak trees stand again, victory will be ours.

"It didn't happen as we thought it would, but victory was ours."

Othniel left Boaz in the fertile land of young Oaks. He reflected on his journey. Armani was the flower; she was sweet and gentle. She was there to patch him up and she supported his endeavors. Fayruz was the flame; she was bold and courageous. When he wasn't sure if he could keep going, he endured because she was there. She wouldn't let him break. He cared about both of them, and he'd level the earth if anyone dared to harm either of them.

I know who I'll ask to the wedding.

GLORIOUS HEAVENS

Aqila was looking at herself in the mirror as her mother smiled, putting on her completed headdress on her long wavy hair. Her braided crown and bun had been released, allowing her full hair length to be seen. She saw the tears in her mother's eyes.

"Does it look alright, mother?"

"My beautiful girl, you look lovely. I'm so proud of you." She touched the dangling crystals from the silver headdress with delicate hands.

"Thank you for working so hard on this," Aqila sighed.

"Of course, love, it was an honor. You look nervous."

"I'm nervous and excited all at the same time. You can't count how many times I've imagined this day. Kavi will be the ruler of Kashmala with me by his side. If we do this together, I know we can handle it."

"Yes, you can," she wiped her tears as she cried, "Don't worry, love, it's tears of joy."

Aqila embraced her mother, "I know. I just thank the Universe that you, Father, and Athens could be here with me."

Aqila looked at herself in her shimmering silver wedding dress. Hand-sewn crystals completely covered the satin dress. The sleeves were detailed with lace, allowing glimpses of her sugar-brown skin to be seen. The train was neatly wrapped around her feet, just waiting for her to take her wedding steps.

She smiled at herself in the mirror. The dressing room door opened.

"Whoa, Aqila, you look like a queen! Kavi struck gold! I can't wait to tell Saar how I predicted this from the first day of school!!!"

"Thanks, Hova, you look wonderful!"

Hova's hair was neat for once, pulled into a neat bun, with gentle gray waves framing her face. Her dress was a floor-length silver and white satin dress. It had a wide jeweled band separating the upper and lower bodice that tied into a large bow in the back.

Ruler Sufa entered the room in a dress matching Hova's and gasped when she saw Aqila. "My beautiful lady, are we ready? All the guests have arrived and are seated."

"I'm ready," Aqila smiled, blinking back tears at the reality that, in mere moments, she would be Kavi's wife. Her mother grabbed the end of her elaborate train as Aqila followed Ruler Sufa. They were headed to the Temple of Harmony, where all rulers were married and crowned. The moment she stepped outside, her skin was kissed by the sun. Her headdress reflected the sun's light into a magnificent display of radiant colors. She and her wedding party walked with grace and dignity as they approached the Temple of Harmony. The temple was built out of white marble and was intricately crafted. The song of birds could be heard as she approached. Ruler Sufa and Hova blocked her view just as she glimpsed Kavi, Saar, with their father, Ruler Akash.

Her hands began to tremble a bit. Ruler Sufa handed Aqila's hairpin and a cage with two white doves to Hova.

Aqila's mother patted her back to soothe her like a mother putting a newborn baby at ease.

Aqila took a deep breath. Ruler Sufa looked back at her, "It's our time."

Her mother extended her ten-foot long train. Afterward, Brisa entered the temple to take her seat for the ceremony. Hova walked to the end of Aqila's train with the doves in the cage.

Kavi, Saar, and Ruler Akash had already gone inside. Suddenly, Ruler Sufa began to walk inside the temple. Once she was several paces ahead, Aqila smiled. She knew it was time. She walked inside the temple with smooth, rhythmic steps to a harmonic melody. She stifled a gasp once inside. There were silver and crystal decorations everywhere. And all the seats were occupied, and some people were standing just to have a spot. Her eyes instinctively looked for people that she knew in the audience. She saw her mother crying, wiping her eyes on her father's robe as he beamed at her with pride. Then there was Athens, grinning from ear to ear as he caught her eye.

There was Boaz with Fayruz, Tiber with Cove, and several of the Flamethrowers. The DragonLord family was present, as well as Cahya. She even caught a glimpse of Zuriel. Then her silver eyes landed upon gold ones, and she nearly cried. The expression, a silent apology, and forgiveness were exchanged with nothing but a look as Jai sat beside Arin.

Gathering herself, she steeled her nerves to look straight ahead at her handsome groom. Kavi's eyes reflected a deep and intimate love. They smiled at each other. Ruler Sufa guided Aqila to stand in front of Kavi. As usual, she couldn't look away from him. Those charcoal-gray eyes encompassed her soul. His silver robe only accentuated his masculine features. At that moment, Aqila's knees trembled. It was like falling in love over and over again.

The audience clapped at the pair standing before each other. Ruler Akash cleared his throat, "Kavi, take Aqila's hands in yours."

Kavi gently claimed and caressed her hands, making her heart flutter. They never looked away from each other.

"Glorious Heavens, before an audience of stars bearing witnesses, two souls offer themselves to the other in Your Name. We all thank you for guiding us to this glorious day. Heavens, keep this couple; guide and exalt them to your destiny. Bless them with health, good faith, and fortune until your set expiration. We bow our heads and send our prayers to the Universe for the couple." All heads bowed as Ruler Akash continued, "Grand Universe, bless this union that it exemplifies faith through love and commitment. Bless a great future to be brought to life from this union spiritually and physically. We sing praise to all of your glory, Oh Grand Skies."

Everyone looked up.

Ruler Akash continued, "Present a dove to the groom." Hova walked to Kavi and presented a dove to him. "Present ribbon to groom." Saar gave Kavi a thin red ribbon from his robe.

Ruler Akash smiled, "Kavi, present your vows to Aqila."

Kavi nodded and smiled as he began to tie the ribbon around one of the dove's legs.

"I still remember the day we met. Your footsteps were quick and feathery. Your eyes glimmered like a full moon on a starless night. And your voice could sing melodies that commanded the stars. These things have never changed, for I am always in awe of you. Beyond your beauty, I glimpsed into your soul and praised the Heavens over what I found. I found a dutiful and sacrificing woman seeking knowledge and pursuing change. Everything I learned about you made me love you more."

"Then, one day, I realized that I could not accept a future for myself where you were not my wife. On that day, I married your soul to mine. Aqila, daughter of Cirocco and Brisa, Legend and Seer, please accept my vows to you. I vow to be likened to the sun, to nurture and provide for you. Allow me to serve as your light and bring you consistent love and happiness. Just as the sun rises every day, I vow to protect you with my life and never jeopardize your safety for selfish desires. I vow to love you tomorrow as I do today and pray that time only makes me evolve into a better husband for you. I thank the Universe for guiding our stars together, for the Great Skies deemed that we are meant to be."

A tear slipped from Aqila's eyes upon hearing Kavi's sentiment to her. Kavi placed the dove back into the cage. "Present dove to the bride." Aqila accepted the dove from Hova. "Present ribbon to the bride." Saar walked over to her and gave her a thin red ribbon. "Aqila, present your vows to Kavi."

She smiled as her long fingers began tying the ribbon to the dove's leg, "The Exalted Heavens always blesses one with what they need. I am thankful that the Universe ordained a great love to breathe through us. From day one, I felt your acceptance of me and all I am. I admired you for your wisdom, bravery, and strength. And I stay wonderstruck by all of the fascinating things you do. I didn't really know what it meant to love someone, but I trusted your wisdom, relied on your bravery, and leaned on you for strength. Then the Universe intertwined our souls like the seasons; you're the neutrals, and I'm the extremes for us to paint a lovely picture like summer, winter, fall, and spring. Your heart became my palace."

"Kavi, son of Rulers Akash and Sufa, please accept my vows to you. I vow to sustain you, be a pillar in your victories, and weather every storm beside you. I vow to maintain harmony in the home, to listen, trust, and respect you, as well as to cultivate a blessed atmosphere of peace and happiness. I vow to love you, evolve, and fall more in love with you every day. Take my love, my heart, my soul, claim it, and make it your paradise. I thank the Universe for guiding our stars together, for the Great Skies deemed that we are meant to be."

She finished tying the ribbon and placed the dove in the cage with the first dove and her hairpin.

Ruler Akash smiled at the couple. "Present the hairpin to me." Hova gave the ruler the hairpin, in which he placed two white gold bands on the pin before passing it back to Hova to put in the cage. "I pronounce this couple husband and wife before the Heavens."

Everyone in the audience jumped up in exclamation, clapping and celebrating. Ruler Sufa opened the cage in Hova's hand, and the doves flew free. They danced in the sky with red ribbons flowing behind them. Kavi brought his face closer to Aqila's until they were breaths apart, then they closed the gap. The kiss was simple and chaste.

"I love you," he whispered.

"I love you too," she kissed him again. Then, the newlyweds walked down the aisle hand in hand, waving to the guests as they exited. A horse-drawn carriage was awaiting the pair. Kavi offered his hand to Aqila, helping her inside, and Hova handed him the hairpin with the gold rings.

"I'll see you two at dinner!" She squealed while clapping her hands. Hova took a deep breath and regained her composure before Kavi stepped inside the carriage and closed the door.

"Well, how does it feel to officially be husband and wife," he asked before kissing Aqila.

"Better than anything I could have imagined."

Kavi took her left hand and placed the gold band on her ring finger. Then she put his ring on his ring finger. He wrapped his arms around her as she slowly leaned into him. The carriage took them on a long ride through Kashmala and Wyndham. Cheering and celebration could be heard, but the couple did not mind as they relaxed in each other's embrace. The afternoon seemed to fly by as sunset approached, and the carriage brought Aqila and Kavi to the wedding reception. The guests were awaiting their presence. The couple was escorted to their seats at the head table. Their parents were already there.

"Congrats to the newlyweds," Aqila's father roared as the bride and groom took their seats at the table.

"Thank you," Aqila smiled at her father.

As Aqila and Kavi sat for dinner, Boaz and Fayruz walked up to them and paid their respects, "Congratulations, Aqila and Kavi," Boaz beamed with pride.

"Thanks, Bo," Aqila smiled.

"How's the training going," Kavi asked.

"Relatively well, I'm picking it up fast."

Kavi smiled and placed his hand over Aqila's.

"We're going to grab some seats for dinner. Congrats again," Fayruz pulled Boaz away.

Kavi sighed, "It's nice that someone knows how to take a hint."

"Kavi, you asked him how it was going," Aqila groaned.

He made an embarrassed expression, "Oh yeah," he remembered.

Before Aqila could laugh, Jai and Tiber walked up to their table. Tiber was giddy, "I'm so happy for you, Aqila!!!"

"Thank you," she smiled at her friend. She turned to Jai, and he smiled, "I'm glad you could make it."

He chuckled, "We're friends. I wouldn't have missed this for anything."

"It's good to see you again," Aqila murmured.

"Same here. If you two ever need anything, just let me know." He pulled Tiber away from the couple's table as their food was being served to them.

Kavi leaned over to whisper in Aqila's ear, "Seems like you're on good terms again."

"I think we are, and I'm relieved."

The evening was an elaborate event with dinner and music. A palpable happiness was exuded from everyone in attendance. The evening ended with all the guests being given a lantern to write their well wishes. Once the sky was dark, all the lanterns were lit and released into the sky. Kavi and Aqila were escorted to the carriage to take them home. This time, they watched as the lanterns looked like radiant stars in the night.

"It's so beautiful," Aqila whispered.

"It is, but not nearly as beautiful as you," he caressed her face.

Kavi stifled a yawn.

"Somebody's sleepy," Aqila joked with him.

"It's been an eventful day. I am a bit tired. Oh," he handed her a small box, "the Legends gave me this to give to you."

Aqila gently grasped the small black box and opened it. It was a ring with four stars, one red, white, green, and blue in a delicate enamel coating. The center of each star held a gem matching the star's color. It was a lovely gift. She unfolded the note in the box:

Aqila,

Congratulations on your wedding! This has been an incredible journey, and we are only at the beginning. We cannot wait to experience more triumphs together. We made four different accessories with our unique "Legend Emblem" to remind us of our commitment to unity. And thank the Universe that when we come together, our stars indeed become legendary. We love you!

Jai, Tiber, & Boaz

Aqila looked out the window and watched as the lanterns grew more distant, Kavi was beginning to nod off to sleep, and she smiled.

I love you, too.

Blinding white lightning crashed against the black sky. The moon nor the stars dared show themselves tonight. Her eyes, hazel with gold flecks near the irises, held an unrelenting gaze. Suddenly she raised her hands beside her head, fingers stiffening as she commanded the sun into the sky. She screamed. The sun trembled at her calling. Balls of fires descended from the sky. Chaos and blood curdling screams could be heard in the distance as civilians fled the area. She smiled at what her hands had wrought. The heavens split and glorious purples, pinks, and gold of ethereal glory swallowed the darkness. The fire ceased; the deafening crash of thunder married with hundreds of lightning bolts coursed through her body at once. Her body shook and convulsed and those beautiful eyes glazed over with tears as she collapsed lifeless to the ground.

Cyra's hands gently pulled the lifeless body until she was completely embraced. Cyra rocked back an forth as tears fell.

"Cyra!"

"She's gone, Basir," Cyra stifled a sob.

Basir took a breath before crouching down beside her. He didn't have children, he couldn't imagine the pain Cyra was in. Unfortunately Soleil reached a point of no return and the Heaven ended her.

"I'm sorry Cyra. I truly am." He rubbed her back.

"I am a terrible mom! I lost both of my babies! Selene died trying to be free of me, now Soleil . . . she needed me to be better."

"Selene's death was an unfortunate accident and you did everything you could to help Soleil from the dark path she was on. Soleil decided her fate. The power consumed her, that wasn't you. That was her."

"What do I do?"

"We bury her. Grieve, heal and then we come back together to try to heal the world. Our people still need us to end this war that we started."

"That I started," Cyra groaned.

Basir turned her face toward him, "We."

"What about the curse? Zeroun said that the solution exceeded our lifetime."

"Then we can't afford to focus on that. Our successors will do their best when the time comes. The only thing we can do about that now is to pray for them. Pray for them to be better than us."

Basir gently closed Soleil's eyes and pulled her from Cyra's arms. "Let's get her buried."

Though she knew Basir's words were true, Cyra could not shake the feeling of failure. All the people she loved died a brutal death. Her mind danced with the thoughts of her parents, Aenon, Selene, and now Soleil. She didn't feel like a Legend, but a bringer of death.

"What about right here?"

Cyra's dark thoughts were disturbed by the sound of Basir's voice. "Yes, thank you. Basir, I appreciate all that you've done. But, I want to bury her alone. Please."

Basir laid Soleil on the ground. Slowly he walked over to Cyra. "I respect your wish." He placed a hand on her shoulder, "Bury, grieve, heal, then send for me. Be strong Cyra."

She turned to see him walk away. Her eyes didn't look away until she could no longer see him. Slowly, she looked down to see her deceased daughter. She sobbed, "I am so sorry, my love."

Aqila's silver eyes opened. The glimmering daylight danced against the sheer curtains. She flinched in bed at the sensation of being pulled from the sight. Kavi groaned against her neck.

"What's wrong?"

She tried to recall the vision. However, it was already slipping away from her.

"Hmm," he hummed.

"It's nothing," she sighed as she settled into the cozy embrace of his strong arms. The steady sound of his heartbeat was lulling her back to sleep. "Yes, it was nothing."